I0736618

A Moonlit Path of Madness

A MOONLIT PATH OF MADNESS

CATHERINE McCARTHY

NOSETOUCH PRESS

Chicago • Pittsburgh

MMXXIII

A MOONLIT PATH OF MADNESS

© 2023 by Catherine McCarthy
All Rights Reserved.

ISBN-13: 978-1-944286-30-9
Paperback Edition

Published by Nosetouch Press
www.nosetouchpress.com

For more information, contact Nosetouch Press:
info@nosetouchpress.com

Cataloging-in-Publication Data

Names: McCarthy, Catherine, author.
Title: A Moonlit Path of Madness
Description: Chicago, IL : Nosetouch Press [2023]
Identifiers: ISBN: 9781944286309 (paperback)
Subjects: LCSH: Gothic horror tales—Fiction. |
Paranormal—Fiction. | GSAFD: Horror fiction. |
BISAC: FICTION / Gothic | FICTION / Ghost |
FICTION / Occult & Supernatural.

Cover & Interior Designed by Christine M. Scott
www.clevercrow.com

Engraved images created from photographs by Tony Evans.

To Tony, the love of my life.
May we walk The Pareog
many more times together.

"Remembrance of things past
is not necessarily
the remembrance of things
as they were."

Marcel Proust

PART
ONE

⊰ CHAPTER ⊱

I

Fair Haven, Vermont, 1902

I AM IN THE HALL, WINDING THE GRANDFATHER CLOCK, when I hear Mother's desperate cry. My foot catches in the hem of my skirt as I dart up the stairs, causing me to stumble. The thud of my fall momentarily halts her wailing, but it is not long before it starts again.

I pause outside her bedroom door to gather my breath, fearful of what awaits me within. The doorknob issues a groan of consternation as it turns.

"Grace, is that you?" Mother's rasping voice fills me with dread. Lungs that rattle and a larynx that crackles and wheezes with each breath.

The bed is empty, sheets thrown back and blankets crumpled in a heap. The air is tainted with the scent of lilac and fear. Mother cowers in a corner of the room, knees to chest, her stark-white nightgown puckered around the hips, exposing more flesh than is proper. But she is oblivious to her state of undress. She stares through me, wide-eyed and open-mouthed, and utters a soft moan as saliva trickles down her chin and pools between her breasts, then she holds out her arms, pleading for help, and as a dutiful daughter I oblige.

"She's come for me," she whimpers, as I help her to her feet. "You must help me, Grace!"

The air seems to chill at her words and I cannot help but cast my gaze around the room, but of course there is nothing to see besides a bed draped in white linen, crumpled by

Mother's distress, and a suite of mahogany furniture, polished to a shine.

"Who, Mother? Who has come?"

She claws at her face and moans, glazed eyes fixed on the far corner of the room.

"Forgive me, Caitlin. God, help me!" Her voice is the lament of the persecuted.

These past few days she has spoken the name "Caitlin" time and time again but offers no explanation as to who Caitlin is. It is not a name I have heard before.

"Come now, there's no one here besides us, Mother. Let me make you comfortable."

Her pupils are pinpricks that dart around the room, and her chin quivers with fear as I help her onto the bed. A sickly-sweet scent hangs in the air, and as I lower her head to the pillow I realize it is the smell of her breath. I administer two drops of laudanum onto her tongue, wipe away the beads of sweat from her upper lip with a handkerchief, and she calms a little.

Her maid, Lilah, bustles into the room, carrying a tray laden with tea and white hydrangea blooms, and Mother stiffens then relaxes when she recognizes her.

"Sorry I wasn't here, Miss," Lilah dips her head, and I wave a hand in dismissal of the apology. "Has she been fretting again?"

"I found her curled in a corner of the room, but she is all right now, aren't you, Mother?"

My question goes unanswered, the tea untouched, and the white hydrangeas appear far too gladsome for the room.

I turn to leave, but Mother whimpers in protest.

"What is it, Mother?"

She clasps my wrist tight with ice-cold fingers and pulls me close, and I cannot help but turn my face away from the sickly smell of her breath. Then she whispers in my ear, her words tickling my cheek.

"You must leave here, before she finds you, too."

"Who, Mother? I see no one."

She points a finger towards the far corner.

"Her."

The word is an icicle that trickles down my spine. Who does she see that I do not? I tell myself she is sick, nothing more, but an element of doubt persists and I cannot help but glance in the direction in which she points.

A shadow lurks there.

A shadow created by the wardrobe.

"You go, Miss. I'll see to her," Lilah says, tucking the sheet beneath Mother's chin. I lean in to kiss her goodnight. Her cheek is a sheet of parchment, powder white, and road-map lined with worry.

She cries softly as I leave, her fear palpable.

This is how it has been these past weeks, but this is not how it began.

⚜ ⚜

Despite a pounding headache, one which rages behind my eyes and causes a zigzag pattern to form in my central vision, I sleep soundly for a few hours, until I am crudely awoken by the sensation of an icy hand on my shoulder. With a gasp, I move to brush it away, but my fingers find my own skin, not the flesh of another. I sit bolt upright and allow my eyes to adjust to the darkness. The grandfather clock in the hall strikes three, each chime thrice slower than the beating of my heart. I am filled with a sense of foreboding.

Has something happened to Mother?

The urge to go to her is strong, but the house remains as silent as the grave. The clock ticks itself back to sleep, and eventually I do the same.

⚜ ⚜

Hours later, a gap in the curtains permits a sliver of light to enter the room, without my invitation, and I wake to a sense of stillness, as if the earth has stopped rotating on its axis. Something has changed, a profound sense of otherness, a shift in the cosmos.

I leap out of bed and approach the window, intending to draw back the curtains and give daylight full rein so that she might absorb some of my fear, but dust motes dance in the sliver of light, and for a moment I am entranced by their weightlessness. If only I were as carefree, but the memory of the previous night persists, the hand on my shoulder tangible, even in broad daylight.

I must go to Mother.

Dignity can wait; she cannot.

I slip a dressing gown on top of my nightdress and pad my way along the landing, barefoot. My heart races and my mouth turns to dust as I approach her room, and I am filled with a deep sense of dread. Before I reach it, the door to her chamber opens and out steps Lilah, carrying a bowl of water from which steam and the faint scent of lavender soap rises.

"How is she?" I ask, but I know the answer before she speaks.

"Not good, Miss. It's her breathing. It's—"

Her eyes are downcast, as are her spirits, and I place a hand on her forearm and give a nod of understanding.

Mother lies prone on the bed. Despite Lilah's best efforts, the room reeks of death. Mother's breathing is the first thing I notice: a rapid pant, like a dog on a summer's day. Her eyes are closed, but her mouth hangs open, like a baby bird's, and her vulnerability is rife. Her pallor is anaemic, the skin on the backs of her hands mottled. I know the signs of imminent death, for I have witnessed it before with Father. I swallow hard, fighting the urge to flee and not return until it is over, but I cannot abandon my duty.

"Mother?"

The word is whispered, barely an out-breath, and receives no response. I take her hand in mine, the skin cool and fragile, and lean forward to kiss her forehead. Her breathing does not change; she does not murmur, but I know she hears me, because beneath the lids her eyes flutter. I am told the sense of hearing is last to leave.

"It is Grace, Mother, I've come to sit with you."

Words skip round my thoughts, there is so much left unsaid, so many questions that need answering, but it is too late. So, instead, I sit beside her, stroking the delicate skin on her hand with a feather-light touch and listen to her short, sharp breaths as she fights for life.

"Doctor Perkins is on his way, Miss," Lilah says with a look of disapproval, and it is then I realize I am still in my nightclothes. Lowering Mother's hand to the bed-sheet, I rise to my feet.

"Have yourself some breakfast while you're at it," Lilah says. "You're all skin and bone. I'll take care of her."

I shall try my best, though no doubt I will manage little, but Lilah is more than a servant, much more, and she knows what is best for us.

By sunset, Mother's incessant panting is so ingrained in my mind that I feel I will never be free of it. I am afraid to leave her side, in fear of the worst, yet willing it to happen so that her suffering might end. My brother, Jonathan, has been sent for and now all we can do is wait.

Eventually, after hours of sitting in the same position, I fall asleep.

I sense the change in her breathing even in slumber and jolt awake. No longer panting, Mother's breaths have slowed, the time between each one stretches until, eventually, she breathes her last. It is the strangest sensation, for in that moment her face relaxes. Lines are smoothed, and it seems as though she is healed.

A wave of emotion washes over me: relief, disbelief, pity, but I can find no tears to prove my grief. It is two in the morning, the world outside asleep. The window is open to allow a little air in, and all at once the room is filled with birdsong.

"Do you hear them, Jonathan?" I say, looking out at the garden which is already in mourning.

"How strange," he says, getting to his feet. "Birdsong, at this time of night."

There is no visible sign of birds from the window, all I see is my gaunt reflection staring back at me, but the cool breeze, come to pay its respects, is a welcome visitor.

And then, without warning, it happens. A rush of turbulent air whips at my face. It smells of Mother's breath and something else, someone else—familiar yet indistinct, and the next thing I know I am on the floor and Jonathan is kneeling over me, willing me to wake up.

⚔ CHAPTER ⚔

II

"**C**AUSE OF DEATH: ORGANIC BRAIN SYNDROME. SEVERE atrophy of the hippocampus and the amygdala is the likely cause of the patient's acute memory disorder and loss of cognitive function." Jonathan glances up at me in order to glean my reaction. His spectacles sit on his nose like a second pair of eyes, and in his left hand he holds Mother's death certificate. The paper on which the words are written appears exhausted—it sags on either side, as though the weight of the words it bears is too heavy. And it is correct in its assumption, for I, too, refuse to believe a word it says. Mother died of fright, not some brain disorder. Pure, unadulterated fear that slowly poisoned her mind and body.

Jonathan prefers the scientific explanation, of course. He imagines my version of events to be a flight of fancy and worries I might up end up drowning in sorrow as Mother did if I am not careful. But Jonathan has not lived with her these past years. He did not witness her steady decline as I did, nor did he experience the inexplicable incidents I witnessed whilst in Mother's company.

As a child I knew no different. I believed my mother to be the same as any other, a little more neurotic, perhaps; a little less inclined to put her trust in others, but nothing untoward. It wasn't until I reached my teenage years that I realized her behaviour was abnormal. I began to doubt her sanity, fretted that something awful might happen to her, that she might do away with herself.

However, this past decade, and especially since Father died, I have come to believe there was more to her erratic, and at times irrational, way of thinking. I believe she was indeed stalked and taunted by something unseen. This is the conclusion I have drawn: somebody—or some *thing*—drove my mother to an early grave.

Why was I not brave enough to tell her so? Why, in her presence, did I insist it was all a figment of her imagination? I convinced myself it would be cruel to encourage her, irresponsible to nurture her wayward thoughts. Was it my way of protecting her, or did I lack the courage to admit, even to myself, that deep down I knew something was amiss?

It is my one regret.

I lean back in the chair and raise a hand.

"Believe what you will, Jonathan. She is gone, and therefore at peace, that is all that matters."

"Would you like—"

He holds the sheet of paper out to me, but I do not take it from him. Instead, I shake my head and get to my feet.

"You keep it. I'll fetch us coffee."

Lilah is busying about in the kitchen when I enter.

"What can I get you, Miss—I mean…Grace?"

She has been more than a maid to our family over the years, a companion to Mother as well as a sick-nurse, and I have lost count of the times I have told her to call me by my Christian name when we are alone. Old habits die hard, I suppose, for my parents would not have allowed any of us to be addressed in the familiar, not by a servant. Now that they are gone, things will be different.

"It's all right," I say, smiling at her slip of the tongue. "I'll get it."

I am grateful for the distraction, glad to escape the intensity of Jonathan's gaze, and besides, I need to gather my thoughts before broaching the subject of the house. As to what will become of this place now that Mother is gone I cannot say, though undoubtedly Jonathan will inherit, what with him being the eldest offspring and male. If I had somewhere else to go, I would. A new beginning, new surroundings, somewhere I might shake off this morbidity that threatens to wrap me in its black cloak until I suffocate.

The coffee cup trembles in the saucer as I pass it to Jonathan, and he relieves me of it as swiftly as he can. Since my fainting spell, he handles me with delicacy, as if I were made of bone china. Mother frowns at us from a photograph on top of the ornate dresser, her expression as dour as this room.

Of course, her own opinion as to who should inherit would have had little sway in Father's decision-making, but still she would want to make sure Jonathan treats me fairly after all that I have sacrificed. He has the house in Rutland and a loving wife and daughter; I have no one but Lilah and this place.

"Jonathan, I must ask——"

He raises a hand to stop me and gulps the coffee that I know will burn his throat. He winces at the pain, or is it the discomfort of having to talk shop that causes him to flinch?

"Listen, Grace, let's not discuss such matters until after the funeral. Rest assured, you have nothing to worry about."

I am not inclined to argue. I do not have the strength to fight my case, not at the moment. I shall put my trust in Jonathan's benevolence and hope he does right by me, though I know that Eva adores this house. My sister-in-law has had her eye on it since her first visit. I am most fond of Eva, and love my niece, Helena, dearly. Perhaps we can come to some arrangement whereby I continue to live under this roof until I marry. There is ample space and it would be wonderful to spend more time with Helena. But what am I thinking? I am twenty-eight-years-old and will never marry, of that I am certain. No man would wish to devote his life to one so melancholic as me, and besides, I am not the marrying kind.

I see Jonathan to the door, promising not to give the subject of my future another thought until after the will has been read. The demands men make of us! He hesitates at the door to the front parlour, wherein lies Mother's body.

"I think I'll say one last goodbye, Grace...before the coffin is sealed." His knuckles are white as he grips the doorknob. "Will you come in with me?"

"No, Jonathan. I said my final goodbye the night Mother died. You heard me say I do not wish to see her afterwards, and I have not changed my mind."

The subtle scent of lilies escapes into the hallway as he opens the door, and I step back, my imagination picturing Mother lying blue-lipped and sunken-eyed. I inhale deeply, picturing her features settled into death. I would prefer to remember her this way.

I have not been myself these past days, though I guess it is to be expected. The house is silent, apart from the ticking of the clock in the hall, which is a constant companion. Standing proud at eight feet tall, its face is as round as the moon. If I close my eyes, I can still hear Father's voice: *My grandfather's clock was too large for the shelf, so it stood ninety years on the floor.* It is a rhyme he would chant as he held me in his arms to study the painted scene on the clock face before carrying me upstairs to bed.

Nowadays, all I need do is stretch my neck a little to admire it, but I can still feel the reassurance of his arms clasped tight about my waist. Before lowering me to the ground, he would pretend to drop me so that I would squeal with excitement.

The face of the clock is a ship's galver; each brass numeral a spoke. Its hands are shaped like arrows on a compass: one engraved with the letter *E*, the other with the letter *W*, east and west, I presume, and its winding arbor is a perfectly formed sea-snail, complete with growth layers.

But it is the painted seascape that decorates its face that holds me captive. Whitewashed cottages line the harbour front, while a grander specimen, built of slate-grey stone, looms above them, its arched windows on the upper storey sleepily watching the comings and goings. A smattering of fishing boats bob in the bay, while, in the distance, a larger vessel sails on the horizon. The colours are as fresh as the day it was painted. It has not faded with time.

That's the ship that brought us here, Grace. Father's words ring clear as a bell. *And one day, it will take us home again.*

We are home, I would counter, to which he would shake his head and smile. *Not really, even this old clock doesn't feel at home here, but no more talk of clocks or ships. It's time you embarked on a voyage up the wooden hill.*

I wish I had pressed him for more information, but even then, I sensed his reluctance to discuss it. Where was *home?* Did Mother want to return, too? Perhaps Jonathan remembers the journey. After all, he is eight years older than me. I must remember to ask him.

Suddenly exhausted, I climb the stairs, intending to go to my room and lie down, but instead of turning right at the top of the landing I find myself turning left and heading towards Mother's room. I have not been inside since the morning after her death and only did so then to help Lilah choose the clothes Mother was to be laid out in: a fine-linen gown, the colour of bone, with a high neck and full sleeves, and a pair of ivory-silk slippers to match, which Lilah later told me had been abandoned because Mother's swollen feet refused to fit into them.

I pause in front of the door in case Lilah should hear me, but she is likely taking a nap since it is three o'clock.

An icy chill greets me as I enter. The room is bathed in light from the window that has been left open to help encourage the smell of death to leave and fresh air to enter. It is a welcome relief, indeed. It is eerily silent, though I am not afraid. Why should I be? A profound sense of emptiness fills both the room and me, the realization that I will never see her again suddenly overwhelming. I step inside and close the door behind me with the stealth of a thief.

Mother's hairbrush sits on the dresser, clinging on to fine, fair strands that belie her age, for there is hardly a grey one amongst them, despite her angst. Gently, I tease out a single hair and hold it up to the light between the pads of my thumb and forefinger. The follicle is intact—it contains cellular matter belonging to her. In this one hair, an element of Mother's life remains. The thought sends a shiver down my spine, but I wrap the hair in a handkerchief and place it inside the pocket of my dress all the same.

Mother's red velvet dressing gown hangs on a stand beside the folding screen. It slips off the stand and into my arms and I find myself immersed in the scent of jasmine and lilac blossom. This is the scent I wish to remember. Not the other one, that which has haunted me even in sleep these past few days.

Her presence is strong now, and I feel like an intruder. Does Mother admonish me for succumbing to sentimentality?

"Do not judge me, Mother," I whisper into air as invisible as her presence.

What is it I seek? To conjure some semblance of her back to life, or answers to questions I was never brave enough to ask while she lived? I suppose, in truth, it is both.

Returning the gown to its rightful place, I turn my attention to the mirrored dressing table, and in particular the little drawer which sits on its own in front of the mirror. I tug at the handle, but it is locked, just as I knew it would be. It has always been locked. I know its secret—a silver trinket box rests inside its wooden coffin. The silver is tarnished, its glory diminished, but I distinctly recall Mother refusing to allow Lilah to clean it, or touch it, even.

I remember the one and only time I set eyes on the box, not long after Father died. Mother held it in the palm of her hand as she wept, though she did not open it. With a sigh, she replaced the box inside the drawer and locked it away, pocketing the key inside her housecoat.

Dare I hope?

The heady scent of jasmine wafts at me as I open the wardrobe door and I am enveloped in Mother's presence. The moss-green housecoat hangs within easy reach, and without removing it from its hanger, I fumble inside the right-hand pocket. The key to the drawer lies in wait, though its greeting is cold.

I close the wardrobe door before returning to the dressing table, unlocking the drawer, and removing the silver box. Though insignificant in size, the box's hinges seem reluctant to open. They issue a whine of reprimand, eager to conceal what lies within. My heart misses a beat as I peer inside, but I am disappointed to discover nothing more than a folded sheet of paper, yellowed with age, upon which something has been written. The letters, *Whe* reveal themselves, but the rest of the word remains concealed beneath a fold.

I lift the paper from the box, and in doing so three small objects are revealed: a pearl-white seashell, which I know is called a baby's ear shell, a jay's feather—striped with bars of bright blue and black, and lastly, something I cannot identify. I lift it from the box, but to my dismay, it disintegrates to the touch. The palm of my left hand now holds faded fragments of something orange and black in colour. With my free hand, I reach for Mother's magnifier and hold it close to my palm. What I discover makes me recoil: six legs, each barbed at the end, a dried exoskeleton. It is the corpse of a sexton beetle, known for burying the dead in order to eat it at a later date.

With a shriek, I drop the remains on the carpet, dismayed to find that two of its legs have adhered themselves to my damp palm. I grab the folded sheet of paper and swipe away the legs, shivering in disgust.

A figure, reflected in the mirror, startles me further, but it is only Lilah. She stands in front of the door, wearing a disapproving frown, though her words are apologetic.

"Sorry if I startled you, Miss, I mean, Grace, it's just that I heard a noise and—"

Despite the fact that she is a servant, I feel the need to explain myself.

"It's nothing…I was just—" Then, without further ado, I hurry from the room, taking the folded sheet of paper with me.

⊰ CHAPTER ⊱

III

I SMOOTH THE PAPER CREASES WITH THE BACK OF MY HAND, taking care not to tear it. The handwriting is Mother's, I am certain, though she must have written it some time ago because it does not evidence the tremble she developed these past few years. It consists of one word:

Wherever.

I turn the paper over, in case there is more on the other side but am disappointed to find it blank. Holding it up to the light does me no favour, either. What on earth could it mean? And why was the note incarcerated with a feather, a seashell, and a desiccated bug? The memory of the fragmented pieces of dried insect sends a shiver down my spine. I am clutching at straws, but cannot help but wonder whether or not Lilah might know something about it.

Lilah's mournful voice seeps through the keyhole of the front parlour as I descend the stairs. She sings a *raudo*: a lament for the dead. I do not understand a single word, but it does not require a linguist to decipher the intent of a tune, whatever the language. She has always reverted to her Lithuanian roots at times of upheaval. I suppose it is her way of coping.

I loiter in the hallway and soon she emerges, arms full of dead blooms and a jug of water.

"These needed changing, Grace," she says, waving a bunch of dead lilies in my direction. She is pleased to have remembered to call me by my Christian name, and in all likelihood is also proud to have demonstrated initiative. If it wasn't for her willingness to attend to Mother post-mortem,

Jonathan and I might have found it necessary to have the coffin sealed earlier.

"Can we talk, Lilah? There are things I wish to ask you."

She eyes me suspiciously, her face flushed.

"Let me rid myself of these and I'll be right with you."

I follow at her heels as she trundles down the hallway and into the kitchen. Once she has deposited the dead lilies, she rolls up her sleeves before proceeding to pump water into the sink.

"What is it you wish to talk about?" she asks.

She busies herself with washing dishes, humming the tune to the *raudo* as she gazes out of the window and beyond into the garden.

"Please, Lilah, come and sit down."

I am already seated at the preparation table and pull out a stool to encourage her to do the same.

Reluctantly, she dries her hands. Red-skinned and coarse, like her they find it difficult to stay still. I sense her discomfort as she swipes away imaginary crumbs before interlocking her fingers in front of her to urge their stillness.

Lilah has been employed at Woodleigh House since as far back as I can remember, and she is part of the furniture. It dawns on me then, perhaps she thinks I am about to dismiss her, that I will have neither the need nor sufficient income to require her help now that Mother is gone. How selfish of me not to have considered this earlier. I am not the only one on tenterhooks about the future. I must try and put her at ease and hope that should Jonathan take over the house he will keep her on, though I know he has his own maidservant.

"I don't know where to start, Lilah…there are things I cannot fathom, things that conjure more questions than answers, and I wonder if perhaps you might be able to help. After all, you spent as much time with Mother as I did."

Her face relaxes a little and she unfolds her hands.

"The little drawer in Mother's dressing table, the one containing the silver box."

Lilah leans an elbow on the table and rests a cheek on her hand. She wears a blank expression and waits for me to offer more.

"I discovered the strangest things inside but have no idea what they mean or how they might be linked to one another. I wonder, did Mother ever speak of the box to you?"

She shakes her head, her lips a tightly-stitched seam.

"Your mother, bless her, wouldn't let me anywhere near that box. Sometimes I'd find her clutching it close to her chest and moaning, but she never said what was upsetting her. I remember asking if she'd like the box cleaned, but she refused, even though the silver was as tarnished as Ivan the Terrible's reputation."

I cannot help but smile at her words.

"So my guess is you have no idea what was inside, then."

"Not a clue."

I describe the contents, and she strokes an eyebrow with her ring finger, lost in thought.

"Well now, there's a puzzle," she says eventually. "You sure it was a bug? Strange keepsake, if you ask me."

"I'm certain, a sexton beetle of all things, the undertaker of the insect world."

"Makes no sense." She shudders. "I can't imagine."

"And the word on the paper, Lilah, *Wherever*. What can it possibly mean?"

She tilts her head to one side.

"Listen, Grace, your poor mother was burdened with fear for most of her life, or at least as long as I knew her. Maybe the things in the box have no particular meaning; perhaps they are not even connected to one another. They could be objects she found, things she considered relevant at the time for whatever happened to be going on inside her head."

She reaches across the table and takes my hand.

"You know how disoriented she could be, how unstable. No offence intended and none taken, I hope."

I sit in silence, considering her words.

"Perhaps you're right. Maybe I am trying to make sense of her thoughts now she is gone, when I should have made more effort while she was alive."

"Oy, you've no need to berate yourself as far as your mother is concerned. She couldn't have found a more loyal daughter if she'd searched the world over."

The sentiment brings tears to my eyes, but I am determined not to let them fall.

"Perhaps you're right, but if you think of anything, Lilah, anything at all, please let me know."

I return to my room and retrieve the sheet of paper from where it rests among more innocent documents: a handmade birthday card from Helena and an invitation to a ball held at the summer home of Cornelius Vanderbilt, addressed to both Mother and Father. As manager of the Granville Slate Company, Father was held in high esteem and often invited to such events.

The date on the invitation read July 5th, 1881. I would have been about seven years old, Mother around the age of forty. I close my eyes and picture her dressed in a jewel-toned ballgown made of the finest silk taffeta, a matching peacock feather in her hair. Reflected in the dressing table mirror, she watches as I enter the bedroom before swivelling to face me, all misty-eyed and porcelain-skinned. Her beauty momentarily makes my breath its prisoner. Could this have been the same night as the Vanderbilt Ball? Why did she keep this particular invitation? My finger traces the elaborate design that snakes its way around the printed lettering—oak leaves and acorns, symbols of strength and endurance, and a coat of arms depicting half an eagle.

A voice from downstairs startles me.

"Then we won't go!"

It is Father's voice. He is furious, though I do not know why. Before I have chance to realize the impossibility of this, something in the room shifts. It is the strangest sensation…

❧ ☙

I tear the peacock feather from my hair, and with it several fine strands that cling to my fingers like vines around a tree. My top lip is beaded with sweat, yet my body shivers. Too afraid to speak, I am rooted to the spot. The figure stands a few feet behind him, her outline sharp, yet her features are indistinct. How does he not sense her presence? I raise an arm and point in warning, mumbling incoherent syllables, over and over.

"You," the figure says, in a voice as smooth as my silk gown. "I come for you, not him."

A steady stream of warm urine flows down my legs, soaking my dress and pooling at my feet, but I am rooted to the spot. He does not see her. He only sees that once again I have ruined what to him would have been a perfect evening.

"This is becoming a regular occurrence, Marta. Can you not do this one thing for me without making such a fuss? Does it always have to be about you?"

But his voice is fading, each word an echo of the previous.

⁂

A severe pain in the abdomen steals my breath. The severity of the pain forces me to my hands and knees and my mouth floods with saliva. The sheet of paper frees itself from my fingers and floats to the ground like a feather caught on the wind. Another vice-like spasm causes me to retch, followed by the sensation of falling, falling, falling. And all the while, Mother's scent envelops me in its warm arms. Then the world turns black.

I wake, soaked in perspiration, head pounding and unaware of my surroundings. Beneath my thighs, a pool of urine turns colder by the second. I do not have the strength to get to my feet, so instead, I turn to lie on my side. Inches from my face the word on the paper taunts me, *Wherever.*

⁂

"Low blood pressure and a racing pulse, sure signs of stress," Doctor Perkins says, pressing two fingers against my wrist. Lilah called him after finding me on the bedroom floor. "Any pain?"

I shake my head.

"Not now, Doctor. It's passed."

"Good, good." He is packing away the stethoscope when I ask the question. "Doctor…is Mother's condition hereditary?" My chin quivers and I run my tongue around my gums in an attempt to moisten them. "It's just that since she died—"

"And there you have it." He interrupts me. "'Since she died.'" You are grieving, Grace, and this is your body's way of telling you to rest. Don't you see, it would be too much of a coincidence if you were to suddenly inherit your mother's condition on the day she died. And besides, there is no evidence that your mother's problems can be passed on."

"But the faint, it has happened twice now, the night she died as well as today. I cannot help but be concerned."

He chews his bottom lip, and I swear I see the cogs of his mind working. He wonders how best to persuade me that I am not about to suffer the same fate as Mother. He takes my hand in his and pats it in a fatherly manner.

"Please, Grace, give it time. You still have the funeral to get through, your mother's belongings to sort. Such things are the cause of great anxiety. Now, I'm going to prescribe a little laudanum, just to get you through the next few days, and we'll see how it goes, all right?"

Lilah brings a tray of tea to my room, along with a slice of fruitcake. "You need to raise your blood sugar. Probably the reason you fainted," she says, but I have no appetite. After a little more fussing, she leaves me to consider what has occurred, which is precisely what I need—time to think. The image of the figure appearing behind Father. The memory belonged to Mother, not me. But *I* tore the feather from *my* hair. How is it possible?

Now I understand why the invitation card remained in Mother's possession: Mother and Father never went to the ball. They would have handed it in at the door if they had done, to prove themselves worthy attendees. My breath is a caged bird, eager to take flight yet trapped. Is it possible that as a child I witnessed the scene and I am simply remembering? Did I spy on my parents as they quarrelled? It is the most sensible conclusion, but if that is the case I have no recollection of it. And the figure of the woman? I close my eyes and conjure the image to mind: a vague outline, devoid of colour or mass and yet as present as Lilah was a few minutes ago. Did Mother see a ghost? Did *I* see a ghost?

Tentatively, I swivel my legs out of bed and sit on the edge, gathering my breath. When my head promises not to bring on another faint, I get to my feet, leaving my slippers behind so that I can proceed as silently as possible. If Lilah discovers me out of bed she will read the riot act.

The loose floorboard outside Mother's bedroom threatens to give me away, so I pause for a few moments, listening to the sound of Lilah raking out the fire in the downstairs sitting room. She is singing again, a cheery folk song this time. I think it must be about a horse because every now and then she issues a little neigh, followed by a snort. I shall miss her terribly if Jonathan dismisses her. I cannot bear to think about it.

I tiptoe past Mother's everyday wardrobe, certain the gown will not be found there. Without so much as a creak, the doors to the second wardrobe open wide, like a welcoming pair of arms, and within seconds, I locate the jewel-toned taffeta gown in shades of peacock blue, the one she intended to wear to the Vanderbilt Ball. I lift it out, surprised by how little it weighs. Testament to the quality of the fabric. I lay it face-down on Mother's bed, a vacant embodiment, before examining the back, smoothing out pleats and ruffles. The light in the room is poor; dusk already knocks at the window, demanding to be let in, but as my eyes adjust, I am certain I detect a disparity in fabric tone close to the bustle.

My heart sinks. Is the memory a reality? Did Mother faint in fear of the ghostly figure, and if so, did she lose control of her bladder, just like I did? Lilah would be certain to know the answer to this, even if the event occurred two decades ago, for she would have been responsible for cleaning the garment. She would also know whether or not my parents attended the ball in question, and if not, why not? But how on earth might I question her about so personal a matter? A maid will remain loyal to her mistress even after death, regardless of how close we have become. I am sure she will be reluctant to paint mother in a bad light, and besides, what excuse can I possibly make for having sought out the gown?

⊰ CHAPTER ⊱
IV

I T SEEMS I AM THE ONLY ONE WHO DETECTS THE PLUMMETING
temperature in the room. I cannot stop shivering and
have to clamp my teeth tight to prevent them chattering.
Black-gloved hands shoved deep in opposite sleeves of my
gown, I attempt to steal some warmth from my skin. Yet the
fire in the hearth blazes, occasionally spitting at the minister's words. Though my eyes are downcast, I sense one or two
mourners pulling handkerchiefs from purses and pockets to
mop their brow. It is not tears they wipe away, but sweat.

Then why am I so cold? Is it anxiety, or something else? I
recall the icy hand on my shoulder the night before Mother
died and my skeleton rattles in its frame.

The minister utters the liturgy with feigned sincerity; he
hardly knew Mother. She had not attended church since Father died and declined to have the last rites read. When he
refers to her as Martha instead of Marta, I flinch but mark
the error down to ignorance rather than malicious intent.

When the minister's part is done, Jonathan speaks a few
words about Mother's dedication to her family, how she and
Father adored one another, and how she never really settled
in Vermont. I raise my eyes at his words, keen to discover if
he might reveal more.

"Our mother left a piece of her heart behind when she and
my father left Wales," he says, glancing at the coffin which
is draped in white lilies, said to restore the innocence of the
soul of the departed. But Mother's soul bears no guilt, not in
my eyes. When the funeral is over, I intend to question Jonathan about Wales to see what, if anything, he remembers.

Instead of listening to the rest of the eulogy, I find myself making mental calculations to decipher what age Jonathan would have been when we sailed to America. Around the age of ten or eleven—old enough to remember.

The clip-clop of horses' hooves alerts me to the fact that the ceremony is over. Outside the window, one of the black horses whinnies, as eager to get this thing over with as I am. Mother's pallbearers raise her casket to their shoulders, Jonathan at the head and Eva's brother on his left, followed by two of Jonathan's colleagues at the rear. Mother was so slight there is no need of six pallbearers, and besides, I am not certain we would have been able to find two more, since, as a family, we are not renowned for socializing.

As they leave the room, solemn-faced and marching in step, I find myself thinking the most morbid of thoughts: Can Jonathan feel her presence through the casket, the physical embodiment of what our mother has now become? The notion makes me shudder.

Gentlemen mourners follow the casket into the street, while several female mourners venture as far as the front door, but I prefer to watch from the window as they lower Mother's casket into the carriage and ride off. A knotted fist forms in my throat, threatening to choke me. The realization that Mother will never again enter her home is hard to bear.

I cannot wait for everyone to leave so that I may mourn her in private, but first Lilah and I will be expected to provide refreshment for the ladies while we await the men's return from the committal.

In the meantime, I am required to sit and listen to cheery anecdotes about how exuberant Mother was in her younger days, and to incidents repeated from dinner parties she and Father held back in the early years. There are no such tales to share about Mother's latter years. Apart from my sister-in-law, Eva, the mourners here-present had not visited Mother for several years, not since her condition worsened.

A profound sense of pointlessness overwhelms me at the thought. This whole charade, the social etiquette associated with death, seems so ridiculous. Eva gazes around the room with a glint in her eye and the hint of a smile on her lips. She is no doubt admiring the wainscot panelling and high ceilings and imagining herself as mistress of the house. I cannot help but feel a little peeved.

"Excuse me a moment," I say, heading for the door, "I must check on Lilah, in case she needs a hand."

The truth is, if I do not get out of this stifling room I fear I might faint again. Either that or I will do something out of character such as declaring everyone duplicitous and shooing them out of the house.

I realize then that Mother must have taken her iciness to the grave with her, because my shivering has been replaced by such dreadful heat that my face burns and perspiration soaks the skin beneath my gown. As I leave the room, I snatch an order of service from the table by the door and fan my face, but I do not go to Lilah. Instead, I creep up the stairs with the stealth of a tiger and spend a few minutes alone in my room.

As soon as the wake is over, I raise the subject of Wales with Jonathan, but he seems reluctant to discuss his memory of the childhood he spent there, using my niece's absence as an excuse for him and Eva to leave soon after the rest of the mourners.

At twelve years of age, I consider Helena old enough to have attended the funeral, but Eva would not hear of it.

"We'll speak at length tomorrow, Grace," he says, both of them edging towards the door. "After we've gone through the details of the will."

As executor, he is already aware of its contents, and yet he sees fit to keep me in the dark a day longer. One more day spent not knowing what my future might entail. Or perhaps one more day of blissful ignorance. It depends on how one looks at it.

Now that the mourners have gone, the house seems eerily quiet. I help Lilah clear the dishes, glad to have something to do. It is strange not having Mother here, even laid out in her coffin, her presence was tangible. Both Lilah and I have changed out of our mourning gowns into something more comfortable, glad to rid ourselves of starched silk and stiff waists.

"I'll rewind the clocks, Grace," she says. "Your mother, when she was in her right mind, would have wanted life to resume." With a reassuring nod, she picks up the chatelaine from where it hangs on a hook beside the range and bustles away.

"Wait, Lilah. I'll see to the grandfather clock if you don't mind. It…it's always been special to me."

Her fingers fumble with the chatelaine, but it does not take long for her to locate the key. Cast in brass, its shank is shaped like an anchor, its bow the head, and I am reminded of the complexity of design that went into making the clock.

I pause in front of it and flatten my palms against each of its sides before studying its face. The wood is cool to touch, yet its familiarity is warm. Without its rhythmic tick, the clock seems bereaved. I believe it welcomes my embrace.

Home…Father's voice resonates as I wind the mechanism and bring it back to life. Did he refer to the seaside harbour depicted on its face, or Wales in general? The clock's heart beats in sync with mine as I admire the scene. The artist has captured the sea so well that I swear I hear the breath of the waves as they break on the shore: a gentle lap that tickles the sand and leaves a gift of salty kelp in its wake.

"Supper, Grace." Lilah's sudden presence causes me to start. "You have not eaten since breakfast. Don't think I haven't noticed."

"Only if you will join me."

My stomach rumbles in agreement and lightens the mood.

We sit beside the fire in the small study, surrounded by Father's books and his cabinet of curiosities. Lilah knows this is where I feel most comfortable. She has prepared some cold cuts of meat, left over from the wake, but I cannot bring myself to eat the flesh of the dead, not today.

Instead, I butter a hunk of fresh bread and enjoy some sharp cheese alongside it, washed down with tea served from a silver teapot, a legacy of my parents' British habits.

Before long, the warmth from the fire and soft candlelight renders me exhausted and I bid Lilah goodnight, thanking her for everything she has done to help the day run smoothly.

Confined in a cave or some kind of underground tunnel, I struggle for breath. Where am I? My fingers claw at loose earth in an attempt to break free, but doing so makes the situation worse as crumbling soil rains down on my head. It mats my hair, invades my ears and nose, so I squeeze my lips tightly to prevent it from entering my mouth. My desperate moans sound muffled in the confined space.

In total darkness, my senses on high alert, I listen—desperate for clues as to where I might be, but my throbbing pulse is the only sound I hear. What little air there is smells of earth: rich and woody. My fingers find purchase in the roots of a plant and I tug gently, fearful of loosening more soil. The strand elongates, pulling me to my feet like a rope, and I follow blindly.

Dim light in the distance, the sound of scratching, I emerge to a circular chamber, though one clearly underground: a roof formed from tree roots, walls of dark soil, and in the centre of the chamber a flattened rock, upon which sits a single candle.

As my eyes adjust to the light, striations in the rock glisten and the walls writhe with the movement of creatures, too small to see individually.

The scratching sound resumes. It comes from up above, so I crane my neck and listen. Movement, quick and sporadic, a pair of sexton beetles scurry along the tree roots, dragging with them the corpse of a shrew, already stripped of its fur.

As they approach, the beetles grow larger in size, the Aztec stripes of their hard wing-cases glow in the candlelight and their long antennae probe the putrid air. Am I to become their next prey? They feed on the dead, not the living, I tell myself, but still I am afraid.

They see me, and in their haste, they drop the dead shrew, which lands on its back with a soft splat. Its paws are hooks that plead for help as it lies facing me. Eyes open, it watches, seeing nothing. Its belly writhes before splitting open, spilling a swarm of maggots that perform a macabre, wriggling march en masse.

I try to scream, but my lungs refuse to comply. A breathy wheeze is all I can manage. The beetles scurry forth, as large as moles and eager to reach their prey. The *click-clack* of wings, a frenzy of excitement that is palpable. I step backwards, they scurry forward. Within three or four paces my back presses against the walls of the chamber, palms pressed flat, eyes fixed forward.

There is no escape.

Then they are on me: blade-like mandibles pierce the flesh of my cheek, before injecting me with a paralysing poison. It courses through my veins, turning my limbs to stone. Only my heart moves, though its beat is erratic and swift. In all my life I have never felt so afraid. The beetles scurry to my bosom, then, with one deft movement, the male mounts the female while her pincer-like legs pin me down. Bile churns in my stomach, but some semblance of sense swallows it, knowing that because I am paralysed I will choke if I allow it to reach my throat. Their copulation is fleeting, yet I am aware of their lust, the male's sudden shudder and the female's warm receptiveness. He dismounts and the pair scurry back to the corpse of the shrew, diminishing somewhat in size as they go.

I watch in horror as the female staggers around the shrew's innards, laying her eggs as she goes. And all the time the male watches me, its compound eyes shining and antennae twitching.

The sensation of life returns to my body and I slump to the ground, spent and sick.

I wake with a gasp, a first-breath. My skin crawls and I am soaked with sweat. The room is shrouded in darkness—a cloak as black as the underground nightmare I have woken from. I am so afraid that I am tempted to call for Lilah, like a child calls for its mother in the dead of night. But it is just a dream. I convince myself of this as I swivel my legs out of bed and light the lamp. I pull back the curtains, in search of dawn, but the moon is a silver dollar against a bolt of black velvet. My breath condenses on the cold pane, and as I wipe it away the moon highlights my hands: my nails are filthy, caked with earth, and a glance at my bare feet confirms the same.

As I turn around I see her standing in the far corner: a figure hidden in shadow, svelte yet steadfast, featureless yet distinct.

"Mother?" No, not Mother, I am certain. A pathetic wail, a whimper, one that starts deep in my bowels and reaches my throat but does not make it past my lips. The dream lives with me still. Its cloying stench lingers in the air; the paralysis once more a reality, for I am frozen to the spot.

"You!" The word is a drawn-out breath. Accompanied by the raising of an arm, it melts the ice, freeing both my voice and limbs.

"Lilah!" The door is an escape route, if only I can make it across the threshold.

⊰ CHAPTER ⊱

V

"SOMEONE IS IN MY ROOM, LILAH!" BUT AS I SPEAK, THE words fade in significance, because the light from her lamp confirms that there is no dirt beneath my nails, and the soles of my feet are clean. "How——"

"Stay here, I'll go and check," she says, guiding me into her own room, and with that she hurries away before I can protest.

By the time she returns I have calmed somewhat, though I am glad to hear her confirm there is no one in the house except us.

Tears stream down my face unchecked as she holds me close and strokes my hair.

"A bad dream, Grace, that's all it was."

I cannot say whether I cry over the dream or the loss of Mother. Is this how it started with her? Nightmares and hallucinations. Or is it simply the culmination of recent events? I touch the skin on my face, remembering the sharp sting of the beetle's mandibles. The skin feels raised and itchy. I spring from the bed and head towards the mirror.

"Fetch a lamp, Lilah. There are marks on my face."

She obliges, though I sense her despair. But I am not mistaken: just below the hollow of my cheekbone are four small scratches, like raised pinpricks.

"You see?" Panic resurfaces. "I did not dream it."

She spits on a handkerchief and dabs at my cheek, frowning all the while.

I describe the dream: the beetles increasing in size, the copulation, the maggots, every single detail. And then I explain about the dirt and the woman who hid in the shadows.

Lilah pales, her eyes turn glassy, and I know she is thinking of Mother. "But don't you see?" she says. "The dream is symbolic of your mother's funeral, Grace, that and the remains of the insect you found in the box."

My hands are tightly clasped.

"Then how do you explain these marks on my face?"

She sighs and rubs her eyes with her knuckles.

"You more than likely scratched yourself, Grace…and by the way, have you taken the laudanum as Doctor Perkins suggested?"

Despite her attempt to reason with me, her expression is full of doubt. Is she afraid of the supernatural as I am, or is she fearful that history is about to repeat itself?

"I will not have my mind chemically altered, Lilah. Not after what it did to Mother." My words are sharp as a blade and she flinches from the cut.

She slumps down on the bed, head in hands.

"What will become of us, Grace?"

Her reaction makes me feel guilty for causing her to worry.

"I don't know, Lilah. Perhaps tomorrow, when Jonathan explains the contents of the will. Perhaps then we can plan the future."

She nods, and I suddenly realize she is getting older. This woman, who until now has seemed invincible, is as vulnerable as I am. She has lived with our family for so long, we are all she has. I stand and draw back the curtains, glad to see the sky has lightened a shade or two. Now might be a good time to ask her about the dress.

"Lilah, think back, do you recall the Vanderbilt Ball?" She glances in my direction, uncertain. "Mother's gown… in peacock silk?"

She heaves a shuddering sigh.

"And what does the Vanderbilt Ball have to do with tonight, Grace?"

I shake my head and look down at my feet.

"I don't know. It might be nothing, or it could be significant. When did Mother's hallucinations start, Lilah? How many years ago?"

She chews her bottom lip and I sense her reluctance to divulge such information.

I take her hands in mine and look into her eyes.

"Lilah, I cannot begin to understand what is happening here until I know more about Mother's problems. Please, for the love of God, if you know the answer then tell me."

I return to the window and she joins me. Both of us gaze at a sky that grows less burdened by the minute.

"Your parents did not attend the ball, Grace. Your mother fell ill…with one of her turns, just before they were due to leave. I remember having to send the carriage away empty, and how upset your father was about the incident, how angry—"

"And the dress, Lilah? Did Mother faint and wet herself?"

She narrows her eyes.

"What makes you ask?"

"Please, Lilah, just tell me."

She seems embarrassed to speak of such a personal matter, or perhaps she feels guilty about discussing Mother's past. Eventually she speaks.

"The stain never came out, not fully. I did my best, but the taffeta bore a watermark that refused to disappear, just like the memory of that night."

I breathe a sigh of relief.

"One more thing, Lilah. Was I witness to what happened? It's just that I seem to remember—"

She interrupts me. "Oh no, Grace. You were fast asleep. I distinctly recall checking on you, in case the quarrel had disturbed you."

She must be mistaken. "But I remember Mother wearing the dress. I recall a peacock feather in her hair. She looked so…beautiful." I need her to confirm I was there, because if I did not witness it then I must have experienced Mother's memory myself. But that would be impossible. "Please, Lilah. It's important to me that you are certain."

She frowns and shakes her head. "I am certain, because it was me who put you to bed, Grace. Not your father, nor your mother. The coach was due at any moment and neither of them wanted to run the risk of you refusing to let them go. You were a bit clingy back then, especially with your father. You liked him to tuck you into bed." She stares beyond me, as if picturing the scene. "And the clock, you liked to look at the clock with him, the familiarity of routine that all children enjoy. I made certain you were asleep before leaving you, but as I made my way downstairs to watch for the coach I heard them shouting."

My heart sinks. "And Jonathan?"

Until now it has not crossed my mind as to whether or not Jonathan might have witnessed the argument. Perhaps he did, perhaps he told me about it. Maybe somewhere, deep in my subconscious, I remember him telling me. That might explain things.

She nods and in that gesture gives me hope. "Jonathan saw what happened. I can picture your father now, red-faced, sending him off to his room. But Jonathan was not like you, Grace. Jonathan was never…sensitive. He took things in his stride, as do most of the male species." She winks and smiles. Downstairs, the grandfather clock chimes six. "Come on," she says. "We might as well get dressed and put the kettle on. I don't think either of us will be getting back to sleep, do you?"

I take my time dressing, going over her words in my head. If Lilah is not mistaken, then either Jonathan told me about the quarrel or, like Mother, I am losing my sanity. I prefer to think the former.

❧ ☙

By the time Jonathan arrives I am exhausted, the memory of last night's events having played over and over in my mind. Lilah and I have spent the day going through Mother's belongings, sorting piles of clothing and personal effects into those I wish to keep and those I wish to donate to charity. Lilah's approach has been pragmatic: it seems that a pot of tea and a decent lunch was enough to revive her to her former self, whereas I have been far less impassive.

Lilah greets Jonathan at the door and takes his coat before scuttling off to the kitchen. Her face is flushed—what Jonathan has to say is of importance to her too, though with her being a servant I doubt he has considered such a thing.

"Eva isn't with you?" I say. Her absence suggests my suspicions will be confirmed. It is likely Jonathan will have inherited Woodleigh House and she would prefer it if he delivered the news alone.

He blinks in quick succession from behind dark lashes.

"No, it's a little late, you see, for Helena." He busies himself with his briefcase, removing papers and arranging them on the table.

"I would love to see Helena, Jonathan. It's been weeks since you last brought her."

He says nothing, but heads straight to the decanter and pours himself a whisky. "Wine?"

"No thank you; Lilah has made tea." The whole scenario seems so official that I want to laugh. "You know, Jonathan, both Eva and Helena should be here. I'm sure what you have to say will affect all of us."

He knocks back the drink and refills the glass. "Of course, you're right. I'm sorry, Grace, I assumed you would prefer it if it were just the two of us, you know, the beneficiaries. I'll bring Eva and Helena to visit this coming weekend, I promise."

"That's good, because I want Helena to choose a keepsake from Mother's belongings. Something to remember her by." Both of us are aware of how absent Mother was in her grandchild's life; her illness had made sure of it. "If things had been different, then I'm sure—"

He raises a hand, and swallows hard. It is the first real emotion he has shown.

"I'm sure you're right, Grace, but at least Helena has a wonderful aunt in you. And of course she has Eva's parents. Now, let us sit and get this over with."

His hand trembles as he picks up the will and begins to read.

"Stop, Jonathan," I say, before he has passed the words, *declare this to be my last will and testament*. "Just tell me…in your own words. There is no need for such formality between us, surely?"

He pauses, mouth agape, then places the document on the table and folds his hands as if in prayer.

"You're right, Grace. I'm sorry."

Is he apologizing for his formality, or the fact that he is about to turn me out of my home?

He casts his gaze around the room, just as Eva did yesterday during the funeral, then looks me in the eye and says, "This house, Grace. It's been left to me." He reaches across the table and takes my hand, and I read the guilt in his eyes. "But you can remain here, if that is what you want."

I steal a breath. "So you don't intend to live here yourself?" I know I am playing devil's advocate, but cannot resist.

He squirms a little in the chair. "That is not what I'm saying, Grace. It's Eva, you see…she loves this house."

I remove my hand from his. "I'm well aware of that, Jonathan. In fact, I've known it since the first time you brought her here."

"But you can live here with us if that is what you want. Keep your bedroom. Nothing much will change, and it will be far less lonely for you. Helena will have her favourite aunt for company and—"

"And Lilah? Is she to stay, too?"

"Lilah?" He shakes his head and frowns. "I hadn't given her any thought. I'm certain Eva will want to bring our maid, Mary-Anne."

So it is just as I thought, then. "But Lilah has been here since the early days, Jonathan. Surely you must see how this will affect her?"

He takes another sip of whisky, flinching at the burn as he swallows. "Grace, I think you forget that Lilah is a servant." He licks his upper lip.

"She is more than a servant, Jonathan, far more." I sense the skin on my throat flush. "I don't know how Mother and I would have managed without her this past year or so."

"You are right, of course. But wait, Grace. I have more to say. We are jumping ahead of ourselves. When you hear what else the will contains, you might not want to stay." He stands and strides towards the door. "Come," he says. "Let me show you."

VI

IN THE HALL, JONATHAN STOPS IN FRONT OF THE GRAND-father lock and points towards its face. "Here, Grace. Do you see the stone house? The one dominating the harbour?"

I nod, puzzled. I know this clock far better than him. In fact, if I were more adept at art I could replicate the scene without the need to copy.

"It's yours."

His face is ruddy, eyes whisky-bright. The clock strikes six, each chime a celebration of his words. I wait for it to stop before I speak. "The clock, you mean?"

"No…well yes, but the house too, it's where we lived as children. Don't you remember? And now it belongs to you."

My legs threaten to give way. "The house in Wales?"

"Of course." He gives a nervous laugh. "As you know, Father hoped to return one day, but alas it wasn't to be."

I take two paces and slump down on the stairs.

"All this time, and they didn't sell it?" The chandelier casts a glow upon the clock face, demanding our attention: the row of cottages, the stone house that dominates the scene, the ship that sails the ocean. I am lost for words.

Jonathan's face falls. He mistakes my reaction for contempt. "But you can sell it if that is what you want, Grace. You do not have to up-sticks and travel halfway around the world just because you own it." He joins me on the stairs and studies my face. "Like I said, you can stay here with us. Sell the house in Wales and keep the money for yourself. You won't have to worry about a thing."

"All these years." My eyes brim with tears. "Father often referred to the place as home, but I had no idea he meant that particular house, and I was too young to remember living there, Jonathan. We emigrated when I was two years old."

"Sorry, Grace. I forgot how young you were when we came to live here." He looks again at the clock. "I knew Father had kept the house, in fact he refused to sell it, even when Mother begged him to. I realize I should have told you sooner." He searches my face for clues as to how I am handling the news, but my expression is blank. I am too shocked to take it in. "Take your time. You need not rush into a decision, not after all you've been through. Decisions made in haste are oft repented."

His words are a blur. All I can think about is the fact that the house depicted on the clock belongs to me. What state is it in after being left alone for more than two decades? "Does anyone live there? Surely it's not been empty all these years?"

"Come," he says, pulling me to my feet. "Let's return to the sitting-room, and I'll explain."

❧ ❦

The house is silent. Lilah skulks out back somewhere and Jonathan has gone, taking his official papers with him, though he has left behind an envelope marked *Grace*. One word, written in Father's hand, each letter precise and bold, void of the sweeping curves of Mother's elegant hand. The buff envelope is immaculate, having lay undisturbed these past years in a solicitor's office, waiting for this day. I pour a glass of Meursault-Perrieres to steady my nerves before reading.

The blade of the letter opener tears at my heart as it glides through the red-wax seal. Inside lies a single sheet of paper, folded once. The faint scent of leather and tobacco lingers on the page, or perhaps I imagine it so, and I look up, half expecting him to be standing in front of me. Father and I shared a bond I never knew with Mother, what with her being so dependent, her behaviour so erratic, and I am unsure as to how his words will affect me...

My Dearest Grace,

First, I must apologize for the predicament you most likely find yourself in. It was never my intention to cause you torment, far from it.

I trust that the grandfather clock in the hall still keeps good time and that you adore it as much as you did when you were a child. If you decide to return to your roots, I hope you will have it shipped, so that it can spend its twilight years marking time at the place in which it truly belongs, for the house in Wales was its first home. Your grandparents commissioned it, Grace, so you will be the third generation to own it.

Grace, whilst I do not wish to force your hand, I ask that you consider the prospect of a new life, in the Old Country, carefully. Do you remember how I would talk to you of returning one day? I knew in my heart it would never come to pass, not with your mother as sick as she was. But you, Grace, you possess a strength that surpasses all of that pain.

I hope you find the courage to return home and live the life intended for you.

Peace awaits you in the house by the sea, the gulls will welcome you with their cry, and the waves will wash away your tears.

Your ever-loving father

I read the letter over and over before replacing it in the envelope. For the time being I shall keep it close, in the pocket of my apron, so that I may read it as often as I wish.

I feel as though a great weight has lifted. For the first time in years, I know what it is to be excited. This is a chance to start over, a new life in a new place, and I intend to grasp it with both hands. I must tell Lilah. No doubt she feels anxious about what Jonathan has had to say, and I need to put her out of her misery.

She turns to face me as I enter the kitchen, her face flushed and her hands clasped in front of her bosom.

"Sit down, Lilah. We need to talk." We face each other at opposite ends of the table. My smile is wide and genuine as I ask the question. "How would you feel about moving to Wales?"

"Wales?" Mouth agape, she raises herself in the seat.

"Yes, Lilah, Wales. I have been left the house by the sea, the grey-stone house on the face of the grandfather clock."

I hear the tremor of excitement in my voice, and she grins. It seems my excitement is contagious. She heaves a huge sigh, which I take to be one of relief.

"And you're asking me to come with you?"

"I would love you to, Lilah. This house is now Jonathan's as I suspected, but the house in Wales is mine. It could be a new beginning, Lilah, for both of us. What say you?"

She gazes around the room, as if seeing her surroundings in a new light. "Well, I guess I've nowhere else to go, so it might as well be Wales."

We are secret conspirators, soon sea-bound, and I have not felt this elated in the whole of my life.

⊱ ⊰

Despite feeling utterly exhausted, I barely sleep a wink. My mind is a whirlpool, my thoughts opposing currents, each eddying the other. Not a speck of doubt remains, though. No reconsidering or procrastination. As soon as possible, I intend to sail the ocean and begin a new life, one unburdened by memories of torment and suffering. The one and only regret I have is that I will miss Helena, though reality reminds me of how little I see of her in any case. If I had chosen to stay, it would not work with Eva as mistress of this house. I would not be happy here under such circumstances. No, I shall carry out Father's wishes and make a new life for myself in the place where a piece of his heart remains.

⊱ ⊰

On Sunday afternoon, Jonathan, Eva, and Helena breeze in the front door, bringing the scent of early autumn with them. I sense a little awkwardness in both Jonathan and Eva, but I attempt to quash it by hugging all three of them warmly.

I believe that in granting them this house Father has done me a great favour, for I have never been truly happy here. These last few years in particular have been torturous. I cannot wait to tell them my decision, though I am dreading Helena's reaction. Still, the young are resilient, and I am certain she will adjust to my absence in time.

Instead of a formal lunch, Lilah has prepared a few hot and cold dishes and has laid them out on the sideboard in the dining room so that we might help ourselves. As soon as we are seated, I broach the subject. "So, I have come to a decision." I glance from one to the other, but cannot hide my smile. "I am emigrating to Wales."

Jonathan blinks in quick succession, as though my words are a fly in his eye, while Eva's bottom lip trembles slightly as she attempts to hold back a smile. But I am unprepared for the ferocity of Helena's reaction. She drops her fork, and it clatters against the china plate.

"Wales?"

"Yes, Helena. Did your father not tell you?" I frown at him. Surely he must have mentioned the inheritance, if only to explain they will be moving to this house?

"Daddy?" The look of shock on her face speaks volumes. As he is wont to do, Jonathan gets to his feet and meanders over to the sideboard on the pretence of helping himself to a second serving of beef.

"Your father and Aunt Grace lived in Wales as children, Helena. Grandpa George kept the house they were raised in, and now that Grandma is no longer with us it has been left to your aunt," Eva says. She turns to me. "But of course, she is welcome to live here with us. You do know that, don't you, Grace?"

"Live here? You mean we are moving house?" Helena's eyes sparkle in astonishment.

I cannot help but feel as though I am being blamed for upsetting her. "You really ought to have explained, Jonathan. Helena is not a child; she is on the brink of womanhood."

Eva bristles in her seat, while Jonathan shakes his head. The pleasant mood we began with is already tarnished.

"Of course we intended to tell you, Helena. We were waiting to see what Aunt Grace's decision was, that's all. What would be the point in upsetting you unnecessarily?" He glowers at me.

I am sure annoyance is written all over my face, too. The last thing I want is for Helena to feel as though I care little for her. She pushes her plate away, her appetite ruined, and I do the same.

I hold out a hand to her. "Come with me. I would like you to choose something to remember Grandma by. You and I can eat later." I stare daggers at Jonathan and Eva, daring them to contradict me, and we sweep from the room.

On entering Mother's bedroom Helena slumps on the bed, clenches her fists and groans.

"They drive me insane sometimes. They treat me like a five-year-old. You're the only one who takes my side in such matters and now you're leaving."

I sit beside her and take her fist in my palm. "Listen, Helena. I understand, really I do. I guess it's because you're an only child and they want to keep you young as long as possible."

"But it isn't fair. I wanted to come to Grandma's funeral, too, but they wouldn't let me."

She pulls her hand away and folds her arms across her chest while staring out of the bay window towards the park. Her throat constricts as she gulps back the tears.

"Grandma loved you dearly, Helena, but she was very sick, especially these last few years. She wasn't always capable of expressing her love, but in her more lucid moments I often caught her clutching your photograph and smiling."

It is the truth. I would not say it otherwise.

"What did she die of, Aunt Grace? Daddy says she suffered some kind of brain fever, but I never realized a fever could last so long."

"Your father believes what he's been told by the medical examiner, Helena, and he may be right. I lived with her though, so I saw how she deteriorated over the years. I guess we'll never know for certain."

She stands and walks over to the window. The sky is cloudless, the air crisp. A sudden gust of wind billows the curtains, causing us both to shiver. Neither of us wants to acknowledge the feeling that Mother's spirit has come to listen.

"Come, I want you to choose a keepsake from Grandma's jewellery box. I know she would want you to."

I take the box from the dressing table and place it on the bed. Helena's eyes brighten as I lift the lid to reveal a cornucopia of colour. I remove the top tray and place it beside her.

"Choose anything, top or bottom. Whatever takes your fancy."

Her eyes settle on a brooch and she lifts it out and places it on her palm. "This one, it's...different somehow."

She has selected Mother's mourning brooch, oval-shaped and edged in gold filigree. On a bed of pearl lie three tiny curls of fair hair, arranged in the shape of a fan and fastened with a small golden clasp. She does not flinch when I explain how Mother had it made from my grandmother's hair after she died. This girl is made of far sterner stuff than either of her parents credit her with.

"How fascinating," she says, tracing the feather-shaped curves with her forefinger. "But I guess you will want to keep this piece."

"No, if that is what you want you shall have it. It's just that I thought you might prefer something a little less macabre." I can't help but smile. "Do you know, Helena, I think you have a lot of me in you, and that makes me happy."

She laughs, then her face falls and she hugs me about the waist. "I shall miss you so much. I know Daddy rarely brings me to visit, but I do love you, you know. I wish I could come to Wales with you."

I embrace her warmth, the lavender scent of her hair. "We'll write often, and one day, when you're old enough to travel, perhaps you can come and stay for a while. How would you like that?"

She releases me from her grip. "I'd like it very much," she says, pocketing the brooch. Then, with a sigh, "I guess we'd better go and eat. They'll only worry otherwise, and we can't be having that, can we?" She rolls her eyes in a mocking manner.

Rather than adult and child, we are soul-sisters on an equal footing. We step onto the landing at the same time as Eva, except she has come out of my bedroom, not Mother's. She appears flustered and stumbles over her words. "Ah, there you are," she says. "We were beginning to think you'd got lost."

I have to bite my lip to stop myself asking what she was doing in my room. In all likelihood she was sizing it up for Helena. It is the second largest bedroom in the house and will, no doubt, be hers when I move to Wales.

"Look at what I chose, Mamma." Helena slips the brooch from her pocket and holds it out for Eva to inspect. "It's

Grandma's mourning brooch. The fan shape is made from my great grandmother's hair. Isn't it beautiful?"

Eva casts me a look of contempt and exaggerates a shiver. "Really, Helena? Couldn't you have chosen something a little less ghoulish?"

Helena smirks. "But that's precisely why I like it, so there."

She may have inherited her mother's looks, but she has also inherited her aunt's morbid nature.

⊰ CHAPTER ⊱

VII

LILAH AND I HAVE DECIDED TO GIVE OURSELVES A MONTH to pepare for the move. Our tickets are booked for the second of November, time enough to make the necessary arrangements, but not long enough to change our minds. Of course, I feel a little trepidation, but the thought of making a new life, in a new country, far outweighs the potential downsides.

It is obvious from Father's letter that he intended me to inherit the grandfather clock, and Jonathan agrees. He has never particularly liked it. He considers it too twee. It will cost an arm and a leg to ship, but I do not care. The clock meant a lot to both Mother and Father and I will cherish it always. Apart from that I shall take very little with me to Wales, except for the necessary personal effects and a few small items such as Mother's silver trinket box. I cannot say why the thing has such a hold on me. It is a puzzle I am yet to solve, and despite the strangeness of its contents I am drawn to it.

Lilah is in the kitchen preparing a bowl of hot water and baking soda so that I can remove the tarnish from the box in preparation for its new life, one untarnished by past stains. First, I lift out the jay's feather, sweeping a finger back and fore along its vane. The barbs on the left side are shaded grey, ranging from the palest cloud to the deepest thunder, while those on the right dazzle with their electric blue stripes. Holding it by the quill, I twist it forward and back, hypnotized by its visual spell. Why a jay's feather? Might the stark contrast between the two sides be the reason Mother kept it?

Electric blue versus dull grey, like the two sides of her personality. I lay it down on the dressing table before taking out the white baby ear shell. So delicate, its curve is like that of a human ear and about an inch in length. What significance could it possibly have?

"Grace, this water is already cooling. Are you coming to clean that silver or not? I'll do it for you if you like." It is Lilah calling from downstairs.

"No, no. I'm on my way." I place the shell beside the feather and pick out the folded sheet of paper before laying it next to the items. No trace of the sexton beetle remains, and I am thankful for that, though the memory still makes me shudder.

The sharp tang of vinegar and lemon makes my mouth water as I enter the kitchen. Lilah is at the sink, scrubbing pots and pans which glint as she holds them up to the window to check they are clean.

"Mother was superstitious of birds, Lilah. Did you know that?"

"Yes, Grace. I remember a sparrow hitting the bedroom window the day before your father died. It knocked itself unconscious on the glass. Shook your mother something awful, it did. Made her physically sick. She swore it was a portent of impending doom, and I guess she was right, though your father was on his last anyway, poor man."

"If she hated birds so much, I wonder why she kept a jay's feather? She refused to have any fabrics or clothing printed with birds in the house. I guess she thought a feather didn't count." I am polishing the silver box as we speak, digging my cloth into the grooves and curves. Lilah sits opposite, armed with her own bowl and several candelabra.

"Who knows, Grace. Now, we Lithuanians believe that if a bird shits on you it brings good luck." She laughs and places a hand over her mouth. "Excuse my language, Grace. Whatever was I thinking?"

I suppress a grin. "Don't apologize, Lilah, there is no need of formality between us." I put down the box and cloth and fold my hands on the table. I yearn to know more about her, the real Lilah. "Tell me about life in Lithuania, Lilah. What was it like?"

She dries her hands on her apron and stares into the distance. "I remember very little. I must have been around the age of seven when my family came to America. They did it to escape poverty and tyranny, you see." She looks at me now. "As Jews, we were as much a minority there as here, so it made little difference." Her expression is melancholic. "It's an awful feeling, Grace, the sense of never belonging. No matter where you go or what you do, you're always considered an outsider."

I nod. "To some degree, Father felt the same when we came here. Even though he established himself on the board of directors at the slate quarry, his heart remained in Wales. As for Mother…I'm not sure she ever felt at home anywhere." The sun shines in at the window and the silver box winks in agreement.

"Like your mother and father, my parents were also very different from one another. Mother was a devout Jew. She studied the Torah, attended the synagogue and observed holy days. She adhered to every dietary law under the sun, whereas my father was a little more…rebellious, shall we say."

She closes her eyes and takes a deep breath, lost in the past. "I can picture his face now. He loved to tell my brother and I tales of witches and *maumai, laumės* and *aitvarai,* though he swore us to secrecy. My mother would have been appalled to discover we were being educated in such things." She grins.

"Do tell me a story, Lilah, please. Tell you what, we'll swap. You tell me one about the *laumė* and I'll tell you about the *coblynau* that haunt the Welsh mines."

"All right, wait there," she says. "First, I have something to show you." She stands and leaves the room, but returns a minute or so later, cradling something in her hands.

"Here…" She places a small object on the table in front of me, concealed beneath a woven piece of tapestry, which she slowly unwraps. It reveals the figure of a woman, bird's claws for feet, the legs of a goat, and pendulous breasts with nipples made of some kind of pinkish gem. The craftwork is exquisite, yet its semi-naked state makes me squirm. Lilah, however, seems far less prudish. She touches a nipple with the tip of her finger, and I feel the heat rise to my face.

"It's a *laumė*, whittled in wood by my father's own hand," she says. "The nipples are made of rose quartz, the stone of unconditional love." She grins at my discomfort. "My father made it for me the year we came to America." She strokes the figure lovingly. "I have so little to remember him by. This'll be coming to live with us in Wales, Grace." She pauses. "Now, let me tell you a story."

For fifteen minutes I am held captive as she speaks of a goddess, half-animal, half-human, whose ample breasts were spliced from her body by a high god after he discovered her breastfeeding her human son.

"Not this particular *laumė*, though," she says with a chuckle. "As you can see, she's well blessed."

Before putting the figure to bed in its tapestry blanket, she smooths out the fabric for me to see. "*Laumės* were renowned for weaving, too, Grace, though it was my mother who wove this fine piece."

I pick it up and examine it closely. The design is made up of miniature menorah, embroidered in gold thread and interspersed with conch shells. "It's exquisite, Lilah. How clever your parents were."

Pride shines in her face and flecks of gold glint in her eyes. "Do you see the contradiction in this, Grace? A creature of myth, wrapped in an orthodox blanket. I'm not sure my mother would have approved, but despite the contradiction they go well together. You see, *laumės* would weave all kinds of objects, even people, and give them as gifts."

"People? How might one weave a person?"

She shakes her head, dismissing my doubt. "They find a way. But beware, they were also known to kidnap babies and raise them as their own and they could be vindictive towards disrespectful men."

The folktale is fascinating, but now it is my turn. She listens intently as I tell of the *coblynau*, the gnome-like creatures that haunt the slate mines of Wales. Father would speak of how men in the mines sacrificed morsels of their lunch to the *coblynau* in return for the promise that they would be kept safe whilst underground. Father's stories were the best, and his voice resonates loud in my ears as I relate his words.

This is something else Lilah and I have in common, though I did not realize it until today. We both knew the love of a father who enriched our young lives through story-telling.

Silverware gleaming, I return to my room in good spirits. Day is fading to evening, so I light the lamps before returning to the dressing table. The folded sheet of paper yawns open, in all likelihood waiting to be tucked back into bed, but as I pick it up I reel in shock. The word *Wherever* has company. I open the note wide and see that someone has added the words, *Remember for me, Grace.*

White noise fills my ears, invisible hands tighten around my throat. How can this be? I snatch the note and flee downstairs.

"Lilah, look." I thrust the paper towards her. She is elbow-deep in soapy water, so unable to take the trembling note from my hand. "Someone has written on the note. It says, *Remember for me, Grace.* Why, Lilah?" I slump down on a chair, the heat of my body still present on the wooden seat. "Who would do such a cruel thing?"

She dries her hands and takes the note from me, then dons her spectacles. "'Remember for me, Grace.'" She repeats the words, her voice soft with surprise.

"Why torment me like this?" I tear at my hair, the ghost of Mother tugging at my heart. Even in death she haunts me. I think back to last Sunday, when Jonathan and Eva visited. "Of course! It must have been Eva."

"Eva?"

"Yes, I caught her coming out of my bedroom as Helena and I were leaving Mother's room." I am close to tears. "But why would she do such a thing? Isn't it enough that she has inherited this house? Does she have to drive me insane, too?"

Lilah has paled. "Now don't go jumping to conclusions."

"But it has to be her. Mother could not have written it from the grave, and you saw for yourself that when I first found it only the word *Wherever* was written there."

She squints closely at the note, and her voice quakes when next she speaks: "I am loath to say it, Grace, but for all the world it looks to me like your handwriting." She holds the note in front of me and points. "See there...you write the letter *b* without closing the loop. Many a time I've struggled to decipher your writing on shopping lists."

I stare at the note, agog. What she says is true. But I have no memory of having written on it. I snatch it from her hand. "For goodness sake, Lilah, surely I'd remember if I'd written it. These past weeks have been stressful at times, I grant you, but I am not mad." Even as I say it I sense the uncertainty. It lurks in the pit of my stomach, curdled and rancid as sour milk.

The day is ruined. Perhaps Lilah's *laumė* has woven a spell on me, one which cannot be undone.

⊰ CHAPTER ⊱

VIII

THE FINAL THREE WEEKS IN VERMONT PASS BY IN A BUSY blur. My trunk is packed, paperwork complete, and the grandfather clock has already been shipped. The hall mourns its absence, the whole house is bereft of its comforting heartbeat. Though the clock has embarked on its return journey to Wales earlier than Lilah and I, it will arrive a month later. Without me being able to rewind it, I doubt it will notice how slowly time passes.

I close my eyes and try to imagine how the inside of the house in Wales might look. How many rooms will it have? What condition will it be in? All I have to go on is the painting of the exterior on the clock face, which suggests the house consists of three storeys—though I imagine there might also be a basement—a door with a columned porch, and eight windows to the front, the top two being arched and the one in the centre of the middle floor having its own small veranda, just like this house.

According to Jonathan, it has been looked after by a caretaker, but other than that has remained unoccupied. The furniture remains *in situ,* exactly as it was the day we left when I was little more than a baby. The fact that Father spent so much money ensuring the house remained habitable goes to prove just how attached he was to it and how he must have hoped to return one day.

The first thing I will do is find the right position for my clock. I hope and pray it survives the journey intact and does not suffer any damage. How tragic that would be.

In two days, I will follow in its footsteps to New York, ready to set sail the next day. My stomach lurches at the prospect, both with excitement and nerves. But today another matter weighs heavy on my mind, for I have decided to visit the grave of my parents one last time. It is right and proper that I say my farewell at their place of rest.

Since Mother's burial, I have put off going to the cemetery. My weekly walks to visit Father have ceased. There are several reasons for this: first of all, I dread seeing his headstone removed. Jonathan and I have agreed on Mother's epitaph, but it will be some time before the stone is engraved and ready to be refitted. Secondly, the thought of seeing freshly-dug earth makes me shiver. It creates an image of the physical reality of their situation, one I do not want to picture. Beneath a bed of warm grass, I was able to imagine Father at peace; a mound of soil might make me want to scratch at it with bare hands, dig them up and summon a necromancer to breathe new life into their lungs. But is that what I really want? To reignite Mother's torment and suffering?

Last of all, I have been reluctant to leave the house of late, so much so that I have not been anywhere since the week before Mother died. The thought of open spaces, people, horse-drawn carriages and those modern devil-wagons, capable of knocking a person to the ground before one sees them coming, terrifies me. Lilah worries that I am becoming agoraphobic and has offered to come with me, but this final farewell is something I must do alone.

I step out into dense fog, a grey blanket of disguise. At least it will render me less visible to the outside world. After three or four steps I stop, compelled to peer inside my purse and check that the key to the clock is safe, a compulsion I have acquired these past few days. But the clock is precious. I dread to think how it might feel if it arrived at its former home, only to discover it could not be resuscitated.

The compulsion to check on the key is nothing new. Since childhood I have been plagued by such rituals. They entrench themselves with ease, worm their way into my daily routines without me even noticing, but are far more difficult to dislodge. For example, whilst eating I cannot bear to have one type of food left alone on the plate. Each forkful must consist of a little of everything: a morsel of meat, a slice of carrot, a sliver of potato. Everything is considered, right down to the final mouthful.

Checking on the key is the latest in a long line of obsessive habits, but at least it is one I should be able to rid myself of once established in the new house. I will determine a safe place for the key, close to its parent, so that the two are never far from one another, and then I shall be free of the habit.

I look down at my feet as I cross the road and head for the park gates, relying instead on my sense of hearing to keep me safe. Thankfully, the park is devoid of people, the fog having held visitors at arm's length. It welcomes me, though. The maples that stand to attention on either side of the pathway have shed their leaves, creating a red carpet for me to walk along. Just as Clytemnestra welcomed her husband back from the Trojan War, a crimson path welcomes me back, though I hope it shall not end in murder as it did in the play. Vermont in the fall: it is one of the few things I shall miss, because her colour show is incomparable.

I hurry through the park and exit the far gate, walking a hundred yards or so along the pavement before crossing the road and heading for the cemetery. Its iron gates loom large, guarding the dead with solid uprights and spear-shaped finials. Its hinges warn its occupants of my approach as I push against them. In contrast to its foreboding entranceway, the cemetery is far more welcoming. No crimson walkway here. Instead, I find myself stepping on paths padded with pine needles, my footsteps hushed so as not to disturb those at rest.

My feet falter as I spy the mound of earth, the funeral flowers unkempt and wilted. Why did I not think to bring fresh? I make a mental note to remind Jonathan to do so soon. Thoughts churn and rage in my head, like the maelstrom of Atlantic Sea water I am soon to cross. I stand beside the grave and take deep breaths in an attempt to calm myself. The sky breaks through the barrier of grey to peep at me through a blue spyglass. Perhaps she is curious about what I have come to say, but unless she is a mind-reader she will glean no gossip from me.

Before I say my farewell, I need to confront Mother about the writing on the note. I have racked my brain over the past few days and still fail to make sense of it. There are several possible culprits, the most likely being Eva.

After all, she was seen coming out of my room and she appeared flustered when she saw Helena and me. The difficulty I have with this, though, is establishing her motive. Perhaps the enigmatic detective, Sherlock Holmes, whose exploits I have been devouring in *The Strand* could come up with one. I, however, cannot.

There is also the possibility that the culprit is Lilah, though I do not believe for one minute it is her. She is only a suspect due to the fact that she had access to the box. I am well aware that the handwriting matches my own, especially the letter "b", but someone who knew me well could easily have forged it.

If neither of these women are culpable, then there are only two conclusions: either I wrote it myself and have completely forgotten doing so, or Mother really did come back from the dead to haunt me. Which, I ask, is the more likely conclusion?

Despite putting all four options to Mother I am none the wiser, for she remains as silent as the grave in which she lies. Father also refuses to offer his opinion, which is out of character for him. As for the sky, which now bears a hole the size of a crater, all I can say is I am glad its head is clearer than mine.

I decide to change the subject and instead speak of my preparations for the journey, reassuring Father that his wish is to come true and Mother that, if by some act of God (or the Devil) she did indeed write the words on the note, then I will do my best to remember whatever it is she wants me to. It does not seem ridiculous, this talking to the dead. I have always considered a graveyard a good place to consider one's options.

A rook eyes me from the safety of the yew, its feathery trousers quivering in the breeze. *Kaah, kaah, kaah* it calls when it sees me watching. Its message translates to:

So you have found no answers, then.

I have stood long enough. The small of my back aches and the balls of my feet protest at being forced to wear heels, having been spoiled for too long in house slippers.

I bid my mother and father a final farewell, promising to keep them close in spirit if not in body, then, ignoring the strained sound my throat makes as it fights back the tears, I walk away with my head bowed low.

PART
TWO

⊰ CHAPTER ⊱

IX

Pembrokeshire, Wales, 1902

"HERE YOU GO, MISS." THE COACHMAN BRINGS THE horse to a standstill in front of a roofless circular building with an open doorway. Next to it stands a single-storey cottage, lime-washed pink, with a little door and one window. Both clearly long abandoned. Prickly gorse sprouts from the roof-space of the circular building, a deterrent to all living things, while the flesh-pink pores of the cottage seep patches of rain. The scent of salty air is rife: briny and green. Gulls circle overhead, screeching in amusement as Lilah and I step down from the coach, stiff as corpses.

"Now then," the coachman says, wringing his hands. "We'll have to make the rest of the journey on Shanks's pony, I'm afraid." He slaps the mare on the flank and beams.

"Shanks's pony?" I say, looking around for a small horse.

"Aye, your own two legs." He finds himself amusing, though I have no idea why. The first of many mistranslations, I assume. He mistakes my frown of confusion for sullenness. "But if you're not up to it, I can drive her round the back lane." He gestures towards the mare. "Just I thought you'd prefer to arrive by the front door, seen as it's your first impression, like. It's only a short walk."

He points in the distance towards an imposing stone house that stands a few hundred yards or so away. I recognize it as the house on the clock face, and my face relaxes.

Seen from this angle the harbour looks very different to how it appears in the painting, but the house itself is instantly recognizable as one and the same.

"Look, Lilah, there's Parrog House, our new home." I can hardly believe the words that tumble from my lips.

Lilah peers into the distance. "Can you believe it? I never thought we'd get here." She rubs the small of her back with balled fists, raises her chin to the heavens, and utters a small prayer. The mare whinnies an amen, which makes all three of us laugh.

The coachman ties the reins to a balustrade before walking around to the rear of the coach and eyeing the trunks.

"Just you wait here a minute while I nip across to The Ship Afloat to get some help."

To our left is an inn, its sign swinging in the breeze. He soon returns, accompanied by three men, all dressed in dark pants, woolly sweaters, and flat caps. One sucks on a pipe and studies me from beneath heavy eyebrows. His lips stutter, *p-p-p*, as they puff on the pipe-stem. The other men stare wide-eyed at the two strange women who have appeared in the harbour as if by magic. I get the distinct impression they are unused to seeing strangers and wonder how long it will take for us to feel at home. I smooth my skirts and wait for the men to make a move.

"Rightio then," the coachman says. "Two to a trunk, if you please, gentlemen."

All four shuffle off towards the rear, taking the faint scent of fish, horse, and tar with them, while Lilah and I reach into the coach and retrieve our hand luggage from the back seat. They heave our trunks up onto their shoulders and head off in the direction of the house.

I stand for a few moments, taking in the vista. Inland, rugged mountains dominate, while the crenellated roof of what appears to be a castle can be seen in the middle distance. I turn back around to face the estuary. Its mouth yawns wide, sleepy in the ebbing twilit tide. And beyond is the sea, with bobbing boats and buoys, and a horizon that defies the viewer to determine where water ends and sky begins. My shoulders drop and I turn to Lilah and say, "Lilah, I do believe we'll be happy here."

We trail behind the men like lost lambs, past the inn and a field of bleating sheep, their woolly outlines indistinct against the darkening sky, then along a narrow pathway, no more than three feet wide with hip-height stone walls either side. Little wonder the coachman would not have got the cart down it. The horse alone would have failed to navigate its narrowness, never mind the cart.

Thank goodness it is low tide, or we would be forced to climb the steps and take an even narrower path to Parrog House. Instead, we hoist our skirts and stumble across a short length of beach, our heels sinking in the damp sand. We have been here less than a few minutes but are already leaving our imprint.

"Here you go," the coachman says, nodding towards the house. "Parrog House. Careful of these steps now. They're pretty steep."

I pause at the front gate, allowing the men to go on ahead. The approach is so steep I have to strain my neck in order to view the house properly. It is magnificent. It towers over the harbour, well aware of its importance. Fifteen stone steps climb towards the path. The men wait for us at the front door, eager to relieve themselves of our luggage. My heart is pounding, for I cannot wait to see inside.

The key is concealed beneath a seagrass mat, as previously arranged with the caretaker. It crosses my mind that this must be a trusting place if access can be so easily gained. It takes longer than necessary for me to turn the key. The lock is stiff, reluctant to grant access to newcomers such as us, but eventually it gives and I stand back to allow the men to enter first.

"Hallway do?" one of them asks, and I nod, fumbling around in my purse and pulling out a few shillings with which to tip them.

"We'll not be taking no money from you, Miss," the pipe-smoker says, thrusting weather-worn hands deep in his pockets so that they cannot be tempted by my offer. "A favour's a favour; nothing more, nothing less." Now that he is free of his burden, he relights his pipe and puffs away. The pungent smell of tobacco competes with the earthier scents of old stone and camphor.

"Thank you. Thank you very much." I am unused to someone refusing a tip and feel myself flush.

"'Tis no bother."

The other two leave with a nod of their caps and the pipe-smoker casts his gaze around the hall and shivers.

"You might want to think about spending the night down at The Ship Afloat, till you get chance to warm the place up a bit. It'll be dark soon, and I'm sure there'll be room to spare at the inn." He takes a long drag, tilting his head back to reveal nicotine-stained nostrils. His words and froth of white hair seem biblical; the smoking less so.

"Thank you, perhaps we should consider it." A warm bed and a good meal sounds quite appealing, but first I must explore the house.

I pay the coachman and they leave.

Lilah slumps down on the second stair, exhausted by the long journey. Beneath her eyes sit two purple sacks, and her whole body sags as if someone has let out the air. Poor Lilah. I have not given enough consideration to our difference in age.

"That inn sounds tempting. What do you say?" She eyes me, hopefully.

"I must look around first, Lilah." I let out a squeal of excitement. "Let's light some lamps before the twilight robs us of the opportunity." It is only five-thirty, but already quite dark.

Somewhat reluctantly, she gets to her feet. I am already considering the grandfather clock and where it might reside. There is a perfect space in the hall, to the right of the staircase. It is not so different a spot to where it stood in the Vermont house, which should help it feel at home. I imagine it is where Mother and Father positioned it all those years ago; indeed, the wood floor appears a little darker and wears a few scratches, as if something large has been removed.

Lilah struggles to light the gas lamp on the wall beside the coat stand. It coughs and sputters, reluctant to wake up after such a long sleep, so instead we make do with candle stubs, our weary complexions softened by the warm glow. Elongated shadows follow us down the hall until we open the first door on the left and enter the front parlour. Items of furniture, draped in white sheets, stand silent as ghosts, and a black watermark along the chimney-breast does its utmost to depress me. But it will take more than a patch of mildew to dampen my spirits.

Lilah sniffs the air. "A few fires is all it needs," she says. "That'll dry the place out."

Alerted by her words, a gull squawks and rustles in the chimney, sending a torrent of soot into the hearth.

"We'll have to call the sweep in first," Lilah says. "Else we'll roast it alive, and we don't want to get off to a bad start, do we? Gulls are said to harbour the souls of old sailors, did you know? It's unlucky to harm one."

"How awful, Lilah." The thought of roasting a gull imbibed with the soul of a dead sailor makes me shudder. "We don't want to do that."

We are losing the light fast. By the time we pay a cursory visit to the remaining ground floor rooms there is more wax pooled in the holder than there is on the candle. Remembering the storm-lamp in the corner of the porch, I use what is left of the candle to light it and the hallway cheers somewhat.

"Just a quick peep upstairs, Lilah, then we'll see if the inn has a room for us, I promise." My enthusiasm refuses to be snuffed, despite the desperate look in her eyes.

"You go on up, I'll wait here." She leans a shoulder against the newel post, exhausted. Her pallor is blanched against her dark bonnet, her lips tinged grey.

"I'll be quick, then we'll get ourselves fed and watered, all right?"

I hoist my skirts and begin the ascent. Each tread protests against my footfall, the carpet is threadbare in parts and has worked loose of the rods like wrinkled skin on old ribs. I pause at the top, uncertain of whether to turn left or right. It is strange to think that the first two years of my life were spent living here. I have no recollection of having done so, but still I try to muster a sixth sense in order to determine which room might have belonged to me.

A huddle of furniture, shrouded in white sheets, awaits me in every room, rendering each the same as the next. Nothing remarkable; nothing to remind me of a past life, and to some degree I am grateful for the fact. A clean sweep is precisely what I need.

"Grace, if we don't hurry it'll be too dark to find our way to the inn." Lilah's voice carries up the stairs.

"Coming!"

On the landing, an arched window faces out to sea. Night has encroached on us these past few minutes and Venus winks at me from her low position in the western sky.

I see you, she seems to say. *All is well.*

CHAPTER

X

RM IN ARM, WE MAKE OUR WAY TOWARDS THE SHIP Afloat. The tide has ebbed somewhat since we arrived, but in the dark it is difficult to see where best to place one's feet on the sand. One by one, the stars pop out to watch as we stumble our way to the inn. We giggle like fools when one or other of us steps in a pool of seawater, and I have not felt this sense of abandon since childhood.

The closer we get to the inn, the easier our journey becomes, as a warm glow from the windows guides the way. We pause at the door, intimidated by the sound of raucous laughter spilling from within.

"You first," I say, nudging Lilah across the threshold and into the tiny entranceway. I have never been inside an inn before and doubt Lilah has either, so am filled with trepidation. To the left stands a door marked *Lounge*; to the right a door marked *Bar*.

"Which one?" Lilah asks, confirming my suspicions, and we chuckle again, drunk on the newness of our situation.

A sudden burst of laughter from the Bar helps make up our minds. Lilah pushes open the door to the Lounge and we step into a room with a welcoming fire that fogs Lilah's spectacles.

A distinguished gentleman sits in the far corner, smoking a cigar. A glass of whisky sits on the table in front of him. He raises his eyes from the newspaper and gives us a cursory nod. Apart from him, the Lounge is empty. No one serves behind the bar, but a brass bell sits on the counter next to a sign that reads: *Ring For Service.* I pick it up and tinkle it timidly.

"Give it here," Lilah says. "No one will hear that, not with the racket in there." She nods in the direction of the Bar before giving the bell a good shake.

Seconds later the landlady appears, still in mid-conversation with someone in the Bar. It is clear, both from her actions and the volume of conversation coming from the other room, that behind the serving area the rooms adjoin. She wears a tea-towel over one shoulder and a wicked grin.

"Cer o 'ma!" she shouts to someone on the other side. Neither Lilah or I have any idea what has been said, though of course I recognize it as Welsh. It has not crossed my mind until now that my inability to speak the native tongue might be an issue. Other than a few words and greetings, I speak none. I wish my parents had taught me; I am certain they were both fluent, though during our time in the States they hardly uttered a word of Welsh. I suppose they did not find it necessary.

The landlady turns to face us for the first time.

"What can I get you?" she says, assuming correctly that neither of us speak Welsh.

I stutter a little, suddenly anxious. "D-do you have any rooms available? Just for one night?"

She shakes her head and puffs her cheeks before blowing out the air, as if in doubt.

"The coachman earlier…he-he suggested you might."

She retrieves the towel from her shoulder and rubs vigorously at a glass. "The American ladies, soon to be occupants of Parrog House," she says, looking us over. If nothing else, my accent will have given us away. "And I suppose you'll want feeding, too?"

Lilah gives me a furtive glance before saying, "We've travelled all the way from—what's the place called again, Grace?"

"Liverpool."

"All the way from Liverpool, so I guess you might say we're pretty hungry."

It is unlike her to be so forthright, and I bite my lip to avert a smile. Perhaps we will have to spend our first night in Parrog House after all, with neither heat, light or food. My heart sinks a little, but is soon brightened when the landlady says, "So long as it's just the one night you're after, I think we can manage it. And dinner is served at seven o'clock on the dot. You can eat down here, in the Lounge. I'll lay the window table for you. Now, follow me and I'll show you to your room." It sounds as though Lilah and I are to share, but I am not concerned, in fact I shall be glad of the company.

She leads the way up a narrow set of stairs, and the smell of ale morphs into one of beeswax which is far more pleasant. Indeed, every stick of furniture is highly polished, and the limewashed walls are freshly coated.

Our room is at the far end of the corridor. "It'll be quieter for you here," she says. "Furthest away from the Bar." Though sparsely furnished, the room is warm and pleasant with clean white linen and fresh towels. The dressing table, though well-worn, is set with a jug and basin and a bowl of dried lavender.

"This will do nicely, thank you," I say.

"Good, good. Will you be wanting anything else?"

"No, thank you. We'll be down for supper at seven. We're both famished."

She nods, then adds, "And by the way, my name's Aelwen. I imagine we'll be seeing more of each other, seen as you'll be living in the village. Might as well be on first name terms, I suppose. You are?"

"Grace, Grace Morgan, and this is Lilah."

"Grace and Lilah; Lilah and Grace," she says, looking us over in turn. "I'll try to remember, though the old memory box isn't what it used to be." She taps her temple with a plump finger and takes her leave.

Over a simple meal of pan-fried sole, served with a tarragon sauce, boiled potatoes, and steamed seaweed, Lilah and I discuss our plans for the following day.

"Perhaps we should ask if she can recommend a chimney sweep, Grace. That'll need seeing to as soon as possible, or we won't be able to air the house." She raises her eyes in the direction of the landlady who busies herself behind the bar. She is humming a tune that I swear Father used to sing.

When she comes to take our plates, I say, "Could you possibly recommend a chimney sweep? We seem to have inherited a few squatters of the feathered variety at Parrog House."

"That'll be those pesky gulls. I can indeed, Siôn Jenkins. I'll send him 'round in the morning."

"That's most kind." I dab at the corner of my mouth with a napkin and turn my attention to dessert, unable to recall when last I felt so hungry.

A minute or so later she returns, armed with two steaming bowls of pudding, scented with apple and cinnamon, and a jug of custard.

"My guess is you're George Morgan's daughter, George and Marta?" She studies my face.

"I am." I shift in my seat, unsure of how much to divulge. Should I tell her my parents are dead?

"Thought as much. If the accent hadn't given you away, those sorrowful eyes would have. Got them off your mother, I see."

I am taken aback by her boldness and feel a little forlorn. It has been a long time since I have felt this happy, so to be told my eyes are sorrowful is disheartening.

"And you must be?" She addresses Lilah, taking in the plainness of her dress.

"My companion," I say, before Lilah has chance to answer. "Lilah has been with us since we moved to the States."

Lilah dismisses the comment and picks up a spoon, eager to tuck into dessert.

"I remember both your parents, your father in particular. He was a good sort. Am I right in assuming he's no longer with us?"

I glance down at the table.

"You are, and neither is Mother. She passed away recently."

"Well, my dear, I hope you'll settle here. It's where you belong, I suppose. Anyway, I'll leave you to finish your meal, that custard's growing a skin. Breakfast at eight?"

Before retiring, Lilah and I treat ourselves to a drop of port, feeling more and more drowsy with each sip. A chorus of male voices in the Bar perform a rendition of *Ar Hyd Y Nos*, the sound of their voices so lulling that Lilah's chin drops to her chest and she gives a little snore. The men need no musical accompaniment—their hearts are piano keys, their souls harp-strings. As they reach the climax, the hair on my arms stands on end and a shiver runs along my spine. I am moved to tears. But tears are short-lived, for no sooner is the song over than I hear them laughing and joking and bidding each other goodnight.

It is time for Lilah and me to turn in. I nudge her awake and off to bed we go, both of us exhausted but in good spirits.

XI

MY BREAKFAST OF PORRIDGE, SWEETENED WITH LOCAL honey, goes down in lumps. I cannot wait to see Parrog House in daylight and have no appetite for time-wasting. The weather, however, has other ideas. Overnight, a blanket of fog has staked its claim on the harbour, making it difficult to see anything from where we sit at the table in front of the window.

Lilah's appetite is not the least bit marred. She battles a plate of bacon and eggs and looks to be the winning combatant.

"Eat up, Grace," she says, pointing at my bowl with her fork. "You'll need your strength today if we are going to lick that old house into shape."

I think about her words and how she has become like a surrogate mother to me over the years and do my best to swallow a few more spoonfuls.

Aelwen appears and takes our plates, bringing a fresh pot of hot water to top up the teapot. "Siôn says he can call around mid-morning, sort those chimneys for you. And my daughter, Lowri, will be free once she's finished here. She can lend a hand, too, if you want."

"That's most kind. Another pair of hands won't go amiss, hey, Lilah?"

"Sounds good to me. We'll have our work cut out for us today and for many days to come, I reckon, but it'll be worth it in the end."

"Then I'll send her 'round later. She's a good girl, my Lowri, hard-working, like her mother." She chuckles and waddles off to the kitchen, balancing the dishes along her arm like a plate-spinning juggler.

Minutes later, we step out of the inn and into a world shrouded in mist. To my left, the row of whitewashed cottages are fast asleep, cocooned in grey blankets, but Parrog House is wide awake. It looms above the mist, refusing to be outdone by the weather.

Blood-red buoys, black-tipped like giant ladybugs, stand proud in the sea, while small fishing boats appear and disappear behind the mist, their chains chiming to alert us of their presence. I am reminded of the lines from Kipling's poem, *The Bell Buoy…*

> *There was never a priest to pray*
> *There was never a hand to toll,*
> *When they made me guard of the bay,*
> *And moored me over the shoal.*

An overwhelming feeling of déjà vu sends a shiver down my spine.

"You cold?" Lilah asks. "Make sure you put on a few more layers when you change into your work clothes, at least until we get those fires lit. You'll catch your death if you're not careful, 'specially with not much meat on those bones."

I nod in agreement, preferring her to think it is the cold that makes me shiver rather than the sense of having been here before.

We amble towards the house, past the field of sheep that bleat us good morning, and along the narrow pathway until we reach the place where the path ends and the beach begins. The tide is high, so it is necessary for us to climb the steps and take the narrower route towards home. But is it home? It does not feel like it yet; I hope and pray it will soon.

Inside the house we are met with profound silence. No ticking clock, no dripping water or creaking floorboards; the house holds its breath, as wary of us as we are of it.

"Now then, where shall we start?" Lilah says, already heading towards the kitchen at the back. Apart from the table and chairs, this room is devoid of white sheets. The wall on the right is dominated by a large dresser, stacked high with plates, cups, and dishes. It would likely have cost more to have such items shipped to America than to replace them, but the fact that they are here reminds me of just how much Father longed for home. Did my parents decide to leave Parrog House in a move-in state so that they might return on a whim? I imagine as I explore other rooms, the answer to this question will become more apparent.

The back wall of the kitchen overlooks a garden, which I see at a glance is woefully overgrown.

"Perhaps we should grow our own fruit and vegetables, Lilah. There's plenty of space out there, and it would be such a waste to give it over to borders and lawn. I'm sure we could find someone in the village who might be willing to lend a hand."

She clasps her hands together. "That would be wonderful, Grace. Imagine…our own vegetables, and with a sea view to the front of the house, I doubt we'd spend time sitting idle in the back in any case. Better to put the back garden to good use."

A cast-iron range nestles inside the chimney breast on the left wall, complete with twin ovens and two hotplates. Above it is mounted a drying rack on a pulley.

"I can't wait to get this beauty going." Lilah places her hands palm down on the hotplate, imagining its warmth, before rubbing them together. "Shouldn't be long if that landlady keeps her word and sends the sweep around."

"I got the impression you weren't keen on Aelwen, Lilah. Am I right?"

She sniffs and scratches her nose. "Can't put my finger on it, Grace. If I'm proven wrong, I'll apologize, but there's something about the woman. Anyway, never mind that, how about we start by removing the dust-sheets from the furniture? Do you want to go through the rooms together, or shall I do downstairs and you do up?"

"Yes, let's split up, it will be quicker that way." I am secretly glad Lilah has suggested this because I would prefer to explore upstairs on my own. Last night's visit was cursory and did nothing to satisfy my curiosity, nothing to reignite subconscious memories, if indeed there are any to reignite.

This morning, the view out to sea from the landing window is even more captivating than it was last night, despite the fog. Because it is high tide, no beach is visible, therefore the view ahead is one of infinite sea. To the right is the estuary, where dunes litter the shore. A ship, shrouded in mist, heads out to sea, just like the one on the clock face, and it isn't difficult to imagine us sailing away all those years ago. Did Father look back with a heavy heart?

Without the view of the beach to ground it, it is possible to imagine the house floats on water. Should it wish, the sea could scoop me up in its arms and carry me back to America, then all my plans would be thwarted. But I should not waste time daydreaming, there is much work to be done.

In an attempt to be methodical, I begin with the first room on the left, the one situated on the return of the landing. It overlooks the garden at the side of the house and the washhouse and is unremarkable. As I stare out of the window, a gull swoops down from above, sending a volley of loud squawks in my direction. Perhaps it is the same gull that nests in the chimney. It senses our presence and knows its days are numbered. I bundle up the dust-sheets and hurry out to the landing to fold them, not wishing to be admonished by the desperate gull.

I ignore the view from the veranda for the moment and instead enter the first room on the right. It is much larger than the previous room. It has a splendid view of the sea through a choice of two large bay windows, each blessed with deep sills, large enough to sit on. I sense instinctively that this would have been my parents' room. I would like to make it my own, but feel uncertain about whether it is the right thing to do. Were Jonathan and I conceived in this room? Is this where we spent the first months of our lives, or did we have a nanny and a nursery? Knowing Mother, the latter is far more likely. Perhaps if I redecorate and change the soft furnishing I can erase the memories of the past and make it feel like mine. I shall have Lilah make seat cushions for the windowsills so that I can sit and read or watch the comings and goings of the harbour in comfort. Or, better still, I shall take up sewing myself. A hobby will fill my time and stop me dwelling.

There are two further bedrooms on this floor: a smaller one overlooking the beach, and a larger one that overlooks the back garden. By the time I have visited each of the four bedrooms, I have amassed a substantial stack of dust-sheets.

Heaped at the top of the stairs, they threaten to topple at any moment. I will need to make several trips in order to carry them safely down. The sound of Lilah singing reaches me as she wanders from room to room.

"How are you doing?" I call, placing one hand on the newel post and the other on top of the sheet stack.

"I'll be washing till Christmas at this rate. Thank goodness there's a washhouse out back. We'll put the dust-sheets in there and I'll wash them a few at a time. It's not as if we plan on using them any time soon, is it?"

"Of course not, we're here to stay, Lilah." The sentiment excites me. "I'll bring these down a few at a time."

It dawns on me then that already my role is changing, and I am glad of it. Glad of the chance to lend a hand and lick this house into shape. How Lilah managed all the work on her own back in Vermont, as well as having to see to Mother, is beyond me, but I suppose it was simply a matter of keeping on top of things, whereas this is a project that will require a lot of work. I shall be eternally thankful to Father for the fact that he had kept the house maintained. Without a caretaker these past years I dread to think what state it might have been in.

It is as I return upstairs for the final bundle that I realize I have not yet explored the upper storey of the house. I turn in a circle on the landing. Why have I not discovered the door that leads to the upper storey?

My thoughts are interrupted by a knock at the front door. I peer over the banister as Lilah opens it to a man who can only be the chimney sweep, for he looks as if he has stepped straight out of a scene from *Oliver Twist*. His face is sooty and he carries an armful of brushes.

"*Shwmae*," he says, which I know means hello. "Siôn Jenkins, chimney sweep. Aelwen the Inn sent me." I remember then, how Father would speak of a habit Welsh folk have of referring to a person by their occupation rather than their name. He does not offer Lilah his hand, for it is covered in soot, just like the rest of him. What he does offer is a toothless grin that follows the curve of his moustache. Should I leave it to Lilah to show him around, or should I introduce myself? I decide to leave him in Lilah's capable hands. She is used to dealing with tradesmen and will call if she needs me. And besides, I need to locate the door to the upper storey.

It does not take long to discover. At the furthest end of the landing is a door, one concealed behind a tall, mirrored cabinet. My curiosity is ignited. Why has it been hidden?

My first attempt to move the cabinet results in nothing more than a wobble. The piece is solid oak and reluctant to divulge its secret. I am tempted to call for Lilah's assistance, but at the same time keen to see the upper storey alone, for so far I have found no evidence that any of the bedrooms on the first floor belonged to either me or Jonathan, therefore we must have been housed on the second floor, or at least Jonathan would have been, since he was that much older.

"Come on, Grace, put your back into it." I chide myself through clenched teeth before gripping the cabinet by the frame and inching it forward. In the mirror, my reflection grimaces back, red from exertion. I hope the beauty of this place will encourage me to get out and about more and improve my strength, for it is pathetic how weak I am for someone so young.

At last the thing moves sufficiently to allow me to access the door. I grip the handle and turn, disgruntled to find it locked. A rummage through the drawers offers up nothing more than a few old coins and a notepad, upon which a string of numbers has been scribbled, separated by commas.

"Grace." It is Lilah calling me. "The kettle's on. Come and have a cup of tea before we start cleaning."

I hesitate for a moment, uncertain whether or not to push the cabinet back against the door, but decide to leave it. Without the key I am unable to access it in any case so must be patient for the time being.

I return to the top of the stairs, bundle the last of the dustsheets into my arms, and head downstairs.

XII

DESPITE A THOROUGH SEARCH, THE KEY TO THE DOOR that leads to the upper storey is nowhere to be found. Lost, I assume, though it does nothing to diminish my curiosity. With some effort, we manage to move the cabinet away from the door and position it against an adjacent wall. Lilah and I agree there is likely a nursery up there, a few small bedrooms and a playroom, perhaps. We have been promised a visit from Ewan Bevan the caretaker in the morning. He sent a message via Aelwen's daughter Lowri, saying he would call at around nine. He is my last hope. Until then, I shall tap my toes and bite my nails to the quick.

As evening descends, it brings with it a fine mizzle, one which blurs the horizon, making it bleed into the sky. It is time to allocate rooms. Lilah's eyes light up when I suggest she takes the smaller of the front bedrooms.

Her face reddens and she wrings her hands which are sore from scrubbing.

"Really? Are you certain, Grace? I never would have imagined having a sea-view, not from my own bedroom."

We set about ransacking the laundry cupboard to make up the beds. The sheets, though clean, smell musty, but we have not had time to launder them. Lilah sprays them with a little lavender water which helps somewhat, then we settle down to a supper of bread, butter and cheese which Lowri kindly brought from the inn. Once Mr Bevan has been tomorrow, we will need to walk into town to buy some provisions. I am told it is no more than a ten-minute stroll up the hill from the harbour and vaguely recall passing through it in the carriage, though I did not realize at the time that it was our home-town.

We turn in early, both of us exhausted from the day's toil, though we are pleased to have made such a mark on the house in so little time. Before closing the curtains, I pause in front of the bedroom window and gaze out to sea. The tide has retreated, leaving behind the gift of seaweed as a blanket for the rocks. A half moon sits low in the sky, seeming to rest its swollen belly on the surface of the water. It casts a long beam of light in my direction, a shimmering silver path that I'm certain I could walk along, should I wish. If things do not work out here, perhaps I will go and live on the moon. How peaceful it would be.

Then, as I am about to pull the curtain, I see her. On the beach stands a young woman, facing out to sea. She sways a little, battling the wind. Her back is to me, so I cannot see her features, only her long dark hair which has escaped her bonnet and waves wild tendrils at the moon as though casting a spell. There is something familiar about her, a feeling of déjà vu, both because of her appearance and the way she looks out to sea. Where have I seen her before? I bite my lip in thought. Her attention remains on the horizon, perhaps if she turned this way it would come to me. Then I blink and she is gone.

Despite my reluctance to let in the cold, I throw open the window and lean out into the night air. The girl is nowhere to be seen. Not on the beach, nor on the pathway.

She has vanished.

Did I imagine it? I am certain I have seen her before, but where? Of course, the night of Mother's funeral, the night I dreamed of the sexton beetles. I remember waking up, soaked in sweat, and sensing someone standing in the corner of the room, watching. Lord in heaven, do not let the visitations start again. Not here, in this place of rebirth. I close the window, shutting out the wind that taunts me with its howl, and draw the curtains against the night sky. Tomorrow will dawn bright, I promise myself. The sun will reveal its gladsome face and douse my fears with its flames.

Blankets tucked beneath my chin, I am about to fall asleep when suddenly I remember where else I saw her. The girl in grey. It was during the voyage, the crossing from New

York to Liverpool. The third night, and the sea a tempest. The closed-in quarters below deck became unbearable, magnifying the ship's movement and making me terribly sick. I had to go up on deck, despite the storm, or else I feared I might faint.

I remember holding onto the railing as the sea roiled and gurgled, foamed and spewed huge waves in all directions. It seemed to mock me, mimicking my insides, and I was close to vomiting. Few passengers braved the night, just myself and a young man who stood in the far distance, closer to the main mast, heaving into the foam. And then she appeared, out of nowhere. Her back had been turned to me, but I remember her profile and the way her hair blew wild and unfettered. She struck a chord, for she did not seem to suffer as we did. She stood firm, holding the railing with one hand, the other relaxed at her side. At that moment, she raised her head and faced the moon which dominated the sky.

And even though her back was turned, I knew she was smiling.

Ewan Bevan knocks on the door at nine o'clock sharp. I am polishing the tiles in the hall and Lilah is in the washhouse, pummelling the sheets with a dolly, when he arrives. I stand and tuck stray locks of hair behind my ears, my face damp with perspiration.

"Ewan Bevan, caretaker," he says, holding out one hand for me to shake while removing his cap with the other. "I've come to see Miss Morgan."

I realize he thinks me a servant because of my appearance. "Pleased to meet you," I say, smoothing the front of my apron. "I am Grace Morgan. Do come in."

"I see," he says, stepping over the threshold. "My apologies."

"Come through to the parlour."

He does as I say. "So how are you settling in? Our little seaside harbour must come as a bit of a shock after the bright lights of Vermont, I imagine."

"First impressions are favourable, and this house feels—I don't know, like home, I guess." I smile and offer him a seat. "I must thank you for looking after it all these years. I dread to think what state it would be in if it had been left to its own devices." I am itching to ask about the key to the upper storey, but must first offer hospitality. "Can I get you some tea? We haven't made it to town yet, but at least we have a little milk, thanks to Aelwen from The Ship Afloat.

"No, no thank you, I shan't stay long. I'm sure you have enough to be getting on with without me taking up precious time. I just wanted to check everything was okay, that's all. I imagine you have a few questions, what with everything being unfamiliar."

"There is one thing…I don't suppose you have the key to the upper storey, do you? The door is locked and I've hunted high and low."

"Ooh, now. That was rather remiss of me. I should have left a note, explaining."

My heart swells with hope at his words.

"Come with me, I'll show you where it's kept."

I follow him back out to the hall where he gestures for me to go ahead of him up the stairs.

"My heartfelt condolences, Miss Morgan, on the death of your dear mother," he says as we ascend. "Your brother wrote and told me about it when he explained you would be coming to live at Parrog House."

"Thank you, Mr Bevan. I am rather hoping this place will mean a new start for me, and Lilah too, my—companion." I no longer think of Lilah as a maid, so will not refer to her as one.

"And I'm certain it will."

We have reached the landing, and I am breathless with anticipation.

"Your mother wanted that particular key to remain in the house at all times, that's why it wasn't on the bunch I left for you. I'm sorry, but I didn't think."

"It's quite all right. I'm delighted to know it isn't lost. I feared we might have to call a locksmith or else have someone remove the door."

He stops at the end of the landing and rubs his hands together. "You found the door, I see."

"Indeed. Tell me, Mr Bevan, why was the doorway blocked by a cupboard?"

He shakes his head. "It was your Mother's wish, and that's all I can tell you. I have checked up there on occasion, lit the odd fire during winter to air the place, but that's about it." He turns to the cabinet, feeling beneath the bottom drawer, where legs meet base. "Now then, place your hand here."

"Is this where the key is hidden?" I ask, feeling about with my fingers.

He hesitates. "It is. Again, it was your mother's wish, in fact she expressed it vehemently, but your guess as to her reasoning is as good as mine, I'm afraid." He glances sideways at me, sheepishly.

"Ah, I think I have it." My fingers have struck a metal object, long and thin, which I assume must be the key. It is pinned beneath the cabinet by a length of string. As I tug, something sharp pierces my finger and I cry out. The finger comes away bloody.

"That damn splinter. I should have warned you. It's happened to me a few times," Mr Bevan says, retrieving a clean handkerchief from his coat pocket and passing it to me.

"It's all right. Now that I'm living here there will be no need to hide the key, so no more injuries, hey? I'd better go and wash this finger." The truth is, I wish to examine the upper storey of the house alone, so now that I am in possession of the key my injured finger is a good excuse to return downstairs.

The sound of Lilah singing can be heard from the hall. I am pleased she is happy. Having uprooted her from Vermont, I feel responsible for her welfare. We follow the sound of her voice to the kitchen.

"You managed to get the range going I see. Not easy; she's a stubborn old devil at times. It all depends on which way the wind's blowing," Mr Bevan says.

"You're not wrong there," Lilah says, arms folded in front of her. "She fought me with everything she had. Little did she know this old Lithuanian has magic right here in these hands." She holds them up, as if expecting us to feel their power.

I introduce them to one another before plunging my own hand into the sink.

"Oy, what you gone and done now?" Lilah says when she sees the blood.

"It's nothing, just a scratch."

Mr Bevan turns to Lilah and says, "Would you like me to give you a little tour of the house and garden? I can point out some of its quirks and foibles and hopefully provide you with some tips."

"What a good idea," I say before Lilah has chance to reply. "We're having terrible trouble with the gas lamps. They don't seem to like us at all. They spit and hiss as soon as we approach." I dry my hands in a towel and tear a strip of linen with which to wrap the wound. "You two go ahead, while I see to this."

My fingers fumble with the lock. The door to the upper storey creaks open. In front of me a narrow staircase curves then disappears into darkness. My shadow accompanies me as I climb, lantern in hand. The last few treads at the curve of the stairs are treacherous: small steps that narrow to a point. They are made for tiny feet, not mine.

I pause at the top to catch my breath. The silence is overwhelming. I feel as if I have stepped back in time and entered another world, one which exists just for me. A corridor stretches ahead, a corridor flanked by dark walls that seem to lean in, and I am surprised to discover no window at the end of the corridor. That would be the side of the house, I realize, where the washhouse stands. I raise the lantern and peer ahead. My footsteps echo on bare floorboards, each step a hollow thud. Wall lamps are dotted here and there, but I have brought no means of lighting them, therefore the lantern I carry must suffice. I take a deep breath before deciding which room to enter first. The furthest one on the right, and from there I shall work backwards.

The door gives and I squint a little, expecting a burst of sunlight, but there is none. The room is as dark as the corridor. The window is shuttered. To protect against storm damage, or prying eyes? It must be the former; no one would be able to see in from outside at this height.

The shutter catch is stiff. It takes some time before I am able to release it, but as soon as I do the sun stretches its long arms into the room, offering it up for inspection. A playroom of sorts, judging by the rocking horse that sits inert and downcast in the corner. I scan the room. The wallpaper, though wearing a few damp patches, is exquisite. A block printed woodland scene in hues of green and purple depicts an abundance of trees and deer that graze the grass or nibble on tree fruits. My fingers trace the flock, outlining the flora and fauna. It summons to mind the Grimm Brother's story, *Snow White,* with its woodland setting, poisoned apple, and glass coffin. I close my eyes and picture the opening scene: a queen who sits at the window during a snowfall, sewing. How easily I could fit the role. Once the seat cushions are made for the windows downstairs, I can sew to my heart's content while watching the coming and going of the harbour. I hope not to prick my finger, though. This house must remain free of curses.

A bookcase stands against one of the walls, filled with delights such as Kingsley's *The Water Babies,* Mark Twain's *The Adventures of Tom Sawyer,* as well as a stack of children's magazines with the title *Good Words for the Young.* How sad that Jonathan never got to take them with him to America. I recall how precious my favourite books were to me as a child, how I would pour over them time and time again. Books such as my collection of *Grimm's Fairy Tales,* Susan Coolidge's series *What Katy Did,* and, of course, Lewis Carroll's *Alice's Adventures in Wonderland,* the like of which I have not read since.

I kneel on the floor, browsing the contents of the bottom shelf, surprised to find copies of *Little Women* and *Marjorie's Quest* among them. They must have belonged to Mother. No doubt she was keeping them for when I grew up.

How much time did I spend in here as a child? Very little I imagine, since I was just a baby when we left. I glance around the room, eager to spot something that might have belonged to me, but apart from a doll that wears a forlorn expression and sits alone on the mantelpiece, there is nothing to suggest my presence. I pick her up. A soft body, stuffed with cloth, that groans a little when I squeeze it, and a china face. I set the lantern down on the mantelpiece and hold her close to the light. She wears a gown of violet silk, faded in parts, though meticulously sewn. The glaze on her face has cracked. A roadmap of fine, dark veins covers the surface. Worse still, the back of her head is smashed. Two of my fingers disappear inside the doll's skull, sensing the emptiness. Painted eyes watch me, judging my reaction, and for the briefest of moments I swear my fingers turn warm and damp, as if they have found brain matter. Enough! I replace her on the mantelpiece and take a step back.

Surely this doll could not have belonged to me? It had to have been Mother's. No two-year-old would be given such a fragile gift. Unless it was me who broke it. I step forward again, admonishing myself for being frightened by a doll.

"My name is Grace," I say, writing the letters in the dust on the mantel next to her. "Perhaps when I next visit, you'll tell me yours."

The rest of the upper storey consists of three further bedrooms: one next to the playroom which overlooks the beach, and another at the back of the house, while the furthest bedroom on the left overlooks the garden at the side. In each room the window shutters are closed, as if it is in mourning, and a bare bedstead and an empty wardrobe are the only contents.

The room at the back of the house is furnished with a single bedstead and a mahogany crib, padded with pale blue velvet. The bed for a nanny; the crib for a baby. It is strange to imagine myself sleeping in here as a young child, and Jonathan before me, no doubt.

Placing the lantern beside the crib, I run a hand over the velvet, enjoying the feel of the nap: smooth in one direction; prickly in the other. The wooden edge bears tiny tooth marks, and as I examine them, saliva floods my mouth. I have a vague recollection of sinking my teeth into the wood. Is it possible to recall something from such a young age? It is likely I was cutting my teeth and enjoyed the sensation of solid wood against soft gum.

The words on Mother's note spring to mind: *Remember for me, Grace.* The puzzle as to who wrote them will never be solved, but is this what Mother meant? Was it her way of expressing her desire for me to move here and relive the past, or did she mean something else?

Lilah's voice carries from the back garden where she is deep in conversation with Mr Bevan. She talks with her hands as well as her mouth. I watch them both from the nursery window, prising it open a little to catch her words.

"Carrots, potatoes, onions, what a delight it would be to grow them right here." She waves an arm over an expanse of long grass, flattened by the damp air. A sorry sight, I must say. It will take some work to lick into shape, but yet again I am cheered by her optimism.

"Now's probably not the best time of year to start a vegetable patch, but come spring it'll be a different matter. I could lend a hand if you like," Mr Bevan says. "Gotta be aware of sodium levels here. The sea'll suck the moisture out good as look at 'em. She's a thirsty devil, despite having all that water."

He laughs and Lilah smiles back, and I think to myself how suited they look: similar age, similar in height and stamp, both erring on the plump side. But it is more than that, they seem relaxed in each other's company, despite having just met.

Why has Lilah never married? And why have I never thought to ask? Was it simply being in service that put her off, or is there another reason?

As if she hears my thoughts, she looks up and waves, her face flushed. We have been here two days and already she appears to have settled. I wish I felt the same. I am desperate to make a fresh start, desperate to escape the morbid thoughts that have dominated my youth, but still there is something I cannot shake off. A sense of impending doom that refuses to leave my side no matter how hard I push it away.

"What have you discovered up there, Grace?" she calls. "Anything of interest?"

"It is just as you thought, Lilah. A few bedrooms, a nursery, and a playroom."

"Listen, I'd best be off," Mr Bevan says. "I'm sure you ladies have enough to be getting on with."

"I'll be right down," I call, before closing the window and heading back downstairs.

❦ CHAPTER ❦
XIII

"SHALL WE CLIMB THE HILL OR GO BY THE LONGER estuary route?" Lilah asks as we don our coats and prepare for town.

"So we have a choice?"

"According to Mr Bevan, we either head right, up the hill from The Ship Afloat, or we continue past the estuary and onto a woodland path. From there, the town is just a short climb, but the route is longer and more scenic."

I pause for a moment, considering both options. "Longer route up and shorter down. Our baskets will be full when we return, no doubt, so we're better off taking in the view while we have nothing to carry."

We pass the inn and the roofless circular building we spotted on our arrival—a disused limekiln no doubt—before bearing left and continuing along the coastal path. A lone ferryman waits for customers in his little boat and turns in our direction as we pass, raising his cap and nodding when he sees we do not intend to cross.

In the silt sits a larger vessel, complete with cargo, which is in the process of being unloaded onto a horse and cart. It has garnered a few spectators: boys and girls who sit on the seawall, swinging their legs and enjoying the entertainment provided by the poor horses that are knee-deep in sludge.

Towering over the town is the castle. From where we stand, its south-eastern tower is visible, along with its crenelated rooftop. I vow silently to discover more about its history. We had nothing like it in Vermont, castles belonged to the land of myth, and I am keen to discover the history of this my place of heritage.

The wind whips our skin raw and does its utmost to remove our bonnets, but soon the woodland trees offer some protection from its merciless bite.

"You can handle the money, Grace," Lilah says, handing me the purse. "It'll take some time before I'm used to this pounds and shilling nonsense."

"Me, too. I guess we'll need some help for a while."

The hill is steep, and what with the wind fighting us all the way, both Lilah and I are breathless by the time we reach the top.

Town consists of a long main street with another steeper street running perpendicular to it. On the street beneath the castle is a church, built of similar stone. From the church tower, a weathercock eyes our approach. It faces north, towards the mountains.

Several hotels and hostelries vie for attention among premises offering professional services such as a physician and a lawyer. But what Lilah and I seek today is far more basic. Health and wealth can wait, sustenance cannot.

"Do they have hardware stores in Wales, Grace? We need to stock up on candles, carbolic, as well as buckets and whatnot."

"I guess. How about we start at the furthest end and work back?"

A blend of nerves and excitement dance in my stomach as Lilah and I browse the wares. The brands are unfamiliar, Wright's Coal Tar Soap and Bird's Custard Powder, but most products are basically the same as in Vermont. Not that I went shopping for groceries back home. Such things were Lilah's domain, though I must say, the experience is enlightening to some degree, especially with having to convert shillings to dollars in my head.

Each store we visit offers something new, something unfamiliar, and I am glad. Repetition destroys the soul, I believe.

In each and every store we are greeted warmly, but I am also profoundly aware of how different our accents are to those of our new neighbours. On a few occasions I am asked to repeat myself, and find it necessary to do likewise, for the Welsh accent is difficult to understand at times. They speak so quickly. What is more, it seems that for the majority of people, Welsh is their first spoken language. Without Lilah by my side I would feel like an alien in this new world.

Our baskets are soon laden with groceries, so we arrange delivery from several stores, including the butcher and grocer. In each shop I am questioned about my background and awarded anecdotes about my mother and father. It seems that most stories have been in the same family for generations. "I knew your father well, a real gentleman, he was," is a common sentiment that pleases me, but I am also greeted with the words, "Your poor mother, how she suffered," from the fishmonger, followed by, "Still, she's at peace now." I cannot help but feel uncomfortable, especially when he adds, "You remind me of her, you know." It will take some time to adjust to the familiarity the Welsh seem to adopt without so much as the bat of an eye.

"Don't let it bother you, Grace," Lilah says as we follow our noses and head towards the bakery. "I'm sure he was only being friendly. Not everyone is as reserved as you. Some folk mind their manners, others mind their tongues, and then there are those who say the first thing that pops into their heads."

"Of course you're right, but it hurts to think that Mother was pitied, Lilah, and the way he looked at me. He said I reminded him of her, but we were not alike, at least not in appearance, were we?"

"Your mother was a good-looking woman, as are you. Sometimes, when people say we remind them of someone they refer to our mannerisms rather than our looks, and besides, you're your own person, so take no notice."

She squeezes my hand. "Look, there's a draper's shop. How about we take a look? You want to refresh some of the soft furnishings, don't you?

We have reached the crossroads, and I peer in the direction in which she points. Above the shop, a purple awning emblazoned with the words, *Ffabrigau pili pala,* flaps gently in the breeze making the butterfly printed thereon dance, as if it attempts to escape. *Pili pala,* the Welsh word for butterfly. I had forgotten until now, but the syllables pop on my lips as I repeat it, "Pi-li-pa-la." I have a vague memory of singing a song about a butterfly as a young child and linking my thumbs whilst flapping my winged fingers. The memory, co-cooned for so long, has hatched.

The fishmonger's words are forgotten as I browse the window display where a variety of autumnal-toned fabrics drape from the reveal, providing an elegant backdrop to an assortment of plump cushions, stacked along the deep sill. In front of the display is a tome of wallpaper samples. I nudge Lilah. "Let's go inside, shall we? I would like my bedroom redecorated as soon as possible."

Our entrance is announced by a tinkling bell which alerts the assistant to our presence.

"Bore da," he says. *"Mae'n oer heddiw."* He shivers and rubs his hands together, so I take it he means the weather is cold.

"I'm afraid neither of us speak Welsh."

"Ah, sorry, sorry. How can I help?" His face is flushed, and he tweaks his moustache as he drinks in my appearance. "You wouldn't be Grace Morgan, would you? George and Marta's daughter?"

I glance at Lilah before replying. It is apparent that from my one spoken sentence he has determined my identity. "One and the same."

"Ah, welcome, welcome. I hear you've taken up residence at Parrog House. Come home at last, *Bach.*" He smiles warmly. "I imagine there'll be a lot to do in that house after all these years, mind you. An empty house soon lets its owner know when it feels neglected."

"You're right." I gaze around the room, eager to change the subject. "I'd like the main bedroom redecorated to begin with. Do you offer a full service?"

"We do indeed. Wallpaper, soft-furnishings, you name it. My wife's the seamstress, and my son's the decorator. I used to do it myself, but these old bones don't like ladders nowa-days." He slaps his thighs as if to punish them for letting him down. "Now then, what did you have in mind?

⚜

"Why don't you let them take care of the bedroom, then you can help make some items for the rest of the house?" Lilah says as we take the short route back to Parrog House.

"You're right, though I really would like to take up sewing. It will give me something to do, but now is not the time to learn a new skill. There are more pressing issues."

My basket digs into the crook of my elbow, so I swap it to my left arm. The fierce north wind has delivered a rain cloud that hangs right above Parrog House. I am certain it waits for us, no doubt intending to soak us to the skin. But I will not allow a little rain to dampen my spirits. The trip to town has been a success, and at least we have introduced ourselves to some of the locals. I have always refrained from making new acquaintances. Father called me shy; Mother called me petulant, though she hardly set a good example when it came to socializing.

"Penny for them," Lilah says, jolting me back to the present.

"It's nothing. I was just thinking about which colour to choose for the bedroom."

"Hmm, not sure I'm buying it, Grace." Lilah always senses when I am not telling the truth.

"Oh, I don't know. I hope I can make new friends here, Lilah, that's all. You know how difficult I find it to trust people, but there are times when I wish…"

"Go on, say it. There are times you wish you were more like your father and not your mother. Am I right? That fishmonger got to you, didn't he?"

"I guess, a little." We have reached the gate and, just as I suspected, the heavens open. "Race you to the door!" I take off, giggling, leaving Lilah to wobble her way up the path.

"Oy, this loaf will turn to mush," she says, protecting the basket with her free arm.

I hold the front door wide to allow her to pass through, and she grins as she shakes off her coat. "Kettle on. The smell of this loaf's been taunting me all the way home."

We hurry to the kitchen and I unpack the groceries, while Lilah makes tea and butters thick hunks of bread and tops them with strawberry jelly.

"Blue," I say, placing apples in a bowl.

"Pardon me?"

"I've decided the bedroom will be blue. I want to bring the sea and sky indoors. Make it feel like one whole space."

Lilah nods, more interested in the bread and jelly. She takes the jar in her hand and spreads its contents on another slice of buttered bread. "Jam," she says, swiping a stray red blob from her chin.

"Hmm?"

She holds the jar in front of me and gives it a little shake. "It's jam, not jelly. Suppose we'll have to speak like the natives if we want to be accepted round here. What d'you call those butterflies again?"

"Pili pala."

"Kind of like the sound their wings make, I suppose. Like pitter patter, but muted." She flaps her free hand and grins.

I envy her cheerful disposition. "Do you think we can change, Lilah? Do we have to be the person we've always been, or can we force ourselves to be something different… someone different?"

"Sure, we can change. We just have to want it enough, it's as simple as that."

"I guess so. At least, I hope so." I vow to myself right then that I shall do my very best to become the person I want to be, not the person I feel I have been coerced into becoming these past few years.

"You haven't seen the second storey yet. Would you like to?"

"Of course, let me see to the dishes and I'll be right up."

"I'll change out of these damp clothes, Lilah, and you should do the same. Call me when you're ready."

❧ ❧

"I wonder why Mother insisted on the door being blocked by a cupboard and the key hidden, Lilah? Mr Bevan said she wanted the key to remain in the house at all times, despite it being hidden. It doesn't make sense."

"Hidden? You never said." She scratches her head in bewilderment.

I slide open the drawer and retrieve the key. "Yes. Remember my bleeding finger? The key was pinned to the underside of the cabinet and my finger caught on a splinter of wood."

As I go to close the drawer, the cream notepaper with the list of numbers catches my attention. I slip it into my pocket, determined to try to make some kind of meaning out of the scribbles at some point in the future.

Once again, the lantern leads the way up the stairs. "Careful there, Lilah, the treads are very narrow on the bend."

"I can see that. I don't think I'll be coming up here very often. It can be your domain."

"But you'll help me turn the playroom into a sewing room, won't you? It will be grand."

"No doubt you'll rope me in, but once it's sorted up here I'll leave you in peace. These old knees aren't keen on narrow stairs."

The rooms welcome us with shadows and dim pools of daylight, and I am glad I did not close the shutters on the previous occasion. "Come and look." I beckon Lilah towards the bay window of the playroom and point towards the sea. "With this view I'm not sure how much sewing I'll get done."

She rests her chin in her hands and takes in the vista before gazing around the room. "Oh, Grace, it's strange to imagine you here as a young child. Makes me feel quite emotional."

The doll eyes us from the mantelpiece, her pallor grey and her demeanour forlorn. I wander over and pick her up. "I think I'll start by making her a new outfit. This dress was once exquisite, but now it's a little moth-eaten," I say, stroking the silk. "And her head is smashed at the back. I wonder if there's any way it can be mended?"

"Well, I guess if you can find the missing pieces you might stand a chance. Other than that, the only thing I can think of is to stuff her head with straw or such like and papier-mâché over the top. Perhaps we'll have a go one day. It'd be a shame to leave her like that, especially when she likely belonged to you, Grace."

"Do you think so? I imagined she belonged to Mother."

She shakes her head. "Maybe. I wouldn't like to say."

⊱ ⊰

It is as I am undressing for bed that I remember the note in my pocket. There is something familiar about the paper. It is impossible to decipher the handwriting, since it is just a few lines of numerals. Of course! The silver box containing the feather, shell and the note written in Mother's hand. The paper remains folded in half, its wings reminding me of the butterfly earlier in the day. If I am not mistaken the paper is exactly the same. I smooth out both sheets and lay them side by side. A perfect match, both in tone and size, and the thickness of the paper is identical. It can only mean one thing: Mother wrote the word *Wherever* on the note whilst living here, unless she found an identical notebook in Vermont and that is unlikely. I examine it more closely. The ink, too, is identical. So what do the numbers mean? Are they part of the puzzle, or am I reading too much into it?

⊰ CHAPTER ⊱

XIV

RAIN HAS FALLEN INCESSANTLY THIS LAST WEEK, BOTH day and night. Lilah and I have kept ourselves busy with household chores, and Parrog House feels fresh and clean, but I am desperate for the weather to improve. I have not yet had chance to explore the harbour properly, or walk the cliff path, both of which I am eager to do. I even bought myself a pair of Wellington boots in town yesterday. All the locals wear them. They do not stand on ceremony when it comes to dress code here, and living in this environment I can see why.

This morning I sense the change before opening my eyes. For the first time in a week, the sunlight granted through the closed curtains is sufficient to penetrate as far as the retina. And there are further clues that the weather has improved. The constant drum of rain against window panes and the gush of water from the gutters has been replaced by the cry of gulls as they celebrate the ceasefire. They trill and whine in quick succession, and are joined by a rhythmic but distant tap, as if someone is hammering on wood.

I rub my eyes and peer at the clock beside the bed: eight fifteen, time to get up, but I am still tired. All night long the sound of barking kept me awake: sometimes an aggressive growl, sometimes the howl of a wolf. I did not dream it, I am certain. I hope it will not become a regular occurrence.

Lilah is preparing breakfast. The delicious aroma of griddled pancakes tickles my tastebuds and provides enough of an incentive to encourage me to wash and dress.

Before going downstairs, I throw back the curtains, open the window, and gaze towards the harbour. The tide is retreating, the dark sand beginning to turn a paler shade close to the sea wall in front of the house. A glorious morning for a walk, if I can summon the energy after last night's disrupted sleep.

Lilah stands with her back to me, drizzling honey on top of the pancake stack before removing a plate of bacon from the oven. "Sleep well?" Before I can answer she turns to face me. "Oh dear," she says, "not by the look of those eyes."

"Did you not hear it?"

"Hear what?"

"The dog…or dogs, I should say. I'm certain there was more than one. Barking, barking, all night long. I hardly slept a wink."

She tuts and shakes her head. "I must be going deaf in my old age. Didn't hear a sound. As a matter of fact, last night was the best sleep I've had all week."

"Lucky you." I heap pancakes onto my plate but decline the bacon. "After breakfast, I'm going to take a walk. See if some fresh air will wake me up."

"You go ahead. It'll do you the world of good, but don't forget the draper is coming at noon. You'll be wanting to look at those samples."

"Of course. Thank you for reminding me."

I do believe I have never looked less glamorous in my whole life. Dressed in a heavy woollen brown skirt and a waxed canvas cape that hangs loose on my slender frame, I appear every bit the plain spinster. At the front door, I pull on the Wellington boots, choosing to ignore the chastisement the hallway mirror wishes to issue, and head outdoors.

The crisp sea air is tinged with the sulphurous odour of seaweed, and I inhale deep into my lungs several times before starting down the path, past the sea wall, and onto the beach. Instead of turning right towards The Ship Afloat, I turn left and head towards the cliff path, scrambling over slippery rocks as I go. A sense of wild abandon quickens my step and I have the sudden urge to throw off my bonnet, lift my arms high, and twirl on the sand. I take a tentative look around to see if anyone might be watching, but the beach is empty.

About to twirl, I spy in the distance a boat, or at least the shell of one. It is moored to a little jetty in front of a rocky bay, and behind it is a boat shed. I stand still and listen. The repetitive sound of hammering comes from that direction. The same sound I remember hearing when I first woke. Not wishing to engage in conversation, I am momentarily tempted to change direction, but if I head towards the harbour instead I am certain to meet at least one neighbour. The thought persuades me to continue along my intended path. For now, I swallow the urge to spin on the sand, just in case I am visible to whoever is fixing the boat.

The shipwright kneels in the hull, his back to me. He hammers away, oblivious of my presence. With any luck, if I sneak around the back and onto the cliff path, I can avoid him altogether.

❧ ❧

The climb to the top of the cliff is not without its challenges. A week of rain has rendered the rocks as slippery as memories, and I am ankle-deep in mud for much of the climb, but the view from the top is breathtaking. The wind is fierce. It is impossible to stand upright without widening my stance and digging in my heels, and the cliff edge, though terrifying, also has a magnetic pull that dares me to inch closer. A wild hedge of prickly gorse does its best to deter the walker from straying too close to the edge, and a squabble of gulls screech in warning above my head. Why does an element of danger make an experience all the more thrilling?

I spy an island in the distance and wonder if it might be possible to visit by boat. Perhaps the shipwright I passed earlier might know. Maybe he offers boat trips. As if I would ever be audacious enough to ask such a thing. The fresh air has gone to my head and made me quite mad.

Down below, the sea pounds the rocks, sending great plumes of spray into the atmosphere. The sea's majesty cannot be outdone. She is mistress to the moon—the two are joined at the hip. Now and then a particularly powerful wave hits, and I stand and watch, counting each one as it rolls in, determined to validate the myth that the seventh wave is the most powerful.

I place my hands against my cheeks, feeling the heat radiate from my skin. If the mirror in the hallway could see me now it might apologize for the sullen remark it made earlier, for I am certain I look the picture of health. And I feel it, too. I am energised beyond belief. This place is where I am meant to be. Little wonder Father hearkened after it his whole life. I turn my face skyward and close my eyes. *Can you see me, Father? I have come home.*

�⚯

When I scrambled up the cliff path earlier, little did I consider how difficult it would be to make my way back down, and worse still is the fact that I can see the shipwright watching me. He stands beside the boat, hands on hips, and stares as if I am some kind of trapeze artist, sent to entertain him. Now my face burns bright with embarrassment, not exertion. How dare he stand there gawping? Could he not at least show some respect and either offer assistance or turn away?

My heart pounds and my legs tremble, and I am forced to use both hands and feet to scramble down the next crop of rocks. My fingernails are caked in mud, and I am sweating profusely despite the bitter wind. Were it not for the fact that he continues to watch, I would take my time and determine the best footholds, but his avid attention makes me feel even more vulnerable. I am tempted to give him a piece of my mind once I reach the bottom, though I know I will not. In all likelihood, I will hurry on by and pretend he does not exist. Instead, I hold an accusatory conversation with him in my head, one which is safe and secret but nevertheless satisfying.

A thicket of gorse temporarily hides me from view as I grow closer to the foot of the path. I am tempted to remain huddled here and wait for him to go home. He might think me an apparition, a figment of his imagination, like a witch from *Macbeth*. But the man from the draper's is due, so I cannot be late, and I also need time to wash and change out of these dirty clothes.

As I round the corner and step down from the final rock, I see him standing there. He has not moved a muscle.

"Thought for a minute you might need some help," he says, grinning as I draw close.

I am lost for words, biting my tongue to quell the outburst that waits at its tip. "I am perfectly fine," I say, avoiding his gaze.

"Nice accent. Grace Morgan, I presume. I heard you'd arrived."

I take a deep breath. The town is full of gossipmongers, it seems. Just then, a Welsh Collie jumps out of the boat, ears pricked and tongue lolling. When it sees the man talking to me it bounds over and runs in a circle as though rounding sheep, then it yaps, loud and sharp.

"Yours, I assume?" I say in a harsh tone.

"Here, Bran." He calls the dog to heel, and it obeys immediately.

It seems I have the upper hand. A perfect opportunity for revenge, I think. "Does it bark at night? I hardly slept a wink last night, thanks to some hound."

My words are sharp, sharper than necessary, but I am still smarting.

His body stiffens, then he bends and ruffles the fur on the dog's chest so that I cannot see his face. "Just the one dog?" He straightens and looks at me. Now I am closer, I see that he is scarred. The skin around his left eye is shrivelled, as though burned. The eye itself stares vacantly. I glance down at my feet.

"Do you have more than one?"

He tugs at the lapels of his jacket and tilts his head to one side, fixing me with his good eye.

"Old Bran here, he never barks at night. Not unless an intruder is in the vicinity." The word *intruder* is emphasized, and I cannot help but wonder if he implies I am the intruder, an outsider, all the way from America. I should not have underestimated his loyalty to the dog. His expression is solemn, his frown deep, and I find myself regretting the words I spoke in haste.

"More than one, I guess. It sounded like a pack." My voice sounds far less confident than it did a moment ago.

He chews his bottom lip in contemplation and nods slowly. "That would be The Hounds of Annwn you heard, then. 'Tis the right time of year."

"Hounds of Annwn? My manner is haughty.

"That's right. But if the bark was loud you needn't worry. It's when you hear a soft bark you should pay heed. Works in reverse, see."

I screw up my face. His unseeing eye seems to gaze right through me, as if it focuses somewhere in the distance, but his good eye pierces my brain as though able to read my thoughts. I do not like this man.

"I must be off." I turn away from him and take a few steps in the direction of home, but he has not finished with me.

"The hounds foretell of death to anyone who hears them, you know, but like I say, if the bark was loud it means they're far away so are most likely on the hunt for someone other than the likes of you."

I turn back around, fists clenched tight. "Are you trying to frighten me? Because if that is the case I consider it a pretty mean act."

He laughs then, but the skin around his blind eye is unable to move in tangent with the rest of his face, so the laugh is lopsided.

"I simply jest, but the legend does state that the further away the bark the louder it sounds and vice versa. Opposite to real life, you know. Look here, Grace Morgan, it's a pity we got off on the wrong foot." He holds out a hand, even though I am at least five paces from him. "Gruff Lewis. Pleased to meet you, and if ever you're stuck on that path," he nods behind him, in the direction I have come from, "Then just shout."

I thrust my hands·in the pockets of my cape, and there they shall remain. I nod, the slightest of gestures, and continue towards home.

⚮

By the time the man from the draper's arrives I am clean and calm, having unburdened myself to Lilah who seems to find the whole thing amusing.

"I wish to bring the seaside indoors," I tell the draper as we browse the wallpaper samples. "I want rid of this dour maroon. It is so depressing."

"Then how about this? It's a brand-new design. William Morris Seaweed, in tones of ecru and silver." He selects a sample from the catalogue and offers it to me.

I stroke the paper, following the sinuous pattern which seems to capture the free-flowing movement of underwater plants. "The colours are gorgeous."

"Let's see how it looks with the light coming in from the bay window." He takes it from me and holds it against the deep reveal. The winter sunlight catches the silver blades of the plant, making them glisten slightly.

"Perfect. I love it." With his help, I select some tonal fabrics for the bedspread, cushions and curtains, then he measures up, promising to start the redesign in two weeks' time. "There are other rooms that need a makeover, but this bedroom must be done first. I've been thinking about taking up sewing. Perhaps I can purchase the fabric from you then make up some of the items myself in the future."

"Of course. Start simple, you know, a cushion cover or such like until you get more confident. Everyone has to start somewhere," he says. "I'm sure my wife will help out if you get stuck."

After he leaves, I climb the narrow stairs to the playroom, hoist myself onto the deep windowsill, and take in the view. In the harbour a boat is moored, reminding me that in about two weeks' time my clock will arrive. I cannot wait to hear its heartbeat again.

The sun sits low on the horizon, admiring its reflection on the sea, and the sky is washed in ripples of indigo and violet. Violet—the colour of inner peace. I place one hand flat against my stomach, sensing the calm within. It is a wonderful feeling, one I do not experience often enough.

"We'll make this space our own," I say to the doll on the mantelpiece. She watches me through painted eyes that offer no insight as to her own feelings. "I'll make you a brand-new gown. You'd like that, wouldn't you? I imagine you're sick of that faded old thing."

I wander over to the bookshelf and take down Mother's copy of *Little Women*. It is years since I read it last, a decade at least. I cannot remember much, other than it being a story about the dynamics of four sisters, one of whom dies far too young. Perhaps now I am older it will seem more meaningful.

"Sleep tight," I whisper to the doll before returning to my room and placing the book on the bedside cabinet. I shall start reading it tonight, but before that I need to write to Jonathan to tell him we have arrived safe and well.

The image of the man with the scar and his tale of supernatural hounds returns to haunt me as I turn out the lamp and tuck the blankets under my chin. I hope not to see him again, though no doubt I will. If he mends boats hereabouts, I am certain our paths will cross. I will not allow his presence to deter me from my walks. I listen hard, hoping not to hear a dog bark. Nothing, complete and utter silence. Even the gulls are asleep.

LILAH AND I ARE UNDECIDED WHETHER OR NOT TO celebrate Thanksgiving. This year, it happens to co-incide with the day on which the haberdasher's son is due to strip the old wallpaper in my bedroom, so the house will be in a mess. And besides, having emigrated to the UK, we think perhaps we should renounce the old ways and just celebrate festivals alongside the locals, none of whom are likely aware that Thanksgiving is about to take place.

On the other hand, a small part of us yearns for home still. Back in Vermont, Thanksgiving was the one day of the year when we got together as a family, or at least that was true while Father was alive. During the last few years of Mother's life the date seemed less important. She was ill at ease with visitors, even close family at times, so we tended to enjoy a small gathering instead.

"I guess we should just have a nice dinner together. There'll be too much disruption with the decorators here in any case," I suggest to Lilah.

"That's probably best, Grace. Oh, and by the way, I've ordered the ingredients for the Christmas pudding. I'm us-ing the recipe Aelwen gave me, so I'll be preparing that on Sunday if you want to join me. The recipe also suggests we add a silver sixpence to the batter. Apparently, whoever ends up with it on their plate shall be granted good fortune for the coming year."

I hide a smile. Aelwen had called 'round earlier in the week to see how we were getting on, and over a cup of tea, she and Lilah had found common ground, albeit in how best to fatten up the family. "I've been thinking…how about we invite Ewan Bevan round for Christmas dinner as a thank you for looking after Parrog House all these years?" The thought has only just occurred, but Lilah will be none the wiser.

She hesitates, knife paused in carrot, then takes a deep breath. "It's a kind gesture, Grace, but I doubt he'll say yes."

"Well, you never know." My stomach churns at the thought of inviting a relative stranger to dinner, but I am determined to be more sociable here than I was in Vermont. I do not want to end up isolated like Mother, and besides, his presence might help us to feel less lonely, estranged from family as we are. "You said he's a widower. Did he say whether or not he has children? If not, he might be glad of the invite."

"He didn't say." She shrugs. "I guess all you can do is ask. The decision will be his to make."

Lilah and I spend the whole of Wednesday morning clearing out my bedroom. Tonight, I shall up-sticks and move into the small room at the back while my own is being redecorated. In the meantime, I will try my best not to peek, as I want the transformation to be a surprise. It seems that no sooner have I settled than I am about to be disrupted again, but it will be for the best, because although I love the expanse of this room and its view, I sense the ghosts of Mother and Father lurking in every corner. I wonder if they are the reason the barking hounds stole my sleep? If so, their portent of death has come rather too late.

It is hard to believe Father has been gone almost six years and Mother less than three months. I feel his loss more keenly than Mother's, and the accompanying guilt is never far away. But that is life, I suppose. It is not because of Mother's ill health that I miss him more, it is because of the relationship we had. The love between Father and I felt deeper, more sincere somehow.

Through the darkened window, a full moon nestles amongst a myriad of stars, each one of them twinkling at the moon's majesty. Since the window overlooks the garden at the back, it is completely private. Therefore, tonight I shall sleep with the curtains open so that the moon and stars can watch over me.

The copy of *Little Women* rests on the makeshift bedside cabinet. As yet it remains unopened. Last night I was not in the mood for young women lamenting their poverty, and, if I remember rightly, there is much talk about Christmas at the start of the book and I was not in the mood for that, either. However, having spoken to Lilah about Christmas earlier today I decide to make a start on the book. Perhaps it will put me in a festive mood, especially with a view of the dark sky and twinkling stars.

My eyes grow heavy as I reach the end of the third chapter, so I close the book and lean to the side in order to place it on the cabinet. Misjudging my reach, it falls to the floor, sending a sheet of paper spiralling in the air. I drape across the bed to retrieve both. It is another leaf from Mother's notebook, I am certain. She must have used it in place of a bookmarker. Eight numbers are scribbled upon the paper, again separated by commas. I can determine no pattern to the numbers; they are not ranked in order, nor is the gap between them exactly the same. Why did Mother persist in writing lists of numbers?

A scratching sound rouses me from a deep sleep. For a moment I am reminded of the dream I had back in Vermont just after Mother died, the dream about the sexton beetles, except this time I am awake. I sit up and look out of the window. The moon has retired for the night, leaving my eyes to adjust to what little light the few remaining stars offer. Silence, my heartbeat is my one and only companion. Just as I am about to lie down it comes again, louder this time. A long scraping sound from up above, like something being dragged across the floor. It comes again, each scrape lasting around five seconds. I close my eyes and picture the somewhat unfamiliar layout of the house, the fact that I am not in my own bedroom making it all the more confusing. The nursery, I am sure, is above this room. The nursery with the single bedstead and crib. The little room where I slept for the first two years of my life. Is it possible we have an intruder?

The bare floorboards against my feet send a cold pulse to my bladder, urging me to visit the chamberpot, but there is not one in this room. I don slippers and a dressing gown and light the paraffin lamp before tiptoeing onto the landing. I shall wake Lilah, then both of us can investigate. I pause at her door, fist poised ready to knock, and listen to the soft rumble of her snores. I do not have the heart to wake her.

I stand on the landing and listen. The upper storey is silent now. Either I have disturbed whoever is there, or I imagined it. The most plausible answer is that an injured bird has fallen down the chimney. I should go back to bed and inspect the rooms in the morning. But as I am about to enter my room, the sound comes again.

I stare at the door to the upper storey, willing it to make the decision for me, but it is as unobliging as when it was locked. The metal handle is frigid against my palm, and I shiver. Three treads up and I pause, listening. No sound now, but I am certain I can detect the faint smell of wet dog.

That would be The Hounds of Annwn you heard. Tis the right time of year.

The shipwright's words come flooding back, and I almost turn on my heels, but something urges me onwards.

The scent of wet dog is stronger on the landing. A whiff of wet fur, salty with seawater, and warmed in front of the fire. But the floor is bare. No carpet to retain the smell of dog all these years. Did we have a pet dog when we were children? Jonathan would know, and if we did, is it possible that the scent of a dog could last for more than twenty years? I doubt it. It must be some other animal, a bird, no doubt. I creep towards the nursery with a pounding heart and dry mouth. This part of the house is damp, Grace, I tell myself. That is the reason for the smell, but with every step I take I fear that at any moment I will be pounced on by some wild animal.

The door to the nursery swings open with ease, and I step into the gloom. My shadow looms large on the wall opposite, the lantern held in my outstretched arm like that of the Grim Reaper. Each breath a wispy wraith; each thought a demon of my own conjuring. A sprinkle of soot tumbles down the chimney to join the grey ash already scattered on the hearth. A bird, I tell myself again. It must have been a bird you heard, nothing more. Another rumble of soot does its utmost to convince me, but the devil on my shoulder whispers, *the chimneys were swept recently, Grace. It cannot be a bird.*

An icy breath on the back of my neck makes me swivel on my heels. A movement outside the door, like the swish of a curtain, then, from on the landing the scraping sound. I want to shout for Lilah. I want to bang on the floorboards and rouse her from sleep, but I am frozen to the spot. Too terrified to move, too frightened of what lurks on the landing. The dog-like smell is replaced by the sweet scent of lilacs, Mother's perfume.

Not here, Mother. For pity's sake, not here.

❧ ☙

Breakfast is such a hurried affair that I do not get a chance to speak to Lilah about what happened the previous night, and perhaps it is best I try to forget. Maybe the move to a different room caused my imagination to run wild.

Before we know it, the decorator arrives and everything is a bustle. The excitement of the day is enhanced by the postman's arrival. He delivers a telegram stating that my beloved grandfather clock is to be delivered in two days' time. The news brightens my mood, and I am determined to make the most of the day. I think I shall start by writing to Helena. In the letter, I will request that she asks Jonathan if we had a pet dog when we lived here. I shall also write a note to Mr Bevan, inviting him to Christmas lunch, and when Lilah and I go to town tomorrow we can post it through his letterbox. After that, if the weather stays dry, I shall go for a walk.

❧ ☙

Which direction should I head in? Dressed in layers to protect me from the bitter wind, I stand in the front garden considering my options. In the pocket of my overcoat rests the copy of *Little Women*. I hope to find a spot sheltered from the wind, so that I can read.

Close to the horizon a vessel sails, my childish fancy imagines it tipping over the edge and hurting into oblivion at any moment. Facing the sea, I look left and right. There is no sign of the shipwright or his boat this morning, therefore I shall head left onto the cliff path. It has not rained for a few days, so with any luck it should be less muddy.

Keeping one eye on the boat-shed in case he happens to be lurking inside, I approach the start of the climb. The gorse does its best to protect me from the wind until I reach the clifftop, then it clings to the cliff-edge for dear mercy, mindful of its own predicament. But, oh, what a view! Nothing but sea, cliffs, and coastline for miles. Breathtaking. The sailing vessel I spotted from the beach has disappeared, no doubt it has plunged into some watery pit of hell. To the right of me, the estuary, with its snaking, grey tendrils. To the right, the island I spotted the last time I came, or is it a headland? I cannot be certain.

I continue a mile or so along the clifftop, enjoying the roar of the waves and the squall of gulls, until the path veers inland a little before descending onto a tiny cove of pebbled beach, through which a stream trickles to join the sea. I stand in the stream, the icy temperature of the water penetrating through my Wellington boots. Closing my eyes, I enjoy the sensation of the current around my ankles. The stream is determined to join the sea. No rock, driftwood, or human can deter its course. It simply wends its way around the obstacle and continues on its journey. Perhaps I should take a tip from it and do the same, then I might achieve far more in life than I have so far.

At the farthest end of the beach, I spy some large rocks. A great spot to sit and read. The cove is protected from the worst of the wind by its curved shape. I sit for several minutes, enjoying the view and breathing in the salty air. I eat a sandwich and drink some water, throwing a few scraps to eager gulls that swoop above my head, waiting for easy pickings. They squawk their thanks, then return to swoop and dive in the sea.

This place is so peaceful, utterly devoid of the trappings of life. I could convince myself I am the only person alive on the planet right now. I slip the novel from my coat pocket and begin to read. It does little to inspire me. In fact, I find it rather tedious—too much frippery and not enough depth, until one particular sentence speaks to me:

"You are the gull, Jo, strong and wild, fond of the storm and the wind, flying far out to sea, and happy all alone."

I read the sentence several times, the words on the page a blur of emotion. I could be Jo, though am I really strong?

I suppose in some ways I am. I have survived the loss of my parents, and have been brave enough to sail halfway round the world to begin a new life, but could I have done it alone? I am not so certain. As for the rest of the sentence…well, yes, I am all of those things. Why else would I be sitting here, all alone, with only the gulls and the wind for company?

The steep ascent from beach to clifftop is a challenge, which goes to prove how little exercise I took back in Vermont. Every now and then I stop to catch my breath. I am halfway up when I see her. Atop the cliff—silhouetted by the afternoon sun—stands a girl, or rather, a young woman. Tendrils of hair fly in the wind, and her arms are outstretched as if she is about to dive into the sea. My instinct is to call out a warning, but then I realize she is just enjoying the power of the wind against her body.

Her face is turned skyward, and because she is side-on, I cannot see her features, though she looks to be around my age and of similar height. I continue to climb, mindful of where I place my feet, but when next I look up, she is gone. I hasten my step, expecting to see her ahead of me when I reach the top, but she is nowhere to be seen. The coast-path stretches ahead, visible for some considerable length. She could not possibly have walked so fast as to have made it around the bend. And then I remember: the girl I saw from the bedroom window the night we moved into Parrog House. The girl facing out to sea as we sailed the Atlantic. They are one and the same, I am sure. I summon to mind the image from my memory: dark, wild hair, rather like my own, and a coat, fitted at the waist that outlines her lean frame.

A ghost girl in grey.

"That you, Grace?" Lilah calls, as I hang my coat in the hall.

I go straight to the kitchen, where she is basting the turkey for tonight's Thanksgiving dinner, her cheeks flushed from the heat of the oven.

"Smells good. Lilah, did you see anyone pass by the house just now? A young woman, dressed in grey?"

She shakes her head.

"Can't say I've had time to stand in the front room and watch the comings and goings, not with preparing our dinner."

"Of course not." I untie my bonnet and set it down on the table.

"The decorator's just left." She nods towards the kitchen door, as if he stands behind me. "You'll not want to go into the bedroom. It's a mess with the walls stripped. He said he'll be back first thing in the morning."

She seems a little harassed. Perhaps I should have stayed and helped her prepare the meal. "Anything I can do?"

"No thank you, potatoes and carrots are peeled, and the cornbread's in the oven." She wipes her hands on a towel before sitting at the table. "Now then, what's this about a young woman?"

"Oh, it's nothing. I thought I saw someone on the cliff top, that's all."

She glances away. "You'll never guess who came by: Mr Bevan. He dropped in to check on us, make sure we were settling in. Anyway, I knew you'd left the invitation on the hall table, so I hope you don't mind, but I gave it to him. It'll save us calling at his house when we go to town tomorrow."

Ah, so this is why she seems flustered. She has had company, and a gentleman at that. "Did he stay long?"

"No, no, just a quick cup of tea, but he seemed delighted by the invitation and accepted there and then." Her face is as red as the cranberry sauce that simmers in the pan on the stove.

I refrain from adding to her discomfort by changing the subject. "You know, I was thinking while I was out…isn't it strange that Thanksgiving started because a group of Pilgrims sailed from England to America in the hope of a new life all those years ago, and now here we are, celebrating it in reverse in a way. I think we should make this our one and only Thanksgiving, Lilah. We'll celebrate tonight as a means of marking our new life, and after that, we'll let go of the old ways. What do you think?"

"That's fine by me. It'll mean less work for these sore hands." She laughs, and I sense her relief in having told me of Mr Bevan's visit.

⊰ CHAPTER ⊱
XVI

I HARDLY SLEPT A WINK LAST NIGHT, KNOWING THE grandfather clock is arriving today. If the tide is high, will the delivery men be able to carry it all the way around the back of the house without dropping it? What if it has already been damaged en route? These and other questions haunted my thoughts during the night.

Mrs. Jones, the draper's wife, arrives just after nine, arms laden with cushions, curtains, and other soft furnishings, all of which are concealed within white cotton sacks. It seems as if all my Christmases have come at once, and I am both nervous and excited. Her daughter assists her in decorating the room, while I wait downstairs in the front parlour, scouring the harbour for signs of the Pantechnicon van's arrival.

Just after eleven, the tide starts to turn, and although I am eager for the delivery, I pray the clock will not arrive for another hour or so, otherwise the sand might be too wet for the men to walk on whilst carrying such a large piece of furniture.

Lilah calls from the landing.

"Come and see, Grace. The bedroom's ready."

I leave the window and hurry up the stairs. All three women stand outside the bedroom door, nervous with anticipation.

"You ready?" Lilah says, and I take a deep breath before nodding.

What a transformation. The room my parents once slept in is unrecognizable. The colours are subtle, calm. The bed is draped in sumptuous cushions and a bedspread that carries the same muted tones of silver and ecru as the walls. The furniture has been rearranged, too, to make the most of the light from the large, bay windows. My dream of extending the room into the seascape beyond has come true.

"Oh, my! It's exquisite. Even more beautiful than I imagined." I clasp both hands to my mouth and gaze around in awe. "Thank you. Thank you so much."

"I'm so pleased you're happy with it," Mrs. Jones says, beaming from ear to ear.

"I'm more than pleased. It's—" I turn to Lilah. "Can you believe it? It's like a different room."

"My husband tells me you're thinking of taking up sewing. I'd be happy to help if you're stuck."

"I'll take you up on that offer if you don't mind, and soon, I hope."

No sooner are the words spoken than we are interrupted by a loud knocking at the front door.

"The clock!" I dash from the room, leaving Lilah to see to the seamstress and her daughter.

A short and stout man stands cap in hand at the door. He gestures towards the harbour. "You're expecting delivery of a clock, I believe?"

"I am indeed." I crane my neck to look over his shoulder. In the distance, six men are struggling to remove the clock from the horse-drawn van.

"Sign here, please." He hands me a note, and I hastily scribble my signature, eager to continue watching the men's progress. Their manner is solemn, focussed on the task in hand, and I am reminded of the men who carried Mother's coffin, only this time their burden requires the strength of six men, not four.

"Where do you want it positioned?" he asks, nodding towards the hallway.

"Just here." I step a few paces into the hall and indicate the spot before returning to watch the clock's progress from the door.

The clock is wrapped in white sheets and looks lifeless as it is borne horizontally over the sand. It seems that time stands still as I watch the precious cargo brought closer and closer to its former home.

"It began life here, you know," I say to the man in the cap. "And now it's come home again." He looks at me quizzically before hurrying down the front steps to help guide the men on the final leg of their journey. I turn to see that Lilah has joined me.

"I sent Mrs. Jones out the back way. Thought it best, as I didn't want them to clash."

Both of us are as nervous as we appear, our hands clasped and continuously wrung. We wait with bated breath as the men negotiate the steps, then stand aside to allow them to enter.

"Just there," the delivery man says, and together they lower it to the ground before unwrapping it, one sheet at a time.

Its round face appears first, and I glimpse the painted seascape I have missed so much. Once it is devoid of all wrapping, the men manoeuvre it into position while I stand by, key in hand.

"Go on then," says the man in the cap. "Let's see her working."

"What time is it?" I ask, and he removes his pocket watch.

"Ten minutes to twelve."

All seven of them gather 'round as I slowly position the hands, tensing at each click and pausing at each quarter chime to allow the clock to gather its breath. What if its beating heart refuses to tick once wound? My hand trembles with anticipation as I turn the key on both of the winding points. Like a surgeon at the operating table, I restart its heart.

Tick, tock, tick tock.

A slow and steady rhythm that I have sorely missed. The familiar sound brings tears to my eyes, and I have to stop myself from wrapping my arms around the clock and giving it a hug.

"There you go," the man says. "She's right as rain."

The men traipse from the hall, one by one, except for the stout man, and I breathe a sigh of relief.

"Thank you, I am most grateful."

After my experience with the coachman who brought us here, I am uncertain whether or not to offer a tip, but Lilah nudges me with her elbow, purse in hand, and I oblige.

No sooner have the men gone than the clock chimes twelve, each gong resonating around the hall. I feel like the mother of a newborn, relieved to hear their infant's first cry.

I clasp it round the middle and hug it tight, unembarrassed now that only Lilah and I are present.

"I've missed you so much. How was your journey? It's good to have you home," I say, and Lilah chuckles with relief.

"Oh, Lilah. If only I could get the moon phases restored. She'd be as good as new."

"Ask around. There might be someone local who repairs clocks."

I nod. "What do you have planned for this afternoon, Lilah? If you're not busy, how about we spend some time planning the rooms on the upper storey?"

"Fine by me, but lunch first. Don't think I didn't notice that you skipped breakfast."

Nothing passes her scrutiny. She is right, of course, but I was too pent up to eat.

Between us we finish off what is left of the Thanksgiving turkey with pickles and wash it down with root beer. Truth is, I have not ventured to the upper storey these past few days, not since my experience a few nights back. I am glad Lilah has agreed to come with me. If the dog-like smell persists, we can check it out, and if there are signs of a trapped bird or a dead rodent, then at least I won't have to deal with it alone. But what of the lilac scent? Lilah would surely identify it as Mother's, too. I shall have to wait and see.

"You go on up if you like. I'll see to the dishes, then I'll join you."

"No, I'll lend a hand. We'll go together." Much to Lilah's surprise, I pick up a tea towel and roll up my sleeves.

"Turning over a new leaf, I see," she says, with no hint of sarcasm. She understands all too well the privileged life I have led and how I am trying to adjust. It does not come naturally, but I hope it will in time. I do not wish to live my whole life like a child, dependent on others to meet my basic needs.

"Careful here," I say as we approach the narrow treads. Each of us carries a gas lamp in order to navigate the stairs, and I have brought matches to light those in the rooms if necessary, though the daylight is sufficient at present, and we should have at least two or three hours before twilight.

As we climb, I sniff the air, but detect nothing more than a damp, musty odour. No wet dog, no lilac, and no sound of scratching, either. Did I imagine it the other night?

"Let's start in the nursery." I do not add *the room in which I heard something the other night.*

Inside the room there is no hint of anything untoward, the traces of ash remain on the hearth, but apart from that there is nothing to suggest that a bird has come down the chimney.

"Did Mother ever mention having a pet dog when we lived here, Lilah?"

She scratches her head.

"Not that I remember, and I would think it unlikely. You know how she was with her allergies. Why do you ask?"

"Oh, it's nothing. The other day, when I came to look at the books, I thought I could smell a dog, that's all."

She sniffs the air. "Maybe a mouse got in and died. It's likely rotting beneath the floorboards."

She sees my expression and laughs. "I'm teasing. I can't smell anything. Now, what plans do you have for this room?"

I shake my head. "I'm not certain." The room is uninspiring. Facing the back of the house it has no sea view and far less light than the rooms at the front. "Let's take a look at the playroom again. I'd like to make it my sewing room-come-library. The light is fabulous in there, and I love the sea view."

The doll on the mantelpiece watches us enter.

"Oh, you poor thing," Lilah says, picking her up and cradling her in her arms. "We need to find a way to fix that poor head of yours, don't we?"

The question spills from my lips before I can stop myself.

"Lilah, did you ever think to marry and have children?"

Seeing her nurse the doll reminds me how great a maternal instinct she seems to have, and I cannot help myself.

She wanders over to the deep windowsill and sits, doll in arms, then, with a sigh says, "There was a man once. A very long time ago. He let me down." She looks at the doll as she speaks, rather than at me, and I sense the hurt that lurks in the shadows. "But that's enough about me. Now you, Grace, you're still young enough to fall in love. Take my advice: don't leave it too late. The older you get, the more set in your ways you become, and the more you get used to your own company."

I shake my head, vehemently. "Not me, Lilah. I'm not the marrying kind."

"Whyever not? Attractive young woman like you. You could take your pick, you know."

I feel the heat rise to my face, and kneel in front of the bookcase, pretending to browse the selection so I do not have to face her. "I don't know. It's hard to explain, but somehow I just know it's not for me. Gut instinct, you know? Anyway, let's not talk about such matters. I'd rather discuss what we came up here for, and that's how best to transform this room."

"So, what do you have in mind?"

I gaze around the room before wandering over to the mantelpiece. "I like the wallpaper. The forest scene and deer make me feel as if I am in a fairy tale, but the curtains will have to go. They're so drab."

"I agree. It could do with lightening up a bit." Lilah points up at the ceiling which has yellowed and bears a large water stain, most likely the result of some past roof damage. "Get Mrs. Jones's boy to paint the ceiling white, then take down these maroon drapes and replace them with pale green, perhaps, to tone in with the wallpaper."

"And I'd like to turn this bay window into a seat. Imagine, I could watch the comings and goings of the harbour whilst reading or embroidering. Wouldn't that be nice?"

"A few comfy chairs in front of the fire, some more bookcases on the far wall." Lilah continues to speak, but I am no longer aware of her words, because as I look out of the window, I see the shipwright and his dog. The man leans an elbow on the seawall in front of the house and looks up towards me. I duck behind the curtain, causing Lilah to stop mid-flow.

"Grace?" She ambles over to the window and peers out.

"Don't look, Lilah!"

She pays me no heed. Instead, she leans forward, her nose almost touching the glass. "Well, unless you're able to see something I can't, I don't know what the fuss is about. All I see is a man with his dog and a ruddy great cloud on the horizon."

I step from behind the curtain. He no longer stares at the house, instead he ruffles the dog's fur and offers him a tidbit, concealed in the palm of his hand.

She eyes me suspiciously. "Do you know him?"

He walks away without so much as a glance, leaving me feeling foolish for making such a fuss.

I shake my head. "I'm not sure. I think it's the man I told you about, the one with the dog."

⚔ CHAPTER ⚔
XVII

T HE FOLLOWING THURSDAY, WE MAKE A SECOND VISIT to Jones the Draper to choose the fabric for the play-room remodel, and no sooner are we out the door than we bump into Mr Bevan, stepping out of the butcher's.

"How nice to see you both," he says, reaching for my hand, "and thank you for the invite to Christmas lunch. It'll save me having to cook a turkey for one." He laughs, then turns to Lilah and says, "I've just ordered us a nice bird." He nods towards the butcher's. "My little contribution."

Lilah's face is flushed. "Oy, whyever did you do such a thing? Invited as a guest, and you end up paying. Oh dear, oh dear."

"There really was no need, Mr Bevan, but thank you all the same," I say, in an attempt to put an end to the argument. "Shall we say two o'clock?"

"Two o'clock sounds good." His face is ruddy with pleasure, and I bite my lip to stop myself from declaring that he looks as if he has stepped straight out of Charles Dickens's *A Christmas Carol.* Mr Fezziwig, that is who he reminds me of.

"Will I be seeing you at church on Christmas morning for the Carol Service?" he asks.

Lilah and I glance at one another then down at our feet.

"Grace?" she says, putting the onus on me.

"Perhaps. We haven't yet decided." What excuse can I make? "We assumed there would be a midnight mass on Christmas Eve and didn't relish the thought of walking home in the dark."

Still, he fails to take the hint. "Yes, yes, there will be, but everyone attends the morning service. I'm sure you'll enjoy it. Not all of the hymns will be in Welsh, you know, so you can join in the singing. Puts you in the Christmas spirit, it does."

The truth is that neither of us attended church back in Vermont, not since Father died, and what with Lilah's Jewish background and her Father's religious rebelliousness she, too, has her own beliefs.

"We'll think about it, Mr Bevan. Might be nice to hear some Welsh Carols, hey, Grace? Put us in the spirit, I suppose."

"If you think you can spare the time, Lilah. You'll be busy preparing lunch, remember." I am not sure I could cope with the church being full of worshippers. Would all eyes be on me, the newcomer from America? I need to give the matter some thought before agreeing.

"Well, whatever decision you make I'll look forward to coming for lunch," he says, shaking both our hands in turn, though I notice that when he takes Lilah's hand he holds it for several seconds. I am nothing if not astute.

"What do you think?" Lilah says as soon as we are out of earshot.

"Church, you mean? I'm not sure, let me think about it." She knows better than to press me for a decision. Not only am I astute; I am also stubborn.

"Not church, I mean the sewing lessons. Something to look forward to after Christmas," she says, changing the subject.

"Indeed." Mrs. Jones suggested Wednesday afternoons, once we have transformed the playroom.

She grips my arm as we descend the steep hill towards the harbour. Last night's frost clings to the road, refusing to relinquish its diamonds, and yet again I am reminded of the fact that Lilah is getting older. What would I do without her? I cannot bear to think about it. She chuckles, and her eyes glisten like the frost. "Hey, Grace, what if Mr Bevan finds the silver sixpence in the pudding? I wonder if he wears dentures? I'm sure I detected a slight whistle when he spoke." We giggle, and I embrace the joy of the moment. There has been insufficient laughter in my life.

As we round the corner, the postman's bicycle is propped against the harbour wall, and in the distance, I spy his navy uniform, heading up the steps to Parrog House. "I wonder if it's a letter from Helena?" I say, hurrying Lilah along.

In fact, he brings two letters, one from Jonathan concealed inside a Christmas card that features the sweetest robin red-breast on the front, and another from Helena. In the letter, he thanks me for the telegram telling him we arrived safely and informs me that they will be moving into our family home in Fair Haven immediately after Christmas. By all accounts, Eva has been busy modernizing the place, converting the smallest bedroom at the back into a purpose-built bathroom, complete with water closet, and I cannot help but feel a little envious.

Of course, he makes no mention of the dog. Only now would Helena be receiving my letter, so I guess I can expect his answer next time. He ends by wishing Lilah and me a Merry Christmas and offers his regret because we cannot celebrate together. I think back to last Christmas and how Lilah, Mother and I spent it alone because once again Jonathan and Eva celebrated with Eva's parents.

Helena's letter is written in black ink, on the finest cream paper, and once opened I hold it to my nose and inhale the scent of lemon and lavender. It is not her smell, but that of the infused pillow slip she has embroidered as a gift, and I am a little disappointed because I hoped her scent would bring me closer to her.

Helena's handwriting is immaculate, her spelling faultless. The money Jonathan has spent on her education has not gone to waste.

Dearest Aunt Grace,

I hope this finds you well. I miss you already and wish we could spend Christmas together. I cannot remember us having done so in such a long time. In fact, I believe I was around the age of seven or eight when last we did. Grandpa had not long died (I hope you don't mind me using the term. I hate how people skirt around the issue of death, the way they embellish it with flowery language such as "departed" or "passed on"), and Daddy insisted on coming to you for Christmas lunch, much to Mother's chagrin, I might add.

It was not a happy time as I recall, for everyone was still in mourning. Even as a child I felt Grandpa's loss, despite the fact that everyone tried to put on a brave face. He was much loved, wasn't he? How nice it would be to have spent just one Christmas together and not have the weight of death hanging over us. Though, I suppose, even if you were still here, it has not been long since Grandma's death, so the celebration would still have been tainted.

Anyway, that's enough maudlin. I'm beginning to sound like an old woman rather than a twelve-year-old girl, and we can't have that, can we?

I suppose Daddy has told you about Mother's renovations. My goodness, she has had a bee in her bonnet these past weeks! She has spent a fortune. It's a good job Daddy earns as much money as he does, I tell you. I suppose I should consider myself lucky to have the privileges I do, but sometimes I think her ungrateful and even wasteful.

When we move in, I shall be occupying your bedroom, Aunt Grace. I hope this will please you. I refused to allow Mother to change a thing in there. Not only do I love the décor, but I can sense your presence and it brings me closer to you.

I hope you like the pillow slip. I embroidered every stitch myself. I believe you will see an improvement since the initialled handkerchief I gave you last year. I remember how my thread knotted every time I attempted the link between the loop and letter stem, how I got in such a temper over it and Mother needed to come to my rescue. This time, though, I think my embroidery could pass as fancy work.

One more thing before I go…and I know I promised to speak no more of death, but I want you to know how much I adore Grandma's mourning brooch. I look at it each and every day and intend to wear it to the Christmas ball next week. If anyone asks (and I have every faith that they will, because it is so unusual), I shall tell them precisely what it is and enjoy the look of discomfort on their faces. (I think I hear you chuckle at my words. Oh, how alike we are!)

Write soon, Aunt Grace, and think of me on Christmas day.

Your ever-loving niece,
Helena

I take both the letter and pillowslip to Lilah who is in the kitchen, busy ironing. We chuckle over Helena's words as she carefully steams and presses the creases out of the pillowslip.

"Competition for you right here, Grace," she says, examining Helena's handiwork. "How long has it been since you last embroidered?"

I think back. "Too long, but that will be remedied soon, especially after a few lessons from Mrs. Jones. How nice it will be to sit in the window seat and sew to my heart's content."

Pillowslip pressed, I take it to my room and find a spare pillow with which to stuff it before heading to the upper storey. All this talk of needlework has given me the urge to revisit what will soon become my sewing studio.

The landing still smells a little dank, but I imagine the more use these rooms have the fresher they will smell. At least no hint of damp dog awaits me, though it is so gloomy up here that I cannot help but feel a little afraid.

This late in the afternoon, the playroom is bathed in shadows. The rocking horse's shadow looms large as a prize stallion on the back wall, and the doll on the mantelpiece points one arm in its direction, as if in awe of its size.

I visit each of the rooms in turn until I find an old stool which I drag over to the bay window of the playroom. I must remove these maroon drapes. They strip the room of cheer. The stool rocks beneath my weight as I stretch to unfasten the hooks, and I imagine Lilah reprimanding me.

There...the shadow of the rocking horse is a little sharper now that more light has been allowed to enter. I wander over for a better look. Its dappled-grey paintwork has worn smooth in parts, its leather seat cracked and dry. It has been well-loved by the look of it. It wears a surprised expression on its face, its mouth open and teeth showing. One of its teeth is missing which makes it look rather comical, but it also summons to mind the nightmare I had. Poor thing! It is not to blame. I wonder if it will take my weight? Today I feel girlish and carefree, ready to take risks.

Lilah often refers to me as *a slip of a thing*, but despite being lean, I am rather tall. Knees to chest, I hold onto its ragged mane and rock, tentatively at first, then more vigorously when it does not protest. Could I learn to ride a real horse?

Here in Wales, surrounded by farmland and pasture, I am certain I could find someone to teach me. I am reminded again of *Little Women* and of Meg's disappointment at having to give up riding when her father relinquishes his wealth in order to help a friend in need. Perhaps I will learn, then I can ride across the beach at low tide with the sun on my face and the wind in my hair.

A distant sound of the grandfather clock chiming four reminds me that Lilah will have woken from her nap and has no doubt put the kettle on for tea. And besides, winter has stolen the last of the daylight. I bundle the maroon drapes in my arms and return downstairs to keep her company.

XVIII

"I WONDER, MR. BEVAN, DO YOU KNOW OF ANY CLOCK repairers hereabouts?" He stands in the hall, admiring the painted scene on the clock face. It chimes a few bars of *Beethoven's Ninth Symphony* before tolling two resonant chimes which cause him to take a step back.

"She sounds perfectly healthy to me." He checks his pocket watch. "And her timing is spot-on."

"Ah, but you see, the moon phases don't work. In fact they have never worked, and I'd love to have them restored."

"What a shame, perhaps Tomos Evans could help. He has a little shop on Church Street. You might have missed it if you haven't explored that part of town yet."

My cheeks burn red. Is he subtly referring to the fact that Lilah and I decided not to attend this morning's Carol service? She was easily dissuaded, what with her being so busy in the kitchen. I decide to clear the air. I do not want the matter hanging over us during lunch. "How was the Carol service, Mr. Bevan? I hope you enjoyed the singing." I refrain from apologizing, since I do not consider it necessary.

"Wonderful," he says, turning his attention back to the clock. "We missed you though, but perhaps next year, hey?"

"Perhaps. Please, allow me to take your coat. Lilah is busy in the kitchen, but lunch is almost ready."

"And it smells delicious. A slice of toast for breakfast is all I've had. Decided to save myself for lunch." He pats his ample belly. "And please, call me Ewan. No need to stand on ceremony now that we are friends, is there?"

A full moon smiles down on us as we see Ewan Bevan out, though the clouds do their utmost to disguise it. High tide, and the waves lap gently at the sea wall in a soothing rhythm. In the distance, the lights from The Ship Afloat twinkle a warm welcome.

"I might just have a nightcap," he says, nodding towards the inn. "Thank you again for a wonderful afternoon, and remember what I said now, Lilah, once winter's over we can get cracking on that vegetable plot."

"Don't you worry, Ewan, I'll not forget."

"You two go indoors now, we're letting the cold air in."

Our first Christmas in Wales has been a success, far more agreeable than the last few spent in Vermont. Despite the fact that it is just past six o'clock, we wrap the leftovers and wash the dishes before changing into our nightclothes and curling up in front of the fire. No parlour games for us. Instead, we indulge in a tot of brandy and a mince pie, made according to yet another of Aelwen's recipes.

"I'm glad you got the sixpence, Grace," Lilah says with a grin.

"Yes, Lilah, since I'm the only one who still has all her teeth." We erupt in a fit of giggles at the memory of Ewan Bevan swirling each spoonful of pudding around his mouth in case the sixpence was hidden in his portion.

"We'll look for the clockmaker when we go to town on Monday, Grace. Church Street, wasn't it? Do you think Ewan minded us not going to church?"

"I don't think so. Didn't seem to mar the day, did it? And in any case, we'll not be dictated to. Strong women like us."

She winks, and I do my best to return the gesture, though I have never quite mastered it. I take the silver sixpence in my hand and close my eyes.

"What you doing?"

"Making a wish, of course."

She remains silent for a few seconds, until I open my eyes, then she says, "What you wish for?"

"Can't say, or it won't come true."

"Fair enough." She nods, and we sip the last of our brandy in silence, engrossed by the dance of the flames.

I do not tell her that I wish for just one thing: that the sense of peace and contentment I have felt today hatches into a white dove.

❧ ❧

I wake up on the floor of the playroom, next to the rocking horse, though I cannot recollect how I got here. My nightdress clings to my skin and my hair sticks to my forehead, despite the icy temperature. What am I doing up here? A wave of nausea hits as I try to lift my head, and it takes three or four attempts before I am able to sit up.

Outside, a black-velvet sky insists it is still night, and from the window, the constellation Canis Major winks to remind me of the dog-like scent that once again resides up here. Not that I ever studied astronomy; Greek mythology was always more to my taste.

The dream comes flooding back....

Teeth.

A vision of leaning over a basin, spitting blood, and mucus, and teeth that clinked as they hit the white bowl. Saliva trickled down the basin and pooled at the centre in a slimy puddle. With each retch, each cough, I spat another tooth, running my tongue around bare gums, sick with panic.

I shudder at the memory. Taking hold of the rocking horse's mane, I pull myself to my feet. The rocking motion makes my head spin, and I fear I might vomit. My fingers find the gap in its mouth where one of its own teeth is missing.

The second part of the dream forewarned me of this. A horse's skull, its jaw hung open, scraps of flesh and muscle still attached, and the maggots. Maggots that oozed through each and every crevice. Maggots that buried themselves in the crowns of molars before wriggling themselves to sleep. Maggots that stank of ammonia, so pungent it makes my eyes water even now I am awake. The horse's jaw had snapped shut, jolting me from sleep.

I stumble over to the window and perch on the deep sill, but the rocking horse continues to watch me, its head nodding slower and slower as it comes to rest. The doll, too. *What on earth do you think you're doing?* her expression says, though she seems to find the situation amusing, because her painted lips are curled in a smirk.

Turning my face away from her gaze, I take several deep breaths in an attempt to calm myself. It is not the first time I have found myself in another room at night, and in all likelihood, it will not be the last. The snap of bone against bone as the horse's jaw clamped down on the maggots is sharp as a gunshot. I run my tongue around my teeth, reassuring myself they are all there. No blood, no mucus, no loose teeth in the mandible.

The brandy, Grace, I tell myself. *The brandy, and wine, and too much rich food.*

I recall the conversation about Ewan Bevan's false teeth, the way Lilah and I giggled over me finding the silver sixpence. This is what caused the dream, nothing else.

But an aching jaw and the reek of maggots accompanies me all the way down the stairs.

For some time, I lie awake, shivering with cold. I am afraid to go back to sleep in case the dream pursues me. How glad I will be when morning arrives.

THIS CLOSE, THE CASTLE IS MAJESTIC, LIKE SOMETHING out of a fairy tale. A three-storey gatehouse, cornered by stone towers, rampant with ivy. A tiny window at the top of the eastern tower narrows its gaze over the town.

"Rapunzel, Rapunzel, let down your hair!" I say, peering towards its sightless eye, and Lilah laughs and elbows me.

"Oy, hush. Someone might hear you."

The castle, according to Ewan Bevan, is in private hands. "Oh, Lilah, you have no idea how much I would like to snoop around in there."

"Well, in that case you'd better get to know the owner. Who did he say it was? Lord something-or-other."

"I can't remember."

To our left, the smaller tower belonging to St Mary's Church diminishes in importance. I take hold of Lilah's arm and point.

"Church Street, I assume."

Once past the church, the road narrows and bends and we almost miss the clockmaker's. Tucked down an alley, and stood next to a larger house which is fronted by a curved stone wall, is a sign that reads *Gruffyd a'i fab clociau.*

We stumble over the cobbles and peruse the window display, but from the outside there is little to see. A bell tinkles as we enter and seated at a small desk in the corner is the clockmaker. His right eye is closed around a loupe and with his left hand he waves us in.

"Shan't be a moment," he says, still focussed on the pocket-watch resting in his right hand.

The space is filled from floor to rafter with clocks in all shapes and sizes. Longcase clocks line up along the back wall, like soldiers on parade. Some are tall, others short. Some are crafted from rich ebony or dark walnut, while others wear a fairer complexion. Interspersed between them is a variety of wall clocks, encased in everything from brass to birch-wood. An L-shaped worktop, littered with pliers, springs, and wheels separates customer from clocks.

It is a visual feast, but it pales in comparison to the noise. Ticks and tocks, some faint, others defined, beat in rhythm, filling the space with their heartbeats. Then, just as the clockmaker puts down the pocket-watch and stands, the clocks strike the half-hour and the shop becomes a symphony of chimes and tunes. He smiles and pauses to allow them to entertain us before wiping his hands on the front of his leather apron.

"Good afternoon, ladies. How may I help?" he says, finally.

It crosses my mind that Ewan has forewarned him of our proposed visit. Why else would he address us in English?

"Good afternoon," I say. "I have a grandfather clock that needs repairing. That is to say, the moon phases need repairing. Other than that, it's in perfect working order and has even survived a trip across the Atlantic and back, though in all likelihood it would benefit from a little servicing."

He studies me closely, nodding all the while. His hair is white as snow, his expression kindly. "Now, might that be the clock with the seascape painted on its face?"

I glance at Lilah before replying. "Indeed."

"Grace Morgan, I presume?"

"One and the same."

"Then I can tell you that the moon phases are not broken. The clock is simply missing its click spring."

I frown, confused.

"Easy to remedy. If you'd like me to call 'round, it's no problem."

"But how do you know without looking at it?"

His smile widens. "Because, my dear, it was me who removed the spring."

Lilah shuffles her feet and avoids my gaze as though she suspects foul play.

I shake my head. "And may I ask why you did such a thing?" I can imagine no reason for him having done so.

He takes a deep breath then says, "Miss Morgan, how much do you know about that clock of yours?"

I bite my lip. The letter Father left in the solicitor's possession before he died confirmed the clock had been made here in Wales. *Your grandparents commissioned it, Grace, so you will be the third generation to own it.* Those were his words. "Not a lot as far as its history goes. However, I do know it began life here and that it once belonged to my grandparents."

He studies me, a slight smirk playing on his lips, as if he is privy to information that I am not. I sense he is about to say more when the doorbell tinkles and in walks an elderly woman. She is dressed head-to-toe in black and her expression is grim. In mourning, I presume.

The clockmaker glances over my shoulder and gives her a nod, his expression as grave as hers. His voice is sympathetic when he speaks. "Ah, Mrs. Williams. I'll be with you shortly." He turns his attention back to me. "Shall we say Thursday? Around eleven?"

Of course I do not want to discuss the matter further while another customer is present. "Eleven it is, then," I say. "I shall look forward to it."

⊱—⊰

"Why, Lilah? Why on earth would Father have had him remove the spring?"

She shakes her head. "Your guess is as good as mine, Grace."

We are in the kitchen unpacking our wares. The smell of freshly baked bread turns my stomach, the mackerel even more so. Once again, I am overwhelmed. Some mystery lies beneath the surface, I have no doubt, but will I ever get to the bottom of it?

"The clockmaker seemed a little reticent, don't you think?" I say. "He seemed reluctant to give too much away."

Lilah guts the fish as we speak. One swift slit, head to tail before hooking in a finger and sweeping out the innards. The membrane attaching its head to its body gives a slight *twang* as it breaks, making me flinch.

"Perhaps he'll open up a bit when he comes on Thursday. He'll be here a while if he intends to service it." She rinses the fish head and bones before tossing them in a pan. "Make good stock, this will. Waste not, want not." She wipes her hands on the front of her apron and hums a tune.

I wish I were blessed with Lilah's pragmatism. She is so accepting of anything that comes her way, whereas I am the total opposite. I have no doubt other than between now and Thursday I will repeatedly mull over the possible reasons for the moon phases having been stopped on the clock.

XX

M Y DEAR CLOCK'S INTERNAL ORGANS ARE ALL EXPOSED: cables and pulleys, pendulums and weights, cogs and levers displayed for all to see. Tomos Evans has temporarily stopped its beating heart so that he might clean and lubricate the mechanism. He wears white gloves, like a pathologist performing an autopsy. Each breath he takes makes his nose whistle. His tongue protrudes between his teeth, his concentration such that I am loath to broach the subject of the removal of the moon phase spring in case it causes him to make a slip. Instead, I place a cup of tea on the hall table and wait for him to finish.

"There, there," he says, after what seems like an age. He sips his tea before reaching into a leather bag and retrieving a monocle which fits his eye-socket perfectly. "Now I need to check for signs of woodworm or infestation," he says, examining the clock's framework one section at a time.

I take a deep breath and smooth the front of my skirts. "Mr. Evans?"

"Yes?"

Somehow it is easier that he does not look at me. "About the moon phases. Do you know why my father wanted them stopped?"

My question is met with silence. Apart from the continuous wheeze from his nostrils, the hall is an empty chasm.

He nods at the clock, then takes a step back and picks up the teacup. He says nothing until the cup is drained.

"Now then, let me think," he says, replacing the cup on the saucer. The hand that had seemed so steady a few minutes ago trembles a little. "You see, I don't want to go tit-tle-tattling or sticking my nose in where it doesn't belong. You understand?"

"Of course, but there is no one else who can tell me. It is not as if I can ask Father, or Mother, come to that."

He rubs the whiskers on his chin and examines me, as if checking that I, too, am not infested with woodworm. "Can't say as I know the full story, but I do know that the moon phases caused your mother some bother, shall we say."

"What do you mean?" My words are barely a whisper.

He huffs so loud through his nose that the little white hairs vibrate, then he rubs the back of his neck and turns his head to look at the ceiling.

"Look, I don't wish to speak out of turn."

"It's fine, truly. I really would like to know."

"Well, your mother suffered with her nerves, didn't she?"

I nod.

"And your father gave me the impression that she became a bit…well, a bit obsessed with the lunar month. Hence, he asked if I could do something to make that part of the clock stop working."

I cast my gaze downwards. I do not wish him to feel as though he has spoken out of turn, but still I feel embarrassed by such a bizarre obsession.

"Mother certainly had her foibles…but moon phases? I have to admit, that's new to me."

He gives a sympathetic nod. "Well, there you go. You never know what goes on inside peoples' heads. It's easy for the likes of us to consider it strange, but I suppose the poor woman had her reasons. Now then, shall I replace the spring and get it set up? If you've never seen the moon phases work-ing, then you're in for a treat." He grins and bares teeth that are somewhat yellowed from tobacco. "If my memory serves me well, there's a lovely painting of the harbour hidden un-der there." He points to the twelfth digit on the clock face.

"Yes, please. I'm excited to see it working again." My hands are tightly clasped as he takes the spring between thumb and forefinger and fiddles it into position.

"Now then," he says, taking a step back. "I consulted the almanac last night and the last full moon was Christmas Eve." He positions the dial so that the full moon is beneath the number fifteen, then turns the dial clockwise through the relevant number of clicks, one for each day past Christmas Eve. "Do you have the key? All she needs now is a good old wind."

I produce the key from my pocket. Even now, it rarely leaves my side.

"May I?" The key is warm in my hand and within a few seconds the hall is once again filled with its familiar tick. "Thank you, Mr. Evans. Now, what do I owe you?"

"Call it twelve shillings, shall we?" He replaces his tools in the leather bag while I fetch my purse. "Now you know where I am if you have any problems."

"I do indeed, and thank you, Mr. Evans...for everything, I mean."

He places a gentle hand on my forearm. "Don't go reading too much into what I told you." His expression turns sorrowful and he shakes his head. "I mean, after what happened, it's not surprising your mother struggled a bit, is it?"

I frown. "I'm sorry, I don't follow your meaning. After *what* happened?"

He shuffles his feet, looking somewhat embarrassed. "You know...after what happened to your sister."

I shake my head. "You are mistaken, Mr. Evans. I do not have a sister."

He narrows his eyes at me. "Of course...I meant the sister who died. Caitlin, I believe her name was."

⚊ ⚊

"Perhaps he's mistaken, Grace." Lilah passes me the brandy glass, the palm of her other hand placed flat against her heart. It is obvious that she, too, is shaken.

"No, Lilah. He seemed certain. Don't you recall how Mother repeatedly called out the name Caitlin in the days before she died?" I drain the contents of the glass in two gulps.

"But that's not the sort of thing you can keep secret, for Heaven's sake. Were you not tempted to ask him more?" She takes the glass from me and tops it up.

"How could I? What kind of family would he think we were, keeping secrets like that? Think about it, Lilah. It all adds up. The doll, for instance. I knew it didn't belong to me. I would have been far too young to play with such a toy. And the books, too. They were suited to a much older child. Instinct suggested something was wrong, and I should have listened."

Lilah tuts, her complexion is blotchy and her bosom heaves. "But if it's true, then why were you never told? And how come Mr. Evans is the first to mention it? You'd think someone else would have spilled the beans before now. We've met enough of the locals for one of them to have said something. I mean, take Ewan, for example. He spent practically the whole of Christmas Day with us, yet despite all the talk of the past the subject of you having a sister was never raised." She twists her bottom lip between thumb and forefinger. "I still think he could be mistaken."

"I hope you're right, Lilah, but nevertheless. All my life I have felt as though a piece of the puzzle was missing, and this might just be it." I clench my fists and beat them against the arm of the chair. The fire spits at my anger and the flames glow redder. "I am so angry with Jonathan, and Father, too. Why did they not tell me?"

"Huh, men." She shakes her head. "Do you know what I think? Men are capable of seeing a problem and swallowing it whole so that it never sees the light of day. They can't face up to things like us women, Grace. That's the truth of it."

"Perhaps." I am lost in thought. "I shall write to Jonathan at once and demand he tells the truth, but the wait for his reply will be agonizing."

"Then you need to find something to do to help pass the time. Why don't you give the playroom a good clean? The lady from the draper's will be here in a few days' time, and I don't think my knees can take those stairs today, not after I spent so much time on them this morning black-leading the range." She hoists her skirts above the knee and rubs the swollen flesh.

"Oh, Lilah, go and lie down, I'll see to it, and you're right. I need to keep busy."

⚞ ⚟

Although it is only two o'clock, the playroom is dimly lit. To the west, the winter sun dips above the headland. Its lower third is hidden behind a vast cloud, but still it reflects a shimmering silver pathway over the sea and shingle. I collect the lamps from all the rooms on this floor so that I may spend some time up here.

Yes, I shall clean the playroom, but I also need to gather my thoughts so that the letter I write to Jonathan this evening will not sound too accusatory.

I begin by rolling up the large rug, though how I will get it down the stairs I do not know. It needs a good beating though, so I must find a way. It wafts a musty smell as I roll, one I am sure is tinged with the scent of dog. I have not yet received a reply about whether or not we once owned a dog. Damn the post!

All the while, the doll watches me from her fiery mantelpiece throne. Her painted lips have faded with time. Instead of rose-pink they are ash-blue, like something dead, and the crackled glaze gives them a flaky appearance. Lilah instinctively cuddles the thing, I am more inclined to throw it in the rubbish bin.

I heave the rolled-up rug out onto the landing and begin scrubbing the floor. The varnished floorboards are darker where the rug covered them, scuffed and faded elsewhere. In truth, it would benefit from sanding and re-varnishing but the new curtains and soft furnishings are arriving in a few days' time. Perhaps instead of cleaning the old rug I should treat myself to a new one, something lighter in colour to tone with the new curtains.

Next, I wipe down the window frames and shutters and clean the glass before shuffling the circumference of the room on hands and knees to clean the skirting. When I reach the far corner, where stands the bookcase, I am tempted to wipe around it, but instead decide to do a thorough job. *Keep busy, Grace,* I tell myself.

A tall stack of books threatens to topple by the time I empty the top two shelves, so I start a new pile. The pages are steeped with the scent of woodsmoke. It mingles with an earthy, dusty odour that belongs to the books themselves. I shudder at the shrivelled corpses of woodlice that lurk in dark corners and the shed skin of a house spider, stuck fast to the back of Ibsen's *Peer Gynt.* I wipe it away with the cloth, my stomach turning as it disintegrates, piece by piece. I have never had a strong stomach. I wipe my hands on the front of my dress before opening the pages. In an instant I am taken back to a long-forgotten time and place: Father and I, at a music hall in Boston, listening to the orchestra play Grieg's *Peer Gynt Suite.* I must have been around the age of eight.

I sit cross-legged on the floor, eyes closed, embracing the memory. Father's arms are warm and his voice is clear as he tells me the story of a young boy who falls in love with a girl he is not allowed to marry. I recall in particular the piece entitled *In the Hall of the Mountain King.* The music replays in my mind—images conjured of the trolls who chase the young boy through the halls of the mountain. Such a happy memory, but why did Mother not attend the concert, or Jonathan for that matter? Were we ever a real family? Were secrets kept to protect me from the sordid truth, or was there another reason?

I open my eyes and look around the playroom. The lamps cast long shadows on every surface. The sun has all but disappeared on the horizon, but I wish to finish the task I set out to do. Tomorrow is New Year's Eve and Lilah and I will be busy cleaning out all of the fireplaces so that we can usher in the new year with a clean slate, as is customary. She has filled jars with orange marmalade, which we intend to label and decorate as gifts for Ewan and Aelwen before delivering them by hand when we go to town in the morning. I must finish cleaning soon, so that I can write the letter to Jonathan and post it while we are there.

Not a sound comes from downstairs, Lilah must still be napping, but from outside dusk carries with it the wheezy *peewit* of a flock of lapwings returning home to roost, followed by the distant boom of a foghorn.

Now that the bookcase is empty, it can be easily moved. I edge it forward, bit by bit, until there is enough room to allow me to clean behind. As I wipe the section of skirting, my forearm brushes the back of the bookcase. Something is attached to it. I stand again and pull at the frame until I am able to see what it is: a child's drawing, dusty and faded, glued to the wood. I retrieve one of the lamps and hold it close to the paper. Three crudely-drawn figures stand on what appears to be the top of a cliff. One of the figures is small, the other two almost identical, both in height and appearance. The smaller figure is that of a young girl. I know this by the braids in her hair and the fact that she wears a knee-length dress. She holds the hand of one of the figures. I pick at the corner of the paper with my fingernail, attempting to peel it away from the wood, but it is stuck fast. It will tear if I force it.

I grab at the books, knocking a pile over, until I have positioned the stack below the height of the picture. Then, I place the lamp on top, so that I may examine the drawing without a wobbling shadow spoiling my view. In the background, a line of sky fails to meet the line of sea by a mile, and I wonder what it is that children imagine lies within that space. There are V-shaped birds here and there, and a few clumps of grass.

My attention returns to the two female figures. My heartbeat drums in my ears and my hands are clammy. Did Jonathan draw it, or Caitlin? Whichever one of them did, there is no doubt other than the picture is of a girl and two women. And why do the women look so alike? Is it because the child's skills were such that all women might look the same when drawn, or is there another reason? And the figure not holding the child's hand—she stands farther back, as would an outcast.

The girl is smiling. Her mouth curls up at the corners, as does the mouth of the woman whose hand she holds. The other woman, though, looks solemn. Her mouth is turned down at the corners and a single tear rests on her cheek. A perfect circle, faded yellow, shines above the heads of the girl and woman, while a grey cloud sits above that of the woman on her own.

Instinct tells me this was drawn by my dead sister's hand.

⚑ ⚑

I have started to write this letter three times, and three times I have failed. I would like to sleep on it so that I have time to mull things over and perhaps calm the emotional angst I feel, but if I miss tomorrow's post I will have to wait until after New Year.

I shall try again....

Dear Jonathan,

I trust this letter finds you well and hope that by now you are happily ensconced in the old house.

I await your reply regarding the matter of us having owned a dog (Why does international shipping take so long?), but now there is something else I must ask, something of far greater significance.

Please, I beg of you, do not hide the truth from me. It will out in the end, and I would rather hear it from you than a stranger. So, I must enquire…

Jonathan, did we ever have a sister?

I imagine you reeling at my question, but I need a straight answer. Someone from the village has told me we did and that her name was Caitlin. In her final days, Mother called out the name Caitlin over and over again. On one occasion she even begged Caitlin for forgiveness. Also, there are other bits of evidence around the house to suggest that a girl, older than me, once lived here.

I will not discuss my feelings here, Jonathan, not until I know the truth. Suffice it to say, it has come as a shock. I would appreciate you telling the truth. In fact, I would like to know everything. You owe me this much…you all do.

Yours,
Grace

As an after-note I write,

P.S. Does this mysterious sister have anything to do with the upper storey of Parrog House being barricaded by a cupboard and the key hidden? Perhaps not, but somehow, I feel the two are connected.

I resist the temptation to re-read. Instead, I place the letter in the envelope and seal it immediately so that I am not tempted to change anything. I wish to give Jonathan this one chance before I explode in a bout of passion.

⧏ CHAPTER ⧐
XXI

WHEN LILAH CALLS ME DOWN TO BREAKFAST, I WAKE with a start. I feel as if I hardly slept a wink. All night long Mr. Evans' words repeat, over and over: *I mean the sister who died…Caitlin.*

And the drawing. Why was it glued to the back of the bookcase? Did the person who drew it try to hide it? If so, from whom? Surely the bookcase is too heavy for a child to manoeuvre alone, so did an adult hide it there? The whole thing makes no sense. No sense at all.

My head throbs and my mouth is so dry that I cannot even swallow. A crack in the curtains suggests the sun has not yet risen. Midwinter, a time of perpetual night, especially when an army of storm clouds patrol the sky. Lilah is not to be blamed, though. I insisted she call me early so that we can do what we need to in town before preparing the house for the new year. Not that I feel like celebrating, far from it. Why does it seem that despite my attempts to start afresh, to put the past behind me and move on, I am unable to do so? Thus far, I have failed miserably. All I have done is inherited more ghosts.

I wash and dress and drag a comb through my unruly locks before braiding it and pinning it to the nape of my neck so that it does not get in the way of my bonnet. My eyes might be similar to Mother's, but I did not inherit her hair type. Hers was fine and fair; mine is dark and unruly. The drawing on the back of the bookcase springs to mind. Both female figures had long, fair hair, like Mother's. Coincidence? Perhaps.

"Why so glum?" Lilah asks as I enter the kitchen.

"I couldn't sleep. Thoughts spun round and round in my head all night long."

I pick up the teapot and pour. Lilah and I have taken to eating both breakfast and lunch in the kitchen of late. It is only dinner that gets eaten in the dining room. The thought brings a smile to my face. Father would turn in his grave if he could see us.

"That's more like it. A smile is always better than a frown," Lilah says, placing a rack of hot toast on the table. I manage a slice with a spoonful of her orange marmalade.

"Did you finish the playroom?" she asks, her cheeks full of toast.

I nod. "You'll have to help me bring the rug down. I can't manage it on my own. It needs a good clean. Either that, or I might buy a new one. I'm sure the rug's the cause of the doggy smell up there."

Should I tell her about the drawing? She might accuse me of over-thinking, and yes, I am guilty of such a thing. I shall keep it to myself for the time being.

I pause in front of the grandfather clock, glad to see that the moon phase has moved on another step. How nice to see it working again. It displays a third-quarter moon, the eye on the left side is bright, the mouth a painted half-smile. The right side of the moon face is hidden behind one of two globes. I cannot wait for the painting of the harbour to reveal itself, but it will be several weeks until it does so.

Now, Grace, I scold myself. *Do not start obsessing over it, you have been told what happened to your mother.*

❧ ❧

"Reckon it'll snow before the day's out," Lilah says as we stumble across the beach towards the harbour.

The wind screams in our faces and nips at our fingers. As we round the bend, it almost knocks us off our feet. I wish I had remembered my gloves.

"You think so?"

"The moon had a halo around it last night," she says. "A sure sign of snow. Plus, no birds."

"What do you mean, no birds?"

"Well, think about it. Did you hear any birds last night? Because I sure didn't." She points towards The Ship Afloat.

"See the row of gulls on the roof? All huddled they are, sneaking a bit of warmth from the chimney and each other. Sure sign of snow."

She is right, of course. "Well, I hope it doesn't start before we get back. These boots aren't fit for snow. I would have worn my Wellingtons if I'd known." I take her arm in mine and we huddle closer for warmth, just like the gulls.

Our first stop is the post office. The postmistress, an elderly lady with whom I have not previously conversed, regards me with suspicion when I hand over the envelope marked, *United States of America.*

"So soon?" she says.

"Pardon me?"

"You writing to your brother again? So soon after Christmas." She turns her attention to the scales and weighs the envelope. "Must have something awfully important to ask him."

A wave of annoyance surges through me. What business is it of hers? I bite my lip to prevent me from saying so.

The pain in my head has settled right behind my eyes. The intense cold does not help.

"Let's get a move on, Lilah. I can't wait to get home," I say as we step into the bustling street.

The first snowflake settles on my cheek, the second on my nose. By the time we reach the harbour they come thick and fast. Boats donned in soft white blankets and rooftops iced like Christmas cake. The place where horizon meets water is a muted wash of grey. Gulls are perched on balustrades, wondering what has become of the sky.

We slip and slide towards Parrog House. I am thankful for my thick coat, otherwise Lilah's nails would leave marks on my flesh.

"Oh my word, Grace," she says, "I'm frightened of falling on these old knees. Couldn't it have waited a bit longer?"

I open my mouth to answer, but before I can speak, I see her. On the beach in front of the house stands the girl. She faces out to sea, so that she is in profile. Her stance is as steady as the rocks upon which she stands, despite the wind, but the blizzard disguises her features. She is merely a dark stain on a dirty-white sheet. I know it is her, though. The same girl I saw the night we moved in. The same girl I saw when I walked the cliff path, and the same girl I saw on the ship. It is her unruly hair that gives her away.

"Look, Lilah," I say, pointing towards the figure.

She squints in the direction in which I point. At that very moment a huge wave, the colour of granite, surges forth, and in the blink of an eye the girl is gone. No scream, no splash. She simply disappears.

"Oy, Grace! I felt the spray from here." She licks her lips. "I can taste the salt."

There is no point in asking her whether or not she saw the girl.

During the afternoon, I kill time in the rooms on the upper storey. If we are to stay awake till midnight to see in the new year it will be a long day. Already I am fatigued. I visit each of the rooms in turn. In the nursery, I imagine myself as a baby, cradled in the crib. Which room was Jonathan's? I am desperate to find evidence of the existence of a phantom sister, but there is nothing to suggest such a thing, apart from the doll, the books, and the drawing. The bedroom next to the playroom is decorated in a rather dour colour—a deep blue fleur-de-lis design, as is the bedroom at the back of the house, so there is nothing to tell them apart.

The doll and rocking horse pay me no heed as I enter the playroom. I pick up the doll and carry her over to the window. Burying my nose in the folds of her dress, I sniff. It smells of dust, nothing else. Clutched to my chest, we both watch from the window as the snow continues to fall. Monochrome, as far as the eye can see. Steel-grey sky, liquorice rocks, dusted with icing-sugar, the sea a revolving surge of molten iron and chiffon foam.

The girl on the rocks. Is she a ghost? The ghost of my sister? Surely, she is far too old. Though I have not seen her up-close, her stature suggests she is a young woman, not a girl. Given Mother's age, it is impossible. Caitlin could not have been as old as that. And ghosts do not grow up, do they?

My thoughts return to Jonathan. What has he hidden from me all these years? The voice of the postmistress looms large.

Must have something important to ask him, she had said. *Ask, not tell.*

Did she know that in the letter I asked about a dead sister? Had word already spread via Mr. Evans the clockmaker that I seemed surprised when he mentioned Caitlin?

"Who did you belong to?" I ask the doll. "Does the name 'Caitlin' mean anything to you?" Her features remain fixed in a blank expression. She refuses to give anything away. "All right, I'll show you one of her drawings, then perhaps you will remember."

Leaving her on the windowsill, I return to the bookcase. Laden with books, it is far more difficult to move than yesterday, but eventually I manage it. Standing the lantern on the floor next to the gap, I return for the doll.

"There," I kneel and hold her closer to the picture. "Did Caitlin draw this? Is it her work?" And then I see it. In the blank space between sea and sky, words have appeared. My heart is a butterfly, trapped in a spider's web.

The space between sea and sky is home to memories is written in black ink. I drop the doll, and with trembling fingers tear the paper from the wood, leaving behind ragged strips that cling on for dear life. The drawing is ruined, as is my mood, but the words are still legible despite their missing letters. Those that stay behind are the letters: c, a, i, t. The first four letters of her name: Caitlin. A sign or merely coincidence?

Leaving behind the doll and lantern, I race downstairs to find Lilah.

"Good heavens! Whatever's the matter?" she says when she sees me. Tears stream down my face and the drawing trembles as I hold it out for her to see.

"This, Lilah. I didn't tell you yesterday, but I found it stuck to the back of the bookcase in the playroom when I was cleaning."

She takes it from me and squints. Her spectacles peep from the pocket of her apron, reluctant to have anything to do with it.

"The writing. It wasn't there yesterday. Don't you see? It's a repeat of what happened to the note in Mother's trinket box." I sob into my hands as she puts on her spectacles and reads.

"But it's just a child's drawing, Grace. Come on now, don't take it to heart."

"It's not just a child's drawing. *She* drew it—I'm certain. And she must have written on the paper, too."

"Who do you mean?" Her voice falters. She hates it when I get upset like this.

"Why, Caitlin of course! My dead sister! Her ghost is here, Lilah. I feel it."

She slumps down on a chair and examines the sheet of paper.

"The drawing looks old, I'll give you that, but that writing, Grace. It's not the hand of a young child—look."

She hands it back to me, but I put it to one side. "Stay where you are. I'll fetch the note, then you'll see I'm right."

I hurry up the stairs, the hem of my skirts swooshing on the floor. What will it take to persuade her?

We agree that the writing on both the picture and the note look similar. The magnifying glass shows that the letters appear to have been written by the same person. The loop of the letter *b* is once again unjoined; the bridge of the *r* bears a little dip on both samples. And another thing, there is no doubt that the ink appears fresher than the faded lines and colours of the drawing.

Lilah appears downcast. She rests her face in the palm of her hand and looks at me with sympathetic doe-eyes.

"Before you say anything, I did not write it!" Head in hands and teeth clenched, I am desperate for answers. I remember how convinced I was that Eva had written on the note back in Vermont, but my sister-in-law cannot be blamed for this. This time it has to be a ghost, but how can I prove I am right?

Lilah is lost for words, either that or she is too afraid to speak her mind. I cannot stand the silence, so I flee from the room, leaving both note and drawing on the table.

Half an hour passes before Lilah appears with a cup of tea and a smile. She sits on the edge of my bed and moves the hair away from my face. A mother's tender touch.

"Come now," she says, her voice gentle. "It's a mystery, I'll grant you that, but you must try to put it out of your mind. Wait until Jonathan replies to your letter. Perhaps then things will become clearer."

I sit up and look her in the eye. "I'm not mad, Lilah, though something, or someone, is trying to make me believe otherwise." My words retain a sobbing quality.

She sighs. "No one said you were mad, dear girl, and the last thing I wish to do is make the situation worse." She hesitates. "Now, I'm not saying you wrote it, but I wouldn't mind betting the drawing's been on your mind since you found it yesterday."

"And?"

She leans away from me, hands twisting in her lap. "Well, you've always been prone to sleepwalking. You can't deny it." She steals a glance before continuing. "All I'm saying is if the drawing was deep in your subconscious, it's just possible that you went up there last night and—" Another glance. "Well, you know what I'm saying. Don't make me spell it out."

I sip the tea and consider the possibility.

"But surely you would have heard me?"

She laughs. "I'm deaf as a post these days. Once my head hits the pillow, that's me out for count."

I remember then, the night I woke in the playroom. Christmas night, less than a week ago. The dream of spitting teeth, and the horse's teeth. Blood and maggots. I heave a sigh. I must concur, it is possible that it happened again, but could I really have moved a bookcase, stacked with books, in my sleep? Would the hand that wrote words in the pitch dark be steady enough to be read in the cold light of day? I examine the words inked in black once more. It is possible the same pen is responsible for writing these words as that which wrote the letter to Jonathan.

The grandfather clock in the hall strikes seven. Lilah strokes my hair.

"Listen," she says. "Why don't you take a nap while I prepare supper? If we're to see in the new year, you'll need a rest."

I dry my eyes with a handkerchief and try to smile.

"Tell you what," she says, "after supper we'll both change into our nightclothes and have a drop of port. No one will call. Not with the snow as thick as it is. And in any case, who's going to traipse all the way to Parrog House to wish a pair of dames a happy new year?"

She turns down the lamp, leaving the curtains open, before closing the door softly behind her. The moon beyond my window matches that on the clock. Half a face, tilted at an angle that suggests sympathy. Now and then clouds scud across its face, their movement swift. The snowflakes they deliver join together to form large crystals that stick to the glass before melting to tears.

Lilah's cheeks burn red from the heat of the fire and three glasses of port she has consumed. It is almost half past eleven and both of us are struggling to stay awake. After the anxiety of the day, the evening has progressed without a hitch, and I feel much calmer.

"I need a glass of water," she says, pressing the back of her hand against her cheek. "Want anything?"

"No, thank you. I'm as full as an egg."

She hobbles off to the kitchen, taking our empty glasses with her. A knock on the door startles me. I am tempted to ignore it, but I can hardly pretend we are in bed when the lamps are lit. I remain seated, hoping that whoever it is will go away, but the knock comes again, more insistent this time.

"I'll get it!" I call, adjusting my dressing gown so that the belt is wrapped tight.

The clock chimes the half-hour, drowning out the sound of voices outside. I turn the lock and hold the door open a fraction, gasping as freezing air enters without welcome. Nothing. No one. I am about to close it again when a face appears. But it is not a human face.

Instead, I find myself cheek to jowl with a horse, or rather a horse's skull. Laughter and voices speak in a tongue I do not understand. The horse's jaw falls open, just like in my dream. Its eye sockets are black orbs. Blind. Its body is draped in white sheets from which strips of red ribbon dangle like bloody sinew. My hand flies to my mouth as it opens its jaw and thrusts it close to my face before closing it with a *snap*.

"*Y Mari Lwyd yma,*" a gruff voice says, but all I am aware of is the repeated snap of the jaw and the skull's missing tooth.

Their voices grow distant, muffled. My legs are weak as water; my head a spinning-top. I know nothing more until I wake from a stupor, surrounded by strange faces, streaked with soot.

"For God's sake, give her space!" someone shouts, as Lilah's face floats into focus.

✂ CHAPTER ✂

XXII

ALL EXCEPT ONE OF THE MERRYMAKERS HAVE disappeared. The man leans a shoulder against the mantelpiece, propping himself up, and watches me with his good eye.

"You sure you're all right?" he says, his expression sombre and guilt-ridden. I recognize him in an instant. It is the shipwright, Gruff Lewis.

I nod and take another sip of brandy. Lilah holds a cotton cloth, filled with snow, against the side of my head. Ice cold water runs down my face and into my left eye. She removes the cloth and tuts.

"The size of an egg," she says, referring to the lump on my temple.

His shoulders hunch when he sees it. He tugs at his bottom lip and sighs.

"We should have known better," he says, shaking his head. "Of course, you'd know nothing of the *Mari Lwyd.*" He swallows hard, and his Adam's apple bulges in his throat.

"You look like you could do with a drop of brandy yourself," Lilah says. "Here, hold this." She thrusts the snow-filled cloth into his hand before gesturing for him to hold it to my head, then waltzes off to fetch another glass.

Too weak to feel embarrassed, I allow him to hold the compress against my skin. Every now and then he wipes away a stray trickle with a clean handkerchief, gentle as a lamb, though his hands tremble.

Lilah returns and hands him the brandy glass which he accepts without protest, then she resumes her place at my side.

He gulps down the brandy and shudders.

"I'll go and get fresh snow." He takes the cloth from her and hurries outside.

Tentatively, I touch the lump with the tips of my fingers. About two inches long and an inch raised, the lump feels tender. My head throbs, but then it has done all day.

He returns with a fresh bundle of snow and hands the cloth to Lilah before continuing to loom over both of us.

"Sit down, won't you?" she says. "You're stealing the light."

I glance up. She is right. His large frame blocks out the fire as well as the lantern on the wall behind him. I had not realized how tall he was until now.

He does as she says, perching at the edge of the chair as though afraid he might soil it. Either that, or he is eager to take his leave.

"Please," he says. "May I explain?"

"It's all right, Lilah," I say. "I'll hold it."

I take the cloth from her and slump back on the sofa.

"The *Mari Lwyd*—the horse skull," he says, though neither of us have given him permission to speak. "It's tradition, that's all." He pauses for a moment. "Gone on for many years, it has. It's meant to bring good luck. You're meant to welcome the *Mari Lwyd* into your house and ply it with food and drink. Then it'll sing you a farewell song and be off."

"Listen, Mr. Lewis," I say, removing the cloth from my head and fixing him with a steely gaze. "Let's not worry about it, shall we? Your intention was not to frighten me, I'm sure. It's just that coming face-to-face with a horse's skull, draped in red ribbons, one that snapped its jaws at me repeatedly was the last thing I expected to see when I opened the door. It's pitch black out there." I nod towards the window. "You gave me an awful fright."

"Of course, of course," he says, shaking his head. "We should have known better. Anyway, I'd best be off." He stands and hands the empty glass to Lilah. "If there's anything you need, just ask."

"I'll see you out," Lilah says, heading for the door.

"Stay where you are." She points at me, though I have no intention of moving. In fact, I am not yet certain my legs would carry me.

I hear the front door close just as the grandfather clock strikes midnight.

"Happy New Year," Lilah says, slipping back into the room like a fairy godmother. "What a way to start 1903!"

"Indeed. And the same to you, Lilah."

She eyes me suspiciously. "By the way…you and that Mr. Lewis. Do you know each other?"

I shake my head. "Not really. Do you remember me telling you about the incident with the shipwright and the dog a few weeks back?"

"I do. Don't tell me it's him!"

"One and the same."

"Well, well. He's out to get you, Grace Morgan." She laughs. "Ready for bed? I'll help you up. Make sure you're comfortable, and if you don't feel well in the night just call me. A bump on the head can be nasty, you know."

❧ ❧

When Mrs. Jones the Draper arrives the following Wednesday, she takes one look at me and gasps.

"What on earth happened to you? A right shiner you have there."

The swelling has subsided, but the skin beneath my eye is a mottled patch of purple and green.

"She had a quarrel with a horse," Lilah says with a snort, relieving Mrs. Jones of an armful of cushions. "And a dead one at that."

I explain about the incident with the *Mari Lwyd,* attributing my faint to having drunk a little too much port and eaten hardly anything.

"You poor thing," she says. "I suppose it's understandable, especially if you're prone to fainting. Not for the faint-hearted is the *Mari Lwyd,* if you'll pardon the pun. Anyway, let's hope that getting the playroom sorted will cheer you up."

I show both her and her daughter upstairs. At least the smell of fresh paint has masked the doggy odour.

"Ceiling's made a difference," Mrs. Jones says once we are in the playroom. "Really brightened the place. Does a good job, my Rhys, even if I say so myself."

Her daughter, Ffion, looks a little forlorn. "Both your children do you proud, Mrs. Jones." I say. Ffion glances at me and smiles.

"Of course. Proud of them both, I am. There now." She places the new curtains down on the windowsill. "What do you think of the colour?"

"I love it," I say, stroking the fabric. "It's bound to cheer the place up, and I'm looking forward to learning to sew, too."

I have not been up here since the *Mari Lwyd* incident, but the rocking horse in the far corner reminds me of it once again. I put two fingers to my cheekbone and stroke the delicate skin. A rocking horse with a missing tooth, the dream about maggots in the horse's jaw, then the *Mari Lwyd*—a horse's skull snapping in my face. Is it really a coincidence? I shudder, remembering.

"I'll leave you to it," I say, and hurry from the room.

When a letter from Jonathan arrives the following morning, I tear it open, imagining for a moment that it might be in answer to my question regarding the existence of our sister Caitlin, before I realize he could not possibly have received the letter yet. Of course, he writes in answer to my previous letter, the one that mentioned the dog.

> *Dear Grace,*
>
> *First of all, on behalf of all of us, I want to wish you a happy new year. I trust you are well and hope you are adjusting to life in Parrog House as we are in Woodleigh House, though I must say, it is rather strange to be back in the old place.*
>
> *Though I complained a little about Eva's extravagant redecoration, I have to admit I am glad. There would have been too many sad memories if the house had been left the way Mother had it.*
>
> *Anyway, in your letter to Helena, you asked if we had ever owned a dog. I can confirm we did not, though I would*

have loved one. Mother was allergic, you see, or at least that is what I remember being told.

We did, however, have a friend who owned a dog, and on occasion we would smuggle the dog upstairs into the playroom and do our utmost to shush it if it so much as whimpered. We were often discovered and chased out of the house. Such fun!

By the way, when next you write, perhaps you might tell me what you have done with the rooms. I am interested to hear.

Yours,
Jonathan

Such a short letter, so typical of Jonathan. He has always played his cards close to his chest, and yet I do believe there is much that can be learned from it. To begin with, I am not surprised that he doesn't mention Lilah, not even when wishing me a Happy New Year. Such a snob!

Secondly, despite considering himself the man of the house, it is obvious that Eva has the upper hand. She always has, though he would never admit it. Instead, he turns things around so that it seems she has done him a favour.

His point about the dog is interesting and goes some way towards explaining the smell. However, I am not convinced the smell would have lasted all this time.

Of paramount importance, though, is his use of the word *we.* He could not have been referring to me. I would have been far too young to have had a friend who owned a dog. I read the letter several times, looking for clues. *We did, however, have a friend who owned a dog; we were chased out of the house.* I agree, the latter could mean Jonathan and his friend; the former, however, could not. So does it refer to our sister? An unintentional error that reveals the subconscious, perhaps?

The afternoon is spent setting out the playroom, which I must stop referring to as such because it is no longer a child's room. Subtle tones of olive and juniper in the soft furnishings coordinate with the wallpaper and look far less dour than the previous dark maroon.

From the mantelpiece, the doll watches my every move. I talk to her as I work, but she refuses to respond. I have moved the rocking horse into the nursery. Since the dream and the *Mari Lwyd* incident I can hardly bear to look at it.

Padded cushions line the bay window, providing the perfect spot for reading. A small group of children play on the beach, despite the bitter cold. Cheeks flushed red and cloudy breath, they do not seem to notice. The sound of their laughter carries on the wind, and I find myself picturing Jonathan and my phantom sister playing there long ago.

Lilah shouts upstairs to ask if I need a hand.

"Come and see what you think," I say. I know she hates the narrow stairs, but I want her to see how different the room looks with the new décor.

The doll's eyes brighten as she enters. I swear they twinkle beneath the lamplight, and Lilah reaches for her like a magnet to metal.

"What a difference," she says, scanning the room. "Much brighter. It feels calmer, more restful." She smooths the top of the doll's head as she speaks. "You've got rid of the rocking horse, I see." She pokes her tongue against the inside of her cheek and grins.

"It's in the nursery, and it's staying there." I shudder.

Lilah picks up the small bolt of fabric that Mrs. Jones has left behind, opens it out, and holds it in front of the doll. "She needs a new dress. I can help you unpick the old one if you like, then we could use it as a pattern."

"Good idea, and what about her head? I don't like that hole. It's creepy."

"We'll fix that while we're at it." She picks up the doll and looks around the room. "You could do with some sort of desk in here you know, for all your sewing things."

"I thought the same, but how on earth will we get one up those stairs?"

"Well, they managed to get beds and a wardrobe up here in the past, didn't they? Proves it can be done."

I admire Lilah's tenacity. She refuses to allow anything to defeat her. "How about the desk in the back sitting room? It's never used, and it's not too cumbersome."

She waggles a finger. "You'll be the death of me, Grace Lewis." She laughs. "Come on, let's have a go."

It is not so much the weight of the desk that makes it difficult to manoeuvre, but, rather, its awkwardness. Each time we take a step, our legs butt up against the legs of the desk. Progress is painfully slow. Nevertheless, we make it up the first flight of stairs without too much damage to ourselves or the furniture.

Lilah stands half-bent and red-faced on the landing. "Let me get my breath before we go any farther," she says, gulping air.

A loud rap at the front door makes me start. "I'll get it," I say, leaving Lilah to recover.

I cannot hide the shock on my face when I open the door and find Gruff Lewis, the shipwright, standing there, his dog on a leash.

He looks rather sheepish as he shifts from one foot to the other.

"Good afternoon. I just called to see how you were doing on my way home from the boat-shed." He points at the faded bruise beneath my eye and winces. "I hope you've recovered well enough. Looks nasty."

The dog whines and pulls at the leash, eager to be gone.

"That's most kind of you. I'm fine, thank you." I sense the heat rise to my cheeks.

"Who is it, Grace?" Lilah calls from the landing.

"You'll have to excuse me, we're in the middle of moving a piece of furniture," I say, eager for him to leave.

"Grace?" Lilah calls again.

He stands there, waiting for me to answer her, so I step into the hall and shout up the stairs. "It's Mr. Lewis. I won't be a moment."

"Mr. who?"

My fists clench. "Mr. Lewis, the man with the *Mari Lwyd*. He wants to know if I've recovered."

There is a moment's pause while she considers my answer. "Then tell him to come up. We could do with a bit of muscle here."

I bite my bottom lip and frown. I could murder Lilah at this moment.

He raises an eyebrow. "Well? Need a hand?"

I scratch my forehead and look down at my feet.

"I guess so. It's Lilah you see, she struggles with the stairs."

I do not wish to give him the impression that I am some kind of weakling.

"Just let me tie Bran." He secures the dog's lead to the metal fence. "Stay," he says. "I shan't be long." He wipes his feet on the mat as he enters and removes his cap.

"Up here," Lilah calls, and I gesture for him to go up.

"Tell you what, me and Grace will move it and you can be foreman," he says, grinning. "I'll take the back end, all right, Grace?"

We cover the length of the landing with ease and soon reach the stairs to the upper storey.

"Now then," he says, "put your end down, and I'll drag it the rest of the way. There isn't room for both of us on these stairs."

I do as he says, and soon the desk is safely on the landing.

"Which room do you want it in?"

"The playroom, second door on the right."

Lilah squeezes past us and opens the door. Though I am reluctant to admit it, the job has been far easier with his help.

"Where do you want it, Grace?" Lilah says. "Against this wall?" She points to the wall adjoining the landing.

"If it will fit in the alcove, I'd rather it there," I say, pointing to the wall next to the window. "That way I'll have more light and a view."

The desk fits like a glove.

"There you go," he says, swiping his hands. "Made to measure." The sound of Bran yapping reaches us from the front garden. "I'd best be off," he says, gazing around the room. "Changed a bit in here. I wouldn't have recognized it."

"Pardon me?"

He nods. "This room. It's changed a bit since I was here last."

I glance at Lilah who stands in front of the window, mouth agape.

"Your brother and me…best friends we were as kiddies. Used to play up here all the time."

"You…y-you never said." I am lost for words. Gruff Lewis, a man I took an instant dislike to, might just hold the answer to many of my questions.

He grins from ear to ear.

"Well, you never asked, did you?"

XXIII

I MUST KEEP BUSY, OTHERWISE MY NERVES WILL GET THE better of me and I will fall apart. Gruff Lewis has agreed to call at six o'clock so that we can discuss his memories of my family and Parrog House. Lilah, of course, will be present, though she intends to keep a low profile and will busy herself with tea and cake.

We have unpicked the doll's dress and assembled a paper pattern from the pieces, adding a quarter inch seam allowance. My hand trembles as I pin the paper pattern to the fabric. The doll sits on the mantelpiece wearing a forlorn expression. She is likely cold in just her undergarments, but it will be worth the suffering.

Gruff Lewis strikes me as someone who speaks his mind. In fact, I imagine he will open up more readily than my own brother. I am both elated and nervous about what I might discover. I have not yet decided how much to reveal, especially regarding Caitlin. What will he think of us as a family if I admit I had no idea of her existence until recently? On the other hand, he might not mention her at all, this phantom sister of mine, brought to life after a throwaway comment from a clockmaker.

Lilah tells me not to fret. She says I should go with the flow, whatever that means, but I did not sleep a wink last night, nor the night before.

Lilah gives the doll a gentle shake and its head rattles.

"Do you know, Grace, I think the missing piece of porcelain's fallen inside. It that's the case, and we can get it out, it'll be so much easier to fix than trying to patch it with something else."

"Bring her over here," I say. "Hold her to the window and I'll take a look."

I shake the doll gently, certain the piece is inside. I remember back to the day I discovered her, and how my fingers probed the hole in her head, the dampness, the warmth. Brain matter. Even now it makes me wince.

"Hold her upside down, and I'll try to get it out," Lilah says, rummaging about in the sewing box for a tweezer. A delicate operation, but eventually we manage it. The missing part of the doll's skull is recovered in two pieces, both with woven strands of hair still attached. The thing looks rather gruesome and reminds me of an article I read about the Native American practice of scalping.

"I'll take her downstairs and mix up a glue paste. I'll call if I need you to hold her still during the operation," Lilah says, peering over my shoulder as I make tiny stitches on the collar of the new dress.

"What will you use?"

"Starch, egg white, a bit of powdered bone to give it strength."

"Powdered bone?" I wrinkle my nose.

"Yes. I was keeping the lamb knuckle to make stock, but I'll grind a bit with the pestle and mortar and add it to the pot. Bone makes for good glue."

Once Lilah has gone, I take my sewing over to the window seat and stitch while watching the sea. It rolls in on foaming waves that bubble and break before the moon pulls it back. A tug of war between earth and satellite.

Ten to three, yet already the moon sits proud in the sky, watching the fruits of its labour. Gruff Lewis is due at six. He will arrive with the dusk, and the moon will light his way. I recall how Father loathed this time of year with its short days and endless nights, whereas Mother enjoyed the solitude it brought. I, myself, cannot wait for summer and yearn for long walks along the cliff path. These dark days can be so depressing, especially when it rains and daylight sulks behind great swathes of cloud.

With only the sound of the sea for company, the house feels empty. How did it cope during those lonely decades?

Did it sustain itself with past memories, or did it feast on the false promise of hope? Hope that it would once again be filled with the sound of living, breathing people instead of a few insentient toys.

I make the final stitch on the collar of the doll's dress and hold it up to the light. Skull mended and the old dress replaced, the doll will be granted a new lease of life. If only it were that simple with people. For me, a new dress is easily attainable, but repairing my head is another matter.

❦

Lilah answers the door and shows Gruff Lewis into the front parlour before scuttling off to fetch the tea tray. I am already seated on the one and only chair, therefore it will be necessary for him to sit on the sofa, which is lower, thus granting me the advantage of height. How calculating I am.

I stand briefly as he enters and bid him good afternoon. He removes his cap, and by the light of the lamp his complexion shines, likely the result of a close shave. He wears what I imagine is his Sunday best.

"Please, take a seat," I say, sensing the heat rise to my face. I am unused to gentleman callers, no matter the reason.

His good eye acknowledges my offer, whilst the other stares blindly. Like mine, his face is flushed, all except for the scars which stand white and proud as sandworms.

"Did you leave the dog at home?" I ask, as a way of breaking the ice.

"I did, though he wasn't too happy about it. Goes everywhere with me, he does."

Ever since he told me about having visited as a child I have wondered about the dog. Could it be the same one Jonathan mentioned in his letter? I think not. No dog lives that long.

Lilah comes in with a tray laden with tea and leftover Christmas cake.

"I'll be in the kitchen if you want anything," she says. "I'm sure you two have lots to talk about. Would you like me to pour first?" She holds the teapot in her hand.

I rise from my seat. "No thank you, Lilah, I'll manage, though you are welcome to join us." Part of me wishes she

165

would. I might feel less self-conscious with her present, and in any case I keep no secrets from her.

"I have things to do, Grace," she says, "but if you want me, just shout."

She closes the door on her way out, and we are left wondering where to begin. "So," I say, swallowing hard. "Where should we start?"

He stands and unbuttons his jacket. "Do you mind if I take this off? It's sweltering in here." He fans his face with his left hand as if to prove a point, and I can't help wondering if he, too, feels nervous.

"Go ahead," I say.

He removes the jacket, folds it neatly, then places it on the arm of the sofa. His shirtsleeves are rolled to the elbow, as is typical of a man who works with his hands. Along the left forearm and back of his hand the skin is puckered. It forms a pattern like fronds of frost on glass. I tear my gaze away and flush deeper, but he does not seem to notice. I busy myself with pouring tea and serving cake onto his plate, though I take none myself. I could not swallow a morsel at present.

He clears his throat before taking a sip from the cup.

"Well, then," he says. "What would you like to know?"

"Anything…and everything. You see, I have no recollection of this house as a child. None whatsoever, and Jonathan—well, let's just say that Jonathan is not one for idle chatter." I smile in the hope that he will not think I am betraying my brother.

He nods and returns the smile.

"Speaking of Jonathan, how is he? I have not yet enquired about his health."

"He is well, thank you. He is married with a daughter, my niece, Helena."

"And your parents, are they——"

I glance at my feet and shake my head. "Both passed. Mother a few months ago, Father several years back."

"I am sorry." He says nothing for a minute or so as a mark of respect. "Well then, let me begin." He takes a sip of tea and a bite of cake then looks around the room as if seeing it for the first time. "Me and Jonathan were the best of friends as kiddies, though worlds apart in some ways." He nods at the room, first left then right, and in doing so I imagine he infers that he and Jonathan came from different breeding stock.

"When the weather was good, we'd play on the beach or mess about on the harbour, but when it rained, which was often, we'd come here and play upstairs in the room where we took the desk the other day."

"So you two were the same age?"

"Give or take, far as I remember. We went to different schools, see, so were not in the same class."

I believe he refers to class in two ways but does not like to say so.

"Did you bring the dog when you played here?"

"My dog, Bran?" He waits for me to acknowledge his words. "Well, before him I had another. His mother, in fact. Her name was Bronwen. A darling, she was. We'd take her for walks and play ball on the beach. Your brother adored her, but your mother was allergic to dogs by all accounts." He raises an eyebrow, unconvinced. "Anyway, sometimes we'd smuggle Bronwen upstairs and she'd lie in the playroom. But your mother had sharp hearing and an even sharper sense of smell." He laughs. "Somehow, she'd always track us down, and when she did we could look out. She'd give us what for."

I move to the edge of my seat and nod, eager for him to continue. When he says nothing more I say, "And do you remember me? I was two years old when we emigrated to America."

He chews his lower lip and eyes me sideways. I have almost forgotten his scars. I am more concerned with my own, though mine are invisible.

"I remember Jonathan telling me he had a new sister." My stomach twists at the word *new*. "But after what happened I——" He hesitates.

"Well?"

He takes a deep breath.

"Well, after what happened, I was never allowed in again."

My heart is a hammer, beating nails of steel.

"I'm sorry," I say. "I don't understand. After *what* happened?"

He winces and covers the scarred skin on his arm with the opposite hand, as though it causes him pain.

"After what happened to your sister, Caitlin."

My stomach hits the ground, though I try my best to hide it.

"It was me who found her, see, after the accident." He points at the scar on his face before delivering the blow.

XXIV

LILAH HAS GONE DOWN WITH A COLD. EVEN SO, SHE offered to accompany me to the graveyard, but I told her to stay at home and rest. If I am honest, this is something I need to do alone. It feels right, somehow.

Just to the right of the yew tree, Gruff had said. *She's buried with your grandparents.*

The wind is in a temper this morning, so I tie my bonnet tight beneath my chin.

You look as though you've seen a ghost, the mirror in the hall whispers.

The grandfather clock strikes eleven. Thank goodness it is Saturday, not Sunday, or the church would be filled with morning worshippers. I am hoping to have the place to myself, what with the weather being so bad. The last thing I wish to do is engage in another conversation about my dead sister, at least not until I have had time to come to terms with it.

The face on the clock depicts a full moon, one that shines down on the harbour like a mother watching over her children. The clockmaker is right. The painted scene really is special, so serene, and I am privileged to see it restored to its former glory.

I step outside into a gale. Low tide. The sea is a distant sheet of grey, but the water in the estuary bubbles and broils in the easterly wind, displaying its mighty crosscurrents as a threat to those who dare to venture across. Patches of iron-grey cloud scud across the sky, and the air is filled with the whistling wind and the tinkling of anchor chains. Their unease hastens me on, but the limekiln looms close and I cannot bear to look at it. Not today. Not knowing it was the place where Caitlin died.

As I climb the hill towards the castle, I glance up at windows that seem to monitor my approach. No sign of anyone behind them, and yet I feel I am being watched. Thankfully, the churchyard appears empty, except for the robin perched on the gatepost. With a flurry of wings, it darts away as I enter, before disappearing inside the nearest yew. Is this the tree beneath which Caitlin rests?

As far back as the Ancient Greeks, yews have been associated with death and the journey from this life to the next. A symbol of death, yet very much alive: evergreen foliage, sharp needles, and multiple limbs that twist like sinew. Inside the heart of the tree, I spy a red breast and a beady eye. The robin thrusts out its throat and sings, safe in the knowledge that it sits on too high a branch for me to reach.

Beneath its canopy, a few headstones lean towards the tree trunk like children seeking comfort from a parent, but it is not those I have come to see. There, to the right of the tree, stands my family memorial. Caitlin's name is hidden beneath lichen, but the numerals recording her age endure. Eight years and eighteen days old when she died.

The headstone is unremarkable, except for a sailing ship and anchor, one in either corner, which suggests my grandfather's occupation was to do with the sea. It explains the location of Parrog House, I suppose, built right on the seafront. Why did my parents never mention them, and why did I never ask? The relationship must have been a loving one, or why else would they have buried their daughter in the same grave?

I have brought no floral tribute with me today. All I can offer are sorrowful words of regret that we never had the opportunity to get to know one another.

She burned to death, Gruff Lewis had said when I pressed him. *I tried to save her, but she was already gone, hence the scars.* He had pointed to his arm.

And your eye? I hope you don't mind me asking, I had said, a searing heat rising to the centre of my breast.

That, too. It was the lime, you see.

A whip of wind smites my face. It tries to remove my bonnet, so I pull it tighter. But it delivers the gift of a leaf. A leaf that lands silently on Caitlin's grave. But it is not a leaf. Not really. It is the skeleton of one. Intricate spine, delicate veins, but the flesh rotted. Is the wind trying to tell me something? I know that by now my sister's body will be nothing more than a skeleton without the wind needing to remind me.

"I'll bring flowers next time," I say, crouching down to trace her name with my finger. "Which did you like?" Born in December, I imagine she would have liked snowdrops or paperwhite narcissus, both winter flowers.

As I get to my feet, a whisk of movement catches my eye. Someone must have been standing at the corner of the church, watching. Now they have fled. I follow in their footsteps, uncertain of what I might do if I catch up with them. But when I reach the corner no one is there. Nothing but gravestones that would make good hiding places. Hands on hips, I wait a while in case someone appears, but when no one does, I turn on my heels and head for the gate.

⬧ ⬧

The sound of Lilah coughing greets me at the door.

"Find it?" she asks, as I take off my coat. Her voice is a wheeze, a whistle of alarm, but still she smiles.

"Yes." I shake my head. "But I don't think I'm ready to talk about it yet. Do you mind?"

Another bout of coughing bends her double.

"Not at all. Take all the time you want. You know old Lilah'll be here when you're ready. Oh, and by the way, the repair on the doll's head is dry. I've put her in the new dress and styled her hair. She looks so much happier, Grace."

I do not see the doll at first. Lilah has removed her from the mantelpiece and positioned her on the windowsill. Since the new dress is made from the same fabric as the seat cushion, she all but disappears, though I swear she smiles at me. The corners of her mouth turn upwards, her cerulean eyes sparkle. It is the light from the window that does it, of course, but nevertheless it unnerves me. I sit her on my lap and examine the back of her head with the tip of my finger. Lilah has pinned her hair in a bun. It hides the scars, but they lurk beneath the surface still.

I sit a while longer, watching the sea roll in and the wind buffet the gulls until they give up the ghost and settle for the beach, where they pluck lugworms from the sand and quarrel over scraps of dead crab. But the scene reminds me of Caitlin and what has become of her body, so I leave the doll to watch them feast while I open the drawer of the desk and take out the drawing.

I trace the words with a finger: *The space between sea and sky is home to memories.* Those four missing letters that spell c-a-i-t seem even more poignant. Did I write it, or was it the ghost of my dead sister? I am less certain now than ever.

Tell me what she looked like. I had said to Gruff Lewis. *In life, I mean. I want to be able to picture her.*

The child in the picture has hair the colour of sand and eyes as blue as the ocean. A self-portrait, perhaps? Gruff Lewis described her as fair, but so are many other children. *A bit of a tomboy,* he'd said. *She loved being outdoors with us boys and was always up to mischief. That's what comes of having an older brother, I suppose.*

He had traced the scars on his forearm as he spoke, as though they helped him remember her. I didn't tell him I knew nothing of her, the shame of it would have been unbearable. Instead, I allowed him to tell me what he wished and probed him with a question here and there when necessary.

Dusk creeps into the room, so I return downstairs. Lilah has retired to bed with a hot water bottle and a tincture of honey and ginger, and I am in the front parlour, reading, when I sense a presence at the half-open door. I tiptoe towards it and peer into the hall, but no one is there. The wall lantern next to the clock reminds me that tonight the full moon will show its face, and I cannot resist opening the front door and stepping out into the night.

To my right, the row of cottages glows warm from within, and the sign outside The Ship Afloat swings to and fro in the wind. But the moon takes centre stage. Poised above the sea, it is surrounded by a galaxy of supporting stars that twinkle at its majesty. A shimmering path of moonlight stretches towards the shore, stopping in front of Parrog House as though inviting its occupants to walk along it. Strands of stratus soften the moon's middle with a cloud-belt, but still it shines.

It is too cold to stay outside for long, so I close the front door, wrapping my shawl about me with a shiver. The parlour door remains ajar, and I am about to enter when a child's voice startles me.

"For the feather, Mammy. I asked if you had a box for the feather."

My breath is a caged bird as I stand in the doorway. Neither of them see me. It is as if I am invisible. The chair I sat on just a few minutes earlier is now occupied by my mother, albeit a younger version. I gasp and put a hand to my mouth, but still she does not notice. In front of her stands a child. A girl with sandy ringlets that swing as she nods. In her right hand she holds something towards Mother, while her left hand is on her hip. Caitlin?

I am frozen. No sound escapes my lips. I cannot even blink.

"What feather?" Mother puts down her book, the book that I was reading moments ago, and fixes her gaze on the child. "What are you talking about?"

The girl holds the feather by its stem and twists it in front of Mother's face as if trying to hypnotize her.

"This feather. The one you found on the beach."

It is the jay's feather, I am certain. The one that sits inside the silver trinket box in my bedroom.

Mother snatches it from the child's hand and scowls. She puts it down on top of the book, then takes the child's hands in hers. Her grip is tight, and the child winces.

"I did not give you that feather. Please, Caitlin, stop telling lies!"

Caitlin! Now there is no doubt in my mind. This is my sister, long dead. I want to cry out, but my lungs refuse to cooperate. As in sleep, my muscles are paralysed. All I can do is watch the scene play out in front of me.

"But you did!" Caitlin's voice is shrill. "When we were at the beach, just the other day. Don't you remember, Mammy?"

My mother releases her hands with such force that Caitlin is thrust backward. I wish I could comfort her, but I cannot move. She begins to cry.

"I only asked for a box to keep it in. You told me to keep it safe, and I'm afraid I might lose it." She rubs her eyes, but her stance is firm, determined. Mother, on the other hand, seems to deflate. Energy sapped, she slumps back in the chair and covers her eyes with her hand. Caitlin senses victory, so continues the tirade. "The jay's feather stands for Jonathan, you said. A jay will protect its family at all costs, you said. It will never hurt them, no matter what." She scowls, then with one deft movement, grabs the feather and runs from the room, passing by me without so much as a glance.

Once again, my sister is no more than a whoosh of invisible air.

Mother is gone, too. The book resides just where I left it, its page-marker still in place.

Shaken to the core, my first instinct is to run to Lilah, but now is not the time. The poor woman is ill. I must not burden her with my woes, and besides, I have evidence to seek.

⚍ ⚎

The silver trinket box is cold to the touch. The key remains squirrelled inside my dressing-table drawer, precisely where I left it. I half expect to see the jay's feather missing, but it is not. It lies against the note Mother left. The note that reads: *Remember for me, Grace.*

Lantern in hand, I climb the stairs to the upper storey. What do I expect to find? A sister I never knew? The ghost of a girl, lurking in the shadows?

The rocking horse is still as stone; its leather seat cool to the touch. It has not recently been ridden.

The door to the playroom squeals as it opens, and I am glad to see that the doll remains in the exact position I left her—staring out to sea, towards a moon whose celestial craters are shadowed in a pensive expression. There is no evidence of my dead sister having been here recently.

⚍ ⚎

I love this place. I love the house, the harbour, the people I have come to know, but I despise the torment that has followed me across the ocean. Is this what Mother meant when she wrote the word *Wherever* on the notepaper? Did she realize that wherever she went, no matter how far the distance between her and her troubles, this mental anguish would follow?

Was there some part of Mother that knew I would come here, and is that why she wrote the words, *Remember for me, Grace?* Or did I write those words? Does some part of my subconscious sense I am doomed, just like she was?

I smooth out the paper and read those five words over and over again. I hold the jay's feather in the palm of my hand and blow gently. But the quill is strong. The backbone of the family. *A jay will protect its family at all costs,* Caitlin had said. Is that why Jonathan never told me? Is it why he seemed relieved when I agreed to move from Vermont? Perhaps he considers me a bad influence on his daughter, or does he simply want to protect all of us from past hurt? Now, more than ever, I long for his reply.

As supportive as Lilah is, I am certain that if I tell her what has occurred this evening she will suggest I speak to the doctor. But what good would come of it? Doctor Perkins in Vermont suggested my hallucinations were caused by the grief of Mother's death, even though he must have thought it possible that I inherited a tendency to suffer from mental illness. The doctor here knows nothing of my past. How difficult might it be to convince him that I am not sick, that I do not require institutionalizing? But to bear the burden alone feels as heavy as the ship's cargo that accompanied me here.

I return the note and feather to the box and consider the drawing I found stuck to the back of the bookcase. There is no need to fetch it from the playroom; the scene is sharp in my mind.

Why did Mother deny she had given Caitlin the feather? Had she simply forgotten, or did her memory loss start all those years ago? Perhaps she was angry, because deep down she knew something was wrong and the fear made her nerves fraught.

Above all else, why am I experiencing past events as if they are occurring right in front of me? Which am I haunted by: ghosts or psychosis?

The pain in my head is a viper. Coiled inside my brain, it fills its fangs with venom, ready to strike.

Tomorrow, I will walk to the boat-shed and speak once more to Gruff Lewis. There is little purpose in waiting for Jonathan's letter. I am already convinced it will reveal very little.

In the meantime, I check on Lilah, pleased to find her asleep. I have eaten nothing since breakfast, and what I ate then was meagre. I consider waking her to see if she would like me to bring her something, but it is best I let her rest.

A blast of cold air hits as I enter the kitchen. Without Lilah in attendance, the range has gone out and the air is frigid. I make do with some ham, bread and cheese and return to the front parlour, certain it will be warmer there. The door is shut, just as I left it, but still I hesitate. No child's voice now. Why should there be? Stop it, Grace, I admonish myself. You cannot let this house become a prison of fear.

XXV

MY PLAN TO SPEAK WITH GRUFF LEWIS A SECOND TIME is thwarted by Lilah's sickness. This morning, she is too ill to get out of bed. In all the years I have known her, not once has she ever failed to be up and dressed before me.

"Shall I get the doctor?" I ask, propping up her pillows.

She is overcome by a racking cough, one which produces a gobbet of dark green sputum. "Don't you dare," she says, gasping for breath. "Once this muck is off my chest, I'll be right as rain."

"Then I insist you spend the day in bed, and no arguments."

She does not protest, so I know how ill she must feel. If she is no better tomorrow I will call the doctor without telling her.

"I could murder a cup of tea," she says, biting her lower lip and looking at me through glassy eyes. "But you haven't a clue how to light the range, have you?" She eases herself to the edge of the bed.

"What do you think you're doing?"

"I need the chamber pot, Grace. Then I'll come downstairs and show you."

"You'll do no such thing." I take her by the elbow and help her to shuffle a few steps. Never before have I emptied her chamber pot, though she has emptied mine on countless occasions. She will protest, no doubt, but it must be done. "You can explain how to prepare the range, then I will do it myself."

By early afternoon she feels a little better. "Will you be all right on your own for a while? I'd like to go for a walk. I could do with some fresh air, and the rain has stopped."

"Of course. I'll probably just sleep—best remedy there is."

Leaving her with a glass of hot water, lemon, and honey, I wrap up warm and head outdoors. Instead of going down to the beach, I keep to the path that leads all the way to the boat-shed, the place where I first met Gruff Lewis. Perhaps he will not be working in this weather, but I am willing to take a chance.

His border collie, Bran, hears me approach and comes bounding from the shed.

"Here, Bran!" Gruff appears at the doorway and watches me, one hand on the dog's collar. It pulls and yelps and I keep my distance. Dogs have always been wary of me, and I of them. Gruff senses my nervousness and ties the dog to a post where it continues to pull and bark. Conversation will be impossible with this noise.

"Come inside," he says, "he'll quieten down once we're out of sight."

The salty tang of the harbour is replaced with that of kerosene fumes which make my eyes water. Hanging from the ceiling is the carcass of a small rowing boat, its ribs and spine bared for all to see. Pulleys and winches, ropes and chains are strung on hooks or wound around giant nails that jut from the walls.

"Watch yourself," he says, as I edge my way past to follow him deeper into the shed. "I wish I could say I'm surprised to see you, but I'm not." He wears the same grin as he did the first time I met him, the one that made me so irate. This time I let it go. "So, how can I help?" he says, wiping the grease from his hands with a filthy rag.

Now that I am here I do not know where to start. "All right." I take a deep breath. "The thing is, Mr Lewis—"

He raises a hand. "Please, call me Gruff, and I shall call you Grace."

Any timidness he showed when he called at the house has vanished. Is it because he is on his own territory, or because he thinks he has already paid his due for the Mari Lwyd incident by helping me discover my family's past?

He disappears momentarily, then reappears carrying a grubby old stool. "There," he says, plonking it down on the ground. "Take a seat." He folds his arms so that the scarred skin on his left forearm is hidden beneath the other. I guess it is a subconscious action.

"All right, then I'll come straight out with it. I would like to know everything about Caitlin's death." I glance up at him. "Please, do not spare me the detail, Mr—I mean Gruff."

He shakes his head and makes a puffing noise, a vibration of the lips that reminds me of the pipe-smoking sailor who helped carry our luggage the day we moved in. "Well, so long as you're sure. It's not pretty, you know."

I take a deep breath and grip the edge of the stool. "I never imagined it would be, but I need to hear it."

He half closes his eyes, remembering, and the shrivelled skin beneath his left eye fades to grey in the dimming light.

"Wintertime, just a few days before Christmas, it was. Russia had delivered us a blast of bitter air that hung about for days. I remember that particular morning well, because Bronwen's water bowl was a swollen block of ice and icicles hung like daggers from the door lintel, ready to stab anyone who ventured across the threshold.

"The first flake of snow fell as soon we stepped out the gate. I remember pausing to catch the second one on my tongue. Sticks with me that does."

He massages the bridge of his nose between forefinger and thumb, then fixes me with his good eye.

My mouth has turned to sand; my limbs to jelly.

"Me and Bronwen trudged on down to the harbour, just as we did every morning, our feet slipping on ice and our coats hunched up round our necks. Whatever the weather, Bronwen loved her morning walk." His eye turns away now and stares out towards the open door of the shed.

"Seems silly, but it's strange the things you remember. I remember the colour of the sky. Purple, like a bruise, yet beautiful.

"Anyway, as soon as we drew near to the limekiln, Bronwen shot off like a bullet. It wasn't like her. She usually stayed close by till we reached the sand. I called her name, but she'd disappeared. Smoke from the limekiln billowed clouds the colour of anthracite and the stench of coal and sulphur caught on the back of my throat."

He clears his throat, as though still able to taste it.

"The sound of Bronwen yapping came from the entrance. I knew something was wrong. I knew she was trying to get my attention." He takes a deep breath. "Thing is, us kids were warned to keep clear of the kiln, see, especially at night when it was lit, but that's where I found her."

I shake my head.

"Inside the limekiln? But what on earth was an eight-year-old child doing outdoors on a winter's night? It doesn't make sense." Thoughts race round my head like rats in a sewer. Images of Caitlin's burned body; mother and father's neglect. I almost miss his next sentence and ask him to repeat it.

"She sleepwalked…apparently. Must have gravitated towards the heat and fallen back to sleep. That's what the inquest suggested."

❧ ❧

My shoulders are hunched all the way back home, their burden too heavy to carry. I know it is selfish of me, but I need to tell Lilah. I need to share some of the weight to stop it from crushing me.

"That you, Grace?" she calls as I close the front door, and the tension eases a fraction. My face gives me away as soon as I step into her bedroom.

"Come on," she says, patting the bed. "Come and tell old Lilah what's happened."

Her words open the floodgates. I tell the story between her bouts of coughing, holding the bowl for her to spit into, and stroking her hair when each bout subsides. Who is mother here? I comfort her with my hands while she comforts me with her ears.

Like every good story, I begin at the beginning. Except this is not a good story; it is the worst possible kind.

When I speak of Caitlin's charred body, tears stream down Lilah's cheeks.

"How did he know it was her?" she asks.

"By her teeth. She'd lost her two lower front teeth the previous week, her baby teeth, and the gap…well, it was the first thing he noticed when he turned her over."

"Turned her over?" Lilah sits herself up and frowns.

I take a deep breath. "She lay curled on her side, like a baby in the womb."

"Oh, Grace. I don't think he should have gone into detail like that. It'll give you nightmares."

"No, Lilah. I asked him to. I told him to spare me nothing."

She shakes her head and blows her nose.

"His scars…" I close my eyes and picture the puckered skin, the blind eye. "It was the quicklime, you see. Her corpse was covered in it. A fine powder, like the white coating on a newborn baby. When he touched her it got on his skin, too. He grabbed handfuls of snow to try to wash it off, hence the burns."

Lilah puts a hand over her mouth and gasps in horror.

"He said when mixed with water, quicklime produces intense heat." My head is bowed, the bedcover balled in my fist. "And his eye. He was crying, you see, and he rubbed his eyes as children do." I shudder. "He's lucky he isn't blind in both eyes, Lilah."

"Stop, Grace. I can't bear it!" Another bout of coughing turns her face purple and makes her own eyes run. I take a clean flannel and wipe her face before topping up her water glass, and she settles back against the pillows. "I'm sorry," she says, "That was selfish of me." She takes my cool hand in hers. Hers burns hot, just like her head, and a wave of fear washes over me. What if anything should happen to Lilah? And I have unburdened myself to her when she is sick. It is me who is selfish.

Neither of us speaks for a few minutes, then she says, "No wonder your poor mother lost her mind. It's enough to drive anyone mad." She shakes her head and shivers.

"His screams brought people running. He screamed with the pain and the sight he had witnessed. I'm sorry, Lilah. Do you want me to stop?"

"No, no…tell it to the end."

I take a deep breath. "He remembers little else, apart from a gathering crowd and the screech of the gulls…Isn't it strange? It's the screech of the gulls he remembers most, that and the snow falling on his skin and instantly melting. He said he's hated snow ever since."

It suddenly dawns on me, New Year's Eve and the incident with the *Mari Lwyd.*

"I guess the snow was the reason he volunteered to be the one dressed as the horse."

Lilah frowns. "I'm not following you, Grace." Her chest is a rattlesnake.

"The night of the *Mari Lwyd.* Gruff Lewis was the man in the horse's costume. It snowed, don't you remember? He was led by the villagers, so he wouldn't have to look at it, would he?"

"I see." She smooths the creases out of the bedsheet, contemplating my words.

"Isn't life strange? When he tried to help my sister, it was snowing, then he held a cloth full of snow to my head to help the swelling." My voice is a whisper. "It must have taken a great deal of courage for him to do that, don't you think?"

XXVI

HE SEWING LESSONS ARE PROVING TO BE A GODSEND. My overly-ambitious plans to create all kinds of soft furnishings for the house have been traded for delicate embroidery. Most days I sit in the bay window and sew, whilst watching the comings and goings of the harbour. It helps me while away the winter.

A few weeks ago, Mrs. Jones and I began with simple cross-stitch, and the years melted away. I remembered learning it as a child, and with a bit of practice the skills came flooding back.

"I need more of a challenge," I say after a few sessions. "Something that will help me focus and take my mind off things."

"Then we need to go freestyle, though it's much more difficult. It's best if you have a particular design in mind."

"I do…the clock," I say without hesitation. "I would like to replicate the painted scene on the face of the grandfather clock downstairs as a present for my niece, Helena."

She raises an eyebrow and smiles.

"All right, I'll have a look on my way out and we can plan how best to go about it." It is not just lessons she provides but companionship, too.

❧❦

Although the days are beginning to lengthen and the nights to shorten, my nerves remain fraught. Being cooped up too long can do that to a person, but then so can other things. Things such as the untimely and violent death of a secret sister, the denial of a brother, the negligence of a parent.

According to Ewan Bevan, my father was away on business when Caitlin died, so he was not at fault. Perhaps it is unfair, but I cannot help but lay some of the blame at Mother's door.

Since Lilah's illness, Ewan calls every Sunday after church. The first time he came, he brought a floral arrangement of pale pink peonies and Lilah blushed roses. He was sorry to hear she had been sick with bronchitis, and glad she was on the mend. By that time, Lilah had been sick for over a week, and I was so afraid I might lose her. How could I deny her the attention of a gentleman caller? Doesn't she deserve to be happy? When he visits, they speak in the kitchen, making springtime plans for the garden, and the sound of their laughter brightens the house. This week the talk turned to seed potatoes. Never would I have imagined seeing a pair so excited by such a thing.

"Soon as it gets a bit milder, we'll start preparing the ground," Ewan said, thumbing the catalogue. "I've roped two lads in to help. Slip 'em a few bob and they'll work their socks off."

He has been kind to me, too, answering my questions to the best of his ability, whilst at the same time remaining loyal to Mother and Father. His words reaffirm what Gruff said: Caitlin sleepwalked to her death, the heat from the limekiln lulling her back into a sleep from which she would never awaken. Toxic fumes would have rendered her unconscious; the searing heat of calcifying limestone would have done the rest.

If it were not for the fact that the limekiln is no longer in use, I might see fit to barricade myself in each night in case I should succumb to the same fate. I think back to the night I woke up next to the rocking horse in the playroom, the night I dreamed of maggots and horse skulls. And that was not the first time. All my life I have sleepwalked, especially if I am upset about something.

Though terrified of the answer, I asked Ewan about my mother's reaction on hearing the news. His chin had quivered as he spoke. "Ah, Grace, I can picture her now. We tried to keep her at arm's length, but she wouldn't listen."

"But who told her? It was early dawn, wasn't it?"

"I can't remember precisely. A right commotion there was, down at the harbour. Someone must have run to the house and asked if Caitlin was missing." He shook his head. "You could hear her screams echoing up the beach like a siren. Surreal it was, what with the snow coming down and your mother stood there in a white cotton nightgown. Not the kind of thing you ever forget."

I pressed him to tell me such things last Sunday because Jonathan's letter was so exasperating. Despite my request for his candour, his reply was short and to the point. Yes, we had a sister named Caitlin. Yes, she was eighteen months younger than him. Yes, she burned to death in a terrible accident, one he wishes to forget. He was sorry I had to hear it from a stranger but believes there are some things that need to be put to rest rather than dragged through the mud. Those were his words. He asks that I refrain from mentioning it in future and that I never discuss it with Helena. His denial makes me furious, but what can I do? As for my postscript regarding the upper storey being barricaded, he does not even mention it.

I will not betray him, not directly. Instead, I intend to record all of it in a journal, one which Helena will inherit one day. She can learn the history of our family in written form, via her aunt.

There is, however, a little light on the horizon. Gruff Lewis has suggested a boat ride, come spring. "I'll show you the coastal nooks and crannies," he said, when last I saw him. "We can visit Dinas Island if you like. Maybe take a picnic." He pointed towards the headland I had spied on my first coast-path walk, and I must admit, it sounded tempting. I doubt I shall take him up on the offer though. It does not seem proper. Not unless Lilah and Ewan accompany us. If he mentions it again, I shall drop a hint.

I am grateful for one thing—a month has passed since the *ghost* incident, and during the past four weeks I have not seen my dead sister or mother. I have, however, sighted the girl in grey, in fact her presence has become a regular occurrence, yet only when I am alone. I am yet to see her features. Always her back is turned, or she is in profile. Either that or she disappears into the distance. There is a vague quality to her; it is as if she is made of matter that is not quite flesh and blood. Neither transparent nor translucent, yet somehow not quite opaque. She is a mist of a girl, and yet I am certain she is not a ghost. The more often I see her, the more confident I feel about the fact. There is a familiarity to her which is almost comforting, yet her indistinct quality is at the same time frustrating.

The thought that Mother's madness might be hereditary haunts me still. I remain hopeful that everything I have encountered can be explained as the result of trauma, just as Doctor Perkins back home believed, but the more I experience such strange things the less confident I feel.

And then there are the words on both the note and drawing. They mock my optimism.

We were not there, and now we are, they chide.

I will myself to remember writing them; if only it were true, but I cannot admit having done so without feeling like a fraud. Truth is, I do not believe I wrote those words myself, no matter what Lilah or anyone else says.

✻ ✻

The afternoon is spent sitting in front of the grandfather clock in the hall, attempting to replicate the harbour scene on paper. According to the moon phases, just three days remain until the next full moon. I shall embroider the scene at night, then I can include a full moon, sewn in silver thread. A moon that symbolizes new beginnings and enlightenment, both of which I wish for myself as well as Helena.

Transferring the design onto the cotton canvas, however, tests my patience. My brand-new sewing box, ordered from a catalogue on display at Jones the Draper, lies in wait on top of the desk. I put down the canvas and wander over, like a child at Christmas, eager to play with a new toy.

Made of rosewood, the centre of the lid is adorned with a tapestry of spring blooms. Hellebore and anemone, bloodroot and bluebells that make me yearn for warmer days. Sliding the brass hook over the catch, I lift the lid and reveal the contents. It really is a special piece. The inside of the lid is divided into nine sections, each one illustrated. I trace the outline of a peacock butterfly, one so realistic I imagine it fluttering over to the window and escaping.

186

But it is the contents of the box itself that excites me most. In the centre sits a row of threads, all colours of the rainbow. I pick out a deep shade of blue, inky black almost, which will be perfect for the night sky. Three paler shades for the sea and silver for the moon. Golden yellow for the harbour lights and hickory brown for the silhouetted buildings. I am glad the painting on the clock face does not show the limekiln, even though I can see it from the window if I stretch my neck.

How innocuous the limekiln looks now. No one would dare accuse it of murder. I have been told that Caitlin's death was the final nail in the coffin for the kiln, that shortly after it roared its last fiery breath. However, having spent an afternoon at the local library, I realize its closure had little to do with Caitlin's death. Quarrying for limestone was already in decline; the kiln's fate already sealed. Still, I suppose it is kind of people to suggest such a thing.

At the library, I discovered old newspaper reports, too. Stories that made the headlines both in *The Cardigan Observer* and *The Pembrokeshire Herald.* An obituary that outlined the facts surrounding my sister's death along with a fair amount of macabre detail that turned my stomach, as well as a rather weak attempt at a verse which read:

> *A love is lost; our hearts soar*
> *Life is uncertain; death is sure*

When first I discovered its role in my sister's death, I could hardly bear to walk past the limekiln. But that was nigh on impossible, given its dominant position on the harbour. I have since persuaded myself to view it with pity, though if it could speak I am certain it would say it is happier these days.

Though its walls have crumbled over the quarter century, it sprouts a hat of gorse with needle-like leaves that deter the gulls from landing. I guess it prefers to wallow in its own company. Its ageing joints are cushioned by sedum; its veins ripple with creeping ivy. Does the sap from the ivy punish it for past misdemeanour? Does the stone itch or sting from its toxic bite? Of course, this is the rambling of a vengeful mind, nothing more. If anyone deserves to be punished for what happened to my sister, then I guess Mother does. Knowing

Caitlin was prone to night-time wandering, why did she not secure the front door in some way? I suppose the accusation is unjust. I recall my mother's words not long before she died: *Forgive me, Caitlin.* Now I understand the enormity of the weight behind those words.

⊰ CHAPTER ⊱

XXVII

H AVING FINISHED STITCHING THE SKY, I BEGIN WORK on the moon. The bottom half of the picture remains untouched as of yet; it was the sky I wanted to stitch first. A circle of neat stem stitches form the moon's circumference; satin stitches in silver and grey infill the centre.

The real moon appears at the window, a faint grey ball, a ghost of itself. Twilight, the sky is not yet dark enough for it to be seen clearly. It soon will be, though. Today has been crisp and cloudless, so I am certain that once night takes the reins the full moon will make a spectacular appearance.

Caitlin's doll sits in the window judging every stitch, every prick of the finger. The doll makes it difficult to forget the past. At times, I am tempted to put her in the nursery alongside the rocking horse, but I do not have the heart.

An ache above my right eye warns me to stop sewing for today. We have lost the light, and I find myself squinting and straining. The eye of the needle is blurred and impossible to re-thread. I pull the fabric taut and examine my handiwork. Once complete, I intend to add the words from Caitlin's drawing: *The space between sea and sky is home to memories.* Stitched in silver, it should contrast well against the night sky. I shall mail it to Helena without explanation. She will discover the story surrounding its mystery through my journal, eventually.

I light the portable oil lamp and turn down the light on the desk. The room is bathed in shadow, apart from the pool of light that dances to the tune of my footsteps. One last look at the sea, then I shall return downstairs.

The space between sea and sky is cloudless; the sea a shade or two darker than the sky. The full moon shines down on the water, rejoicing in its shimmering reflection. I am about to leave when I see her. Silhouetted against the sky, she stands once more with her back to the house. Wild hair blows freely in the wind, the only thing that moves. Who is she?

And then she turns in my direction, slow, purposeful, as if she knows I am watching, but before my eyes can drink in her features the door to the sewing room bursts open and in steps Caitlin. My hands fly to my face, and I gasp, but she is unperturbed. She enters then stops, as though she is seeing the room for the first time. Hands on hips, she stands frowning in my direction. But it is not me she seeks.

"Ah, there you are!" she says, fixing her gaze on the doll on the window seat. "I thought you'd disappeared for a minute." She wags a finger, and her sandy curls bounce to the rhythm. My breath is held prisoner as she runs towards me and picks up the doll, cradling it in both hands. Does she notice the new dress? It does not seem so. Then, without further ado, she runs from the room, taking the doll with her.

Momentarily frozen to the spot, eventually my feet decide to give chase. By the time I step outside the door she is already at the end of the landing, doll dangling in her hand.

Help me, it seems to say as it swings like a pendulum with its head inches from the floor. If this is how Caitlin treated her, it is little wonder the head was smashed.

Fleet-footed, her descent is silent. She seems oblivious to the fact that she is being followed. Both flights of stairs are covered in seconds. Only once we reach the hall do I realize it is no longer night. No time to consider the ridiculousness of the situation, I pursue her out the front door, down the path, and onto the beach.

Somewhere in the back of my mind is the notion that such a thing cannot be happening, but I do not have time to dwell on it. It is not the first time, and I doubt it will be the last. Nonetheless, the situation is frightening. Blood pounds in my ears, both from the exertion of running to keep up with my sister and anxiety.

I call her name just once, but the wind snatches my voice and it falls on deaf ears. She would not hear me in any case, not even if I were right beside her. She cannot hear me, and she cannot see me. Instead, she is lost in the past, lost in memory. This is not really happening, not now, not at this precise moment in time, and yet all logic is swallowed by the unexpectedness of the situation.

As she reaches the shore, I realize it is no longer winter, not at this point in time. The air is a soft blanket, warm and humid, the sand glistens like diamond dust. I keep my distance, a few paces behind. She wears a pale lemon dress and matching ribbon in her hair. The doll swings from her hand as she flings off her shoes and throws them further up the beach where the sand is dry. Only then do I notice the doll's dress. It has reverted back to the old one. Once again, there is no doubt other than I am witnessing a scene from the past.

She sits the doll on the sand, points a finger at the sea and says, "The tide is on its way out, Violet, so you'll be safe. Just don't you go wandering while I'm looking for shells."

Violet: the colour of the doll's original dress. My stomach flips at the realization that I have dressed her in green. I feel as if I have betrayed her.

The doll sits inert on the sand, facing the sea, and my sister wanders the shore, muttering words I can no longer hear, lost in her own little world. I stand and watch as she bends and picks up sea treasure, discarding most of it and keeping the bits she deems worthy clenched tight in her fist.

She turns and wanders back in my direction, her focus still on the sand. She has inherited my curls, or rather I have inherited hers. It is strange to think she would be older than me if she had lived. I am filled with a jumble of emotions: gratitude that I am able to see her, regret that she is dead, fear that this is not real, and I am going mad, just like Mother did. I want to take her by the hand and shake her. I want to warn her of what is to come. Do not wander out into the night, Caitlin. Bar the door, bolt the windows, beseech our mother and brother to watch over you while you sleep, because I know the shadow that looms over you. The burden of what is still to come is a weight on my shoulders. Nothing I do can prevent its inevitable outcome. Oh, the torture of foresight!

She kneels in front of the doll and spills the contents of her fist into the doll's lap, folding back the fabric to secure it, before once again wandering off, except this time, instead of scouring the shoreline, she rummages among rock-pools.

I turn my gaze from her for a moment and look back towards Parrog House. It appears much the same, a little less weather-worn, perhaps, the garden a little more neat.

The beach is almost deserted, except for a few small children who play in the distance, close to the harbour. Squeals of delight and laughter travel on the breeze before the waves snatch their voices.

I turn again towards Caitlin, astonished to see she has been joined by a woman. For a moment I imagine it to be the young woman who haunts me, but then I realize it is not. It is Mother. She wears a simple dress, full-length and blue-floral. She also wears a smile. The smile is the reason I did not recognize her at first, and of course she is younger than I remember, but then she was young when last I saw the ghost of her in the house. The beast of burden shadowed her then, though, the time she scolded Caitlin over the feather. It aged her, made her the Mother I knew best.

She lowers herself onto a nearby rock and beckons Caitlin to her, smiling all the while. Caitlin, too, seems a little hesitant. It is as though she is wary of the woman who sits before her wearing a smile.

In the palm of her left hand, Mother holds something small and white. At this distance I cannot see what it is. Two paces closer, I hear the words she speaks, words that make my head spin and my stomach sick.

"Take it," she says, holding it out like a sugar cube to a pony. "It's yours."

Caitlin glances up at her, trepidation rife on her face, though the fingers of her right hand hover over the object, twitching with eagerness.

Mother smiles. "It's a special shell, a baby ear shell, also known as a moon snail. Look, see how it curves just like the ear of a tiny baby."

Caitlin takes the shell between thumb and forefinger and holds it up to the sun.

"I can see through it," she says, before laying it in the palm of her hand. "So delicate!"

The smile on Mother's face is replaced with sadness, though she tries to hide it. "Just like you," she says, "but it is made of mineral: calcium carbonate, the same as limestone, almost. Similar to all kinds of matter, Caitlin, both dead and alive."

And I know to what she refers: Caitlin's demise.

There is no doubt in my mind. Mother foresees the death of her own daughter.

The words she speaks are of no interest to Caitlin. She does not understand them. Instead, she continues to peer at the sky through a translucent, white shell.

"Grace?"

One word. A word that darkens the sky and whips-up the wind. In a blink, my sister and mother disappear, and the world reverts to normal.

Lilah waves from the gate, a look of concern on her face. "What on earth are you doing out here at this time of night, and without a coat? You'll catch your death!"

I shake my head, for I cannot answer her in truth.

She remains standing, hands on broad hips, until I return to her side. "I—I thought I saw someone, that's all."

Her face falls. Although I did not tell her of my previous encounter with Mother's ghost and Caitlin's ghost the night she fell ill, she worries still. "Now then, Grace. Who on earth did you think you saw at this time of night?"

I say nothing, just shake my head and make my way up the path.

She trails me. "Whoever it was must have been pretty important. I only knew you'd gone because you left the front door wide open. Freezing in there, it is."

She is using talk of the weather to distract herself from reality. Should I confide in her? My ears burn and my hands are numb with cold. I blow my nose in a handkerchief so that I do not have to look at her.

"Sit down, Lilah. There is something I need to tell you."

She wrings her hands and frowns.

"But first I have to check on something. Please, put the kettle on, or better still, pour us a brandy. I'm certain there's some left from Christmas."

My heart sits in my throat as I climb the stairs. I sweat and shiver, both at the same time. As I reach the landing, I see that the door to the sewing room is closed. If I left the front door open, I doubt I would have taken the time to close this one. I grab the doorknob and hesitate, unsure of what I might find inside.

It gives with a creak. Moonlight pours in through the window, highlighting the doll who sits in the window, precisely where I left her.

"Violet," I whisper, though she wears a pale green gown. She stares beyond me into the distance, unblinking.

I head for my bedroom, eager to check the silver trinket box. But it, too, is as I left it: a folded note, a blue jay's feather, and a tiny white shell, curled as though asleep.

XXVIII

DOCTOR REYNOLDS FIXES ME WITH A FROWN, HIS FINGERS pressed to his lips like a child at prayer. We have only met once before, the day I called on him to visit Lilah.

"I suggest you start from the beginning. You're my last patient this morning, so there's no rush."

My throat constricts and my hands tug at my dress. Lilah persuaded me to speak with him after what I told her, but I am not convinced it will help.

And where is the beginning?

First, I speak of Mother's illness, its progression. It is easier to speak of someone other than myself.

"I was not the doctor here back then," he says, "not when her symptoms began. But even if I were, I could not comment on your mother's illness. You must understand." He casts his eyes around the study as though expecting Mother to materialize through the walls.

"Of course, but it is important you're aware of it because I am concerned her condition is hereditary and that I have been unfortunate in that respect."

"So tell me about you. When did all this start?"

I take a deep breath and lay my cards on the table. From the first faint on the night Mother died to yesterday's incident on the beach, I lay my soul bare, hardly daring to look into his eyes for fear of what I might see.

"Hmm," he says when I have finished. "Let me make a few checks while I think things over. I'd like to be certain there's no physical cause, though I can tell you now, my suspicions lie elsewhere."

"So you think me mad?" I gasp the words.

"That is not what I am saying. I think you are a long-suffering victim of trauma. We underestimate the power of the mind, you know, but as I said, let me do some physical checks first so that I can draw a line under a few things, hey?"

My pulse is a hare chased by hounds. My heartbeat a moth hitting against a light. He gives a little cough before asking me to do the same then says, "Menstruation, Grace… any problems in that particular area?"

My face burns red. "Pardon me?"

He sighs, steps away and busies himself with the stethoscope. "Your monthly bleeding, is it regular?"

"Yes, Doctor."

"And the flow…is it particularly heavy?"

I try to swallow, but my throat is parched. When I speak, my voice is that of a child. "I wouldn't say so."

He sits at Father's desk, elbows on the wood and hands folded. "How old are you, Grace?"

"Twenty-eight, Doctor. I will be twenty-nine this summer."

"And you are unmarried?"

"I am, but I do not see what it has to do with what ails me." His words feel somewhat incriminatory, and I am irked.

"You see, Grace, most women of your age are married with children." Steel eyes, the colour of knife-blades, and they hurt just as much. He sees my face and softens a little. "It is not an accusation, I am merely suggesting that marriage and child-bearing is the natural order, do you understand?"

I manage little more than a nod.

"You see, not only does it help balance the humours, but looking after a husband and children also provides a woman with a focus in life, one which stops her from becoming self-absorbed, if you understand my meaning."

I stand and approach the sideboard. If I do not drink, my mouth will seize altogether. Either that or I will say something I might regret. I pour a glass of water, spilling some onto the tray.

"Well, in that case, Doctor, how do you explain Mother's illness? She was married with children, wasn't she?"

"Now, now," he says, his mouth twitching. "I am only trying to get to the bottom of things. You must understand. Come, sit down, and let us talk."

He waits for me to return to my seat before speaking. "You see, Grace, there are no such things as ghosts. You do realize that, don't you?"

I am close to tears. "Of course, but how is it possible, then, that I see my dead sister—a sister I never knew—and my dead mother?" My voice has risen to almost a shriek. "I can describe my sister to you, and yet I never met her. No photograph, no painted image, nothing. How is it possible if it's all in my head?"

He takes a deep breath.

"Then someone must have described her to you, Grace. Think about it for a moment. I will say it again, there are no such things as ghosts."

I sit for a moment, gathering my breath. Did Gruff Lewis describe Caitlin to me? Did Ewan? I cannot, in truth, remember. And then I remember Caitlin's drawing, the colour of her hair, the dress—pale yellow—just like the one she wore when I saw her at the beach. But did I really see her? Did any of it really happen, or did I make the connection from her drawing?

I feel myself deflate.

"All right, Doctor, you win. There are no such things as ghosts. It is clearly all in my imagination." I am exhausted. This is a pointless exercise. I told Lilah it would be.

"I am not suggesting you imagine it, Grace. What I am saying is this: Your whole life has been spent living under the influence of your mother's illness. An illness I imagine brought about by shock and grief. And then there are the secrets, Grace. I cannot imagine why you were kept in the dark about your sister, but it is my belief that it does little good to bury such things. Better to air it, get it off the chest, so to speak."

I nod in agreement.

"You see, harbouring such trauma does neither the secret keeper nor the person kept in the dark any favour. In coming to Wales you probably imagined that the past would be forgotten, that you could put your mother's sickness to one side and start afresh. Am I right?"

"You are. I did." A stray tear trickles down my cheek. I whip out a handkerchief and wipe it away.

"But then you were confronted by the mystery of your sister, the horror surrounding her death, and once again the spark was ignited."

We are interrupted by a tapping at the door.

"Come in," I call, glad of the distraction.

"I just wanted to know if you would like some tea?" Lilah says, her face pale and drawn.

"Yes please. Doctor?"

"Go on then you've persuaded me." He smiles, and I feel my shoulders drop an inch or two.

Lilah leaves, and he continues. "It is my belief that the visions are your mind's way of dealing with things. After all, it must have come as a shock."

I sag in the chair. "I wish someone had told me what happened, long ago, I mean. I wish it had never been kept secret."

"Some of the visions arrived in the form of dreams, you say. Is that correct?"

"Yes, or at least I think I was dreaming. It's hard to know the difference at times. But what of the memories, Doctor? I mean, the incident I told you about, the Vanderbilt Ball. How could I possibly have experienced it from Mother's point of view? And the faint—" Again I feel the panic rise in my chest. "The accident, you know, wetting myself, I mean. It is exactly what happened to Mother. Lilah confirmed it."

He snorts. "You are reading too deeply into it, Grace. It is not uncommon for someone to lose control of the bladder during a faint. Not uncommon at all." He pauses. "May I suggest something? Of course, you do not have to do as I say."

"You may."

"The drawing." He takes a deep breath. "Has finding it made you any happier? Has it brought you peace, or has it added to your burden?"

In truth it has made things worse. "No, but—"

"Then I suggest you burn it."

"Doctor, it is all I have of my sister. How can you suggest such a thing?"

"I suggest it because I believe that holding on to what hurts us only makes things worse. I am not trying to hurt you, Grace. I am just trying to help you let go of the past. Please, try to understand."

I see the logic behind his reasoning but have no intention of destroying the drawing. Lilah brings in the tea tray, and I am granted a reprieve.

"And how are you now, Lilah?" he asks, cheerfully. "Fully recovered, I hope?"

She places a hand against her chest. "I am indeed. It'll take more than a touch of bronchitis to take me down, Doctor."

She pours the tea, then leaves.

"So," he says, lifting the china cup. His index finger is too large to fit inside the handle, so instead he wraps all of his fingers around it. "Before we go making a diagnosis of hysteria, let's try a little tonic, hey? That and some good nights' rest. I forgot to ask how you are sleeping. Not well, I presume."

"Sometimes. There are nights when I sleep well, but then there are the dreams, and the wanderings." I glance up at him. "Yes, Doctor, sleepwalking is another thing I seem to have inherited, though from my sister this time." The word sister…it still feels strange on my tongue. Alien, somehow.

"Hmm, somnambulism…another common symptom of hysteria." He raises an eyebrow before continuing. "I want you to take the tonic and keep a diary for me. Will you do that?"

I nod.

"I want you to record any disruption to your sleep pattern, how anxious you feel, any mood swings. And, of course, if you experience further…*visions*, shall we say, then record those, too." He takes a swig of tea and swirls it around his mouth. "And dates. I want you to record the dates alongside your notes. It is important to be able to see if there are any recurring patterns."

My thoughts turn to Mother, the lists of numbers and her obsession with the moon phases. I have omitted that bit of information. My stomach sinks again. Could this be another sign? And could her lists of numbers be connected to dates? His words have sparked my interest. I want him gone now, so that I might check.

He replaces the cup on the saucer and stands. "Oh, and record the dates of menstruation, too, please. You'd be surprised how often there is a link between this and the condition I suspect you're suffering from."

Out in the hallway, he pauses in front of the clock. It chimes the hour, proud of its voice. He points at its face. "Moon phases," he says, putting on his hat. "If you're interested, visit the library and see what Charles Darwin has to say about menstruation and the cycle of the moon." He shakes his head. "Fascinating. The man's a miracle among men. I'll see you again in three months' time, all right?"

And with that he is off, leaving me with a prescription for a bitter-tasting tonic that no doubt will come concealed inside a brown bottle, the words, *Drink Me*, printed on its face. And, like Alice, I shall do as it says and hope it will not cause me to shrink.

But this is not all he leaves me with, for he has ignited a spark regarding the lunar calendar, that and Charles Darwin, of course. I shall see what the famous naturalist has to say on the matter.

XXIX

"**W**HAT DID THE DOCTOR HAVE TO SAY, GRACE?**" Lilah's frown of concern is accompanied by frantic dish-drying. She wipes each plate as if it is guilty of serious misdemeanour.

"He does not seem to think there is much wrong with me." The word *hysteria* lurks deep within my chest, kept prisoner behind the bars of my ribcage. It will remain there for the time being. "He is certain Mother's illness is the trigger rather than the cause, and believes it is my mind's way of coming to terms with things."

Lilah breathes an audible sigh of relief.

"Well, that's good to hear."

"He left me a prescription for a tonic and wants me to record anything of concern for three months, then he will see me again. I have nothing much to do this afternoon, so I think I'll take a walk into town and get the prescription made up. Best to start it sooner, don't you think?" In truth, I am desperate to visit the library, but I do not want to tell Lilah this.

She smiles, relieved. "Want me to come with you? I was going to bake a——"

"You carry on. I think I'll visit the library while I'm there, so don't worry if I'm gone a while."

"All right, but before you go, please eat something. I noticed you didn't touch your breakfast. You're as thin as a pin, and you must keep your strength up, Grace."

I sigh, knowing she is right. "I couldn't eat this morning. I was too afraid. Afraid he might declare me insane."

"Silly thing," she says, gesturing for me to sit at the table. Yet I know she feared the same.

We sit awhile, chatting over tea and buttered *bara brith*, another recipe borrowed from Aelwen, and my stomach relaxes a little.

"Lilah, why do you think Caitlin drew Mother twice in the same picture?"

"That's an easy one, Grace. The mother whose hand she holds is smiling; the other one, the mother who stands farther away, is sad. It was her way of expressing herself, that's all."

"You mean it was her way of saying she preferred Mother when she was happy?"

"I think so. At least, that's how I interpret it."

I mull it over. "I guess you're right. Mother did have two sides to her personality, didn't she? Though I have to say, the nicer side was rarely seen in later years, truth be told."

Despite her misgivings, Lilah remains loyal towards Mother, even now, so instead of answering she gets to her feet and takes our dishes over to the sink.

⁂

The street in which the library is situated is deserted. I love this place. The single-storey cottage, the middle in a row of three, has been converted to a library some time in the past. Two arched windows face the street, each with diamond-shaped panes of glass like those often found in a church. I step through the red door, and enter a printed wonderland, one which smells of polish and paper.

There is no one here bar me and the librarian, who looks to be as ancient as the building itself. It is not my first visit, so we greet each other amicably, though a little distant. It crosses my mind to ask whether she knew Mother or Father, my grandparents, even, but that can wait.

"I wonder, do you have anything by Charles Darwin?"

"The naturalist, you mean?" She eyes me with suspicion, but I refuse to give anything away. In all likelihood she thinks it unusual for a young woman to be studying such things, unfitting perhaps.

"Indeed."

She slowly emerges from behind the lamp-lit desk, all creaks and knots. She has become part of the furniture, I think. Well beyond retirement, yet she remains here still, and I understand why.

I follow her over to a bookcase marked *Natural History* and wait as she dons spectacles that hang from a string around her neck. Her hands are veiny and pocked with liver spots.

"There's this one." She pulls out a copy of *The Origin of Species* and passes it to me. "Wait there," she says, walking her fingers along the shelf. "We also have this." Bound in the same green leather is a tome titled, *The Descent of Man.*

"Thank you, those should do nicely."

She waits while I make my way to the furthest table, then hobbles back to her desk.

Diamonds of light reflect from the rear window onto the surface of the wooden desk. The light from the second window stretches elongated fingers across the wooden floor, and for some time I am lost in a world of real magic.

In the pages of *The Descent of Man*, I eventually find what I am looking for. There is surely more than a hint at a link between menstruation and the lunar cycle here, for Darwin seems to suggest that the twenty-eight day cycle of female menstruation is evidence that our ancestors lived on the seashore and thus needed to synchronize with the tides.

Darwin's work is fascinating, and I find myself wandering from topic to topic. It is his work around natural selection that I find most engrossing, particularly the discussion around inherited traits. One particular passage in *The Descent of Man* brings to mind the words that appeared as if by magic, both on Mother's note and Caitlin's drawing. He states:

"There is no more improbability in the continued use of the mental and vocal organs leading to inherited changes in their structure and function, than in the case of handwriting, which depends partly on the form of the hand and partly on the disposition of the mind; and handwriting is certainly inherited."

As Mother's illness progressed, her handwriting grew shaky, almost to the point of being illegible, but if I inherited her handwriting style, then perhaps it was me who wrote the words. Both messages mention memory. I sit with my head in my hands, attempting to follow the reasoning in my mind. It must have been me who wrote the words, there is no other plausible solution. As much as I want to blame Eva, the likelihood of her being the culprit is scant. It is more likely that my jealousy over her inheriting Woodleigh House caused me to lay the blame at her door.

Several hours later an aching neck prompts me to move. I have sat here so long that the shadows no longer flood the desk in diamond patterns, in fact I am beginning to squint. I wish to visit Caitlin's grave before returning home, so it is time I left.

"Find what you were looking for?" the librarian asks as I approach the desk.

"Yes, thank you, quite fascinating."

She peers at me through clouded cataracts, unblinking.

"Your father loved it here, you know. He often visited when he was at home." She nods towards the desk I worked at. "His favourite spot—same as yours."

Pleasure ripples from my stomach to my throat, knowing he sat there. Did he read Darwin? It would not surprise me.

"How wonderful." I pause for a moment. "I don't suppose you remember my grandparents, do you?" It bothers me, the fact that Caitlin is buried with them instead of in her own grave. Surely my mother and father would have wished for all three of them to be reunited one day. Or did they plan on emigrating even then? If so, I can understand the logic of them not wanting Caitlin to be alone.

She gives a little chuckle. "So you think I'm that old, do you?"

"I'm sorry, I meant no offence; it's just that I know nothing about them and—"

She leans across and touches the back of my hand with the tips of her fingers. "Listen, dear, I'm not offended. Not in the least." Her face is a wrinkled sheet of parchment, wafer-thin and smothered in stories. I know that somewhere amongst them lies at least one about my family.

She glances left and right, as if uncertain we are alone despite the fact that no one else has been in all afternoon. "Do you have a few minutes?"

I nod. "Of course."

"Then take a pew."

I glance around. The nearest chair is several paces away. "It's all right, I'll stand. I've sat long enough already."

She shrugs. "As you wish." She fixes her watery gaze on me. "Your grandfather was a lovely man. Worked on the ships, something to do with the slate industry. Boss man, he was," she grins, all gums and blue lips, "Hence Parrog House. You're very fortunate, you know. There's many would give their eye teeth to own such a place."

"Yes, I'm well aware of that. So, if my grandparents owned Parrog House, how did my parents come to live there?"

"Tush," she flicks a hand in my direction. "That house is big enough for several families. Mind you, it wasn't long after your parents married that your grandfather died. Accident, if I remember rightly, something to do with his place of work. I was young back then, so can't remember the detail."

"Oh, I see…and my grandmother?"

Her spectacles dangle around her neck. She puts them on, as if she wishes to see me more clearly. "You resemble her, you know. In fact, you look more like her than your own mother did."

"My grandmother, you mean?"

"'Course. Who else?"

The old woman is brusque, but then I did ask. "And what was she like? Not in looks, in ways. What was she like as a person?"

She frowns. "You want the truth?"

I nod, though I am half afraid to hear it. Something about her manner suggests I will not like what I hear.

"Fierce. Fierce and proud. She was the boss of the household, even when your grandfather was alive. Run your poor mother ragged, she did. But the thing is," she taps her temple, "She wasn't well…in the head, I mean."

She sees my face and stops.

"Listen, I don't want to speak out of turn. Folk can't help being ill, can they? But it's hard for those who live with them, too. That's all I'm saying." She returns the spectacles to her chest, preferring to view me with blurred vision now that she has dropped the bombshell.

I stand a while, contemplating her words. Was my grandmother the cause of Mother's ill health, or was Mother's behaviour inherited? I am back to square one. The more I discover about my family's past, the more it seems we are cursed, or at least the women in our family are.

I close my eyes and picture the gravestone. I am certain my grandmother died just a year or so after Caitlin was born. If that is correct, she would not have been very old.

"Do you know how she died? My grandmother, I mean."

Once again, she glances left and right, then she beckons me closer. "Suicide." Her voice is a throaty whisper, the voice of a magpie. "You heard of *Cnwc-Y-Crogwydd,* on the north side of town?"

I shake my head.

"Gallows Hillock, it means. Site of the town gallows, or at least it used to be. Public hanging ended before then, but the wooden post still stood." She gives me a minute to allow me to deliberate her words. "I'm sorry to be the bearer of bad news, but your grandmother hung herself."

I am so shocked that I cannot help but take a step back. "How awful!" My mind reels. No wonder Mother suffered like she did. So many tragedies in one family. Is this why she kept things from me?

"I'm sorry, dear. It must come as a shock." She shakes her head and tuts, as if it is someone else's fault that I stand before her, face ablaze and shaken to the core.

⚜ ⚜

Crouched in front of the grave, I read the words over and over, deciphering the dates and piecing together the story in my mind. Though I do not believe my sister is here in any real sense, I cannot help but worry that our grandmother might not be looking after her. Our grandfather would, though. The librarian spoke kindly of him. Still, it offers cold comfort.

The headstone states that our grandmother died in 1869, which means she would have had to be buried at night and would not have been allowed a Christian service, not if it was suicide. Such was the law back then. I close my eyes and picture the scene: Mother and Father, dressed in mourning attire, standing on this very spot in the dark, full of shame and despair.

For a family with a reputation such as ours, the event would have been devastating.

"Rest in peace," I whisper, the sentiment meant for all three tortured souls. I straighten and glance around, glad to see I am alone.

What will Lilah make of this when I tell her? Goodness only knows. And what of the tonic? Heat rises to my face as I realize I have forgotten all about the prescription. By now, the chemist's shop will be closed. Lilah will have something to say about that, no doubt. I will have to tell a lie and pretend the chemist did not have the ingredients and that I will need to call back tomorrow.

All the way home, I feel as though I am being followed. But each time I turn around there is no one there. I fear it is the past that haunts me, nothing more.

⊰ CHAPTER ⊱

XXX

"YOU WON'T FIND MANY DAYS AS NICE AS THIS MID-March," Ewan Bevan says as he leans against the pitchfork. His sweater is tied around his waist, knitted arms dangling, and he wipes the sweat off his brow with a handkerchief.

I have stepped outside to see how they are getting on. Perhaps I should offer to lend a hand, but I am eager to analyse the notes with strings of numbers left by Mother to see if I can find a pattern.

Lilah beams from ear to ear. In the palm of her hand is a crop of tan-coloured broad bean seeds that remind me of miniature kidneys. A gust of wind courses through the garden, sending the stink of horse manure in my direction. Ewan sees me squirm, and laughs.

"Good fertilizer that," he says, picking up a lump and crumbling it between his fingers.

"Enough!" I say, pinching my nostrils. "I'm going back indoors."

Knowing I will have a few hours undisturbed, I gather all the evidence and take it to Father's study. Where to begin? Since finding the numbers scribbled on the note inside the drawer on the landing on the day I discovered the key, I have since found at least another dozen notes with similar scribbles. They have fluttered from between the pages of books, like paper butterflies, I have found them lurking beneath scented liner paper in drawers. I even discovered one in a box, hidden beneath a layer of tapered candles.

Knowing that Mother grew obsessed with the lunar calendar, I cannot help but wonder if there might be a connection. Perhaps the numbers are dates, and yet no ordinal indicators have been added: no *st* to indicate the first of the month, no *nd*, *rd*, or *th* to quantify other dates. The lists are merely numerical, separated by commas.

I spread the notes out on the desk in front of me. The task of deciphering a pattern seems monumental, and I sit for several minutes with my head in my hands, not knowing where to begin. If only one of the notes were dated, it would help enormously, because then I could seek out an almanac for that particular year and check my theory. It crosses my mind that I might be wasting my time, that I might sit here for the remainder of the afternoon and discover no pattern, simply because there is none. And yet there must be, because each row of numbers consists of eight digits.

Starting from the principle that there are eight moon phases, ranging from new moon to crescent, there has to be a connection, surely.

The first digit in each line does not consistently have the lowest ordinal number, nor does the last have the highest. What strikes me though, is that they range from one to thirty-one, thus indicating a connection with the calendar.

A closer examination shows there is no precise sequence to the numbers that follow, only that they differ, sometimes by as little as two; sometimes by as much as nine. I groan in consternation. I simply cannot decipher a pattern. Darwin would find one, I am sure. I cannot help but smile at the thought.

Thankfully, when Mother and Father emigrated, they were bound to leave behind many of their books. I wonder if it pained them to do so, or did it make the thought of returning one day seem more real? I am exasperated by my inability to decipher a pattern. Yes, the moon phases on the grandfather clock help, but I do not fully understand how long each phase lasts and therefore cannot determine whether or not a link exists between the seemingly random lists of numbers left by Mother. It crosses my mind that perhaps she started making these lists after Father asked the clockmaker to remove the click spring, since she could no longer rely on the clock to do the job for her.

A search through Father's encyclopedias eventually grants me the information I need. In my ignorance, I had imagined each moon phase might last an equal number of days. That is not the case. Each phase lasts approximately three days, but it is far more complicated than that. In some Gregorian calendar months, the full moon appears twice. Then there are Harvest Moons and Blue Moons. No wonder I struggle to determine a pattern. It makes for interesting reading, though.

But why would Mother need to record such a thing? Unless, of course, it influenced her behaviour. I think back. Did she seem more preoccupied on some days than others? Most definitely, but I cannot be more specific. Remembering back to my childhood, I am almost certain that the gaps between her episodes were longer than they were during her final years. By that time she seemed in a constant state of angst.

If the lists are of dates, then why did she not include indicators? Unless, of course, she was trying to disguise them as something else. If Father had discovered her obsession and had the spring removed from the clock, perhaps she continued to forecast the moon phases on paper. This would also answer the mystery as to why the notes were hidden in various places throughout the house. Meaningful to her, but to anyone else who happened upon them they would present as a list of numbers, nothing more.

My mind is a swirling chasm. All this time and energy spent on trying to decipher the clues has got me nowhere. I pace the study like a caged lion, and still no answer presents itself.

Unless…unless I can draw a parallel from my own experiences. Head buzzing, I pull out a blank sheet of paper and think back to my last episode, a few weeks ago, when night became day and I followed Caitlin onto the beach. The incident with the baby ear shell comes flooding back. Mother's cruel words, delivered with a smile.

The incident occurred during a full moon, of that there is no doubt. I remember watching it appear in the sky while I embroidered, the way it changed from pale grey to bright white. I reach for the desk-calendar and count back twenty-nine days to January 23rd, the date on which the previous full moon would have occurred.

January 23rd? How can I possibly remember what happened on that date? Think, Grace, think! I had been reading in the front parlour when I thought I heard someone in the hall. Lilah was sick, so believing she was in her bed I had been surprised to hear someone. I close my eyes and picture the scene…

An empty hallway, in total darkness except for the light which shone through the glass and illuminated the face on the clock. There had been a full moon then, too. I am certain. I remember stepping outside to look at it, the way it shimmered on the sea. It sends a shiver down my spine, the memory of the crisp air against warm lungs. It had been the night I first saw Caitlin, the night she quarrelled with Mother over the jay's feather.

My breath is short, fingers numb and clumsy. I flick the pages of the calendar again and again, all the way back to December 25th. Christmas Day. My stomach hits the floor. The night I dreamed of teeth. My own teeth, and horse's teeth. Maggots, too. I remember waking in the playroom and having no clue as to how I got there. At the time I had put it down to rich food and wine, but could there have been another reason?

I pick up a pen and paper and start scribbling. November 27th, Thanksgiving. My heart plummets. I can recall nothing unusual from around that time. My mouth is dry as a summer riverbed. Why am I punishing myself like this? This ridiculous obsession. All it does is reinforce my greatest fear that I am turning into Mother, or at least that I have inherited her obsessional, compulsive behaviour.

In a fit of pique, I throw the pen across the room. It lands on the beige rug, spewing a splat of black ink—a stain on the rug, and a blot on my conscience. I get to my feet, whipping out a handkerchief with which to dab at the stain. Surely Lilah will have some remedy to hand? I will pretend it was an accident.

I kneel down and dab, cursing myself under my breath. But wait…I remember now, the noise that woke me the night of Thanksgiving. The dog-like scent and the smell of lilac—Mother's perfume. Gruff Lewis's story of The Hounds of Annwn, the story that frightened me so much because hadn't I heard them barking the night before?

The memory is indelible, just like the stain on the rug, and I cannot remove it, no matter how hard I scrub.

❧ CHAPTER ❦

XXXI

THE IDEA OF THERE BEING A CONNECTION BETWEEN BOTH mine and Mother's behaviour and the moon phases has become an obsession. In fact, it kept me awake last night and I was tempted to get out of bed and work at it again.

I do not write this in my diary, though, because I do not want Doctor Reynolds to know about it. But the journal that Helena will inherit? I write everything in there.

As soon as breakfast is over, I return to the study and surround myself once more with scraps of paper.

The evidence I have gathered thus far is sufficient to convince me of a link. Mother, too, was haunted by the past, though I believe that over time she hardly knew where one month began and another ended, such was the extent of her torment. Like me, she too was pursued relentlessly by another being. She spoke of a woman's presence on so many occasions, yet all of us denied her. Instead of believing her, we repudiated the possibility of such an existence. How cruel we were. Just because one cannot see something with their own eyes, does it mean the thing does not exist?

My thoughts regarding Mother are as turbulent as the sea, and my reflection on our relationship just as much so. There were times when she seemed only to think of herself, her fears and her own needs. And I cannot come to terms with the way she treated Caitlin, her negligence, the foresight she did nothing to prevent becoming a reality. And yet I pity her, too. Whether or not she inherited this sickness from her own mother I cannot say for certain, and yet I believe it to be the case.

And where does that leave me? My obsessional tendencies, those I have had most of my life, have now become burdensome. Here I am, making patterns out of moon phases and memories, even though I know it is a road to self-destruction.

"Grace?" Lilah calls me.

"Yes?" I say, hurrying towards the door. I would prefer to speak to her outside of the study. I do not want her to see my copious notes and scribblings spread around the room like some mad scientist.

Her face is streaked with dirt from the garden, but she radiates happiness. "Don't forget you need to pick up the prescription for the tonic."

"Oh, yes. Thanks, Lilah. I'm writing to Jonathan, so I need to go to the Post Office, too. Is there anything else you need in town?"

"I'll have a think. I suppose you won't be going until after lunch, will you?"

That's right."

"I've plenty of time then." She turns on her heels and heads down the hallway in the direction of the back door.

Of course, I have forgotten the tonic. My research has provided too great a distraction. I regret having called the doctor. Perhaps I should simply have followed my instincts, and yet it was he who lit the spark regarding there being a possible connection between my episodes and the lunar calendar. In that respect I suppose he has done me a favour.

I glance at the clock: eleven thirty. Still time to go back a few months further with my research before lunch. As I count backwards towards October's full moon, my thoughts return to Jonathan. Why did I tell Lilah I was writing to him? I have lied to her too many times in recent days. What is the point in writing again? He said all he had to say in his recent reply. But have I said all that is on my mind? I think not. Perhaps I shall write to him as soon as I finish this task. There are things he needs to hear, like it or not.

The letter to Jonathan, though it weighs less than an ounce, feels heavy in my purse, for it bears the weight of my words.

Our grandmother's sickness of the mind, her suicide. This is the topic I open with, and as if that topic is not heavy enough, I ask if he once knew a boy named Gruff, a boy disfigured for life after trying to save our sister.

I speak of the jay's feather, a feather meant to represent his standing within our family as someone who would protect us at all costs. Is this why he refuses to discuss the ill fortune that burdens us?

And what of the shell? A tiny translucent piece of calcite, gifted to a sister doomed to die. Is he aware of its existence?

I do not tell him of my visions, nor do I speak of the girl in grey who follows me wherever I go.

Is it the breeze from the ocean that makes me shiver, or the thought of how he will handle such openness?

The kindly-looking chemist hands me the tonic bottle, concealed within a brown paper bag as though ashamed of itself. His expression of concern has a different flavour to the one he displayed when I collected Lilah's cough syrup. More aniseed; less marzipan. He pities me, I can tell. And he is old enough to have known Mother. No doubt he had made the connection.

The church is just around the corner, so I head in that direction, eager to tell Caitlin of my latest discovery. I shall talk to her of calendars and tides, moons and memories, though I doubt she will hear.

I love the peace and solitude of this place. Though it is full of the dead, there is life, too. Snowdrops, crocus, even the stems of daffodils that promise sunshine in the coming weeks. And then there are the birds. Robin and chaffinch; sparrow and dunnock. And, of course, the carrion crow with his throaty *kraaa*. Like me, he prefers his own company. This place is more than burrowing beetles and earthworms, far more.

Perched on the curb of the grave, I slip the bottle of tonic from its wrapper and examine the label. *Bromocarpine*, it says,

Nerve and brain tonic, for the relief of Nervous Disability, Depression, Lack of Concentration, and Low Vitality. All well and good, but its name suggests the inclusion of Bromide, an ingredient all too often used on Mother with no benefit. She grew progressively worse despite the chemicals.

The stopper gives with a little *whoosh*, a genie escaping from its bottle. Nose to glass rim, I inhale. Sickly-sweet, a faint tang of orange-flower, and a bitter undertone. I tip the bottle upside-down, on top of the earth. Its contents cannot harm the dead. As soon as I get home, I will rinse it out and fill it with sugared water. Lilah will know no different.

Doctor Reynold's so-called tonics cannot help me. I am cursed. The prospect of being incarcerated in an asylum sits on my shoulder, whispering words of torment and suffering. I shake out the last few drops and replace the bottle in the paper bag, then the purse, before laying both my hands flat on the curb-stone. Cool, calming. I know why I love this place. It is because for all of the people here buried, there is no more suffering. No more thoughts whirring around in their heads, no more having to focus on what they must do in order to stay alive. And for what? At the end of the day we cannot escape the fate that awaits each and every one of us. Death will come for us all, so why do we spend much of our lives trying to avoid it?

I came to tell my dead sister about my discoveries; instead, I find myself saying, "I envy you, Caitlin. Not for the way you suffered, because no child should endure such an atrocity. I envy you because you, too, would have followed in our mother's footsteps if you had lived. You would have inherited the curse that burdens every female in our family."

The crow answers on her behalf. *Kraaa,* it says. *Kraaa, kraaa!* Then it crouches low before lift-off, and with an almighty push it leaves the ground, black-fingered wings and tail-feather working in tandem, until it reaches the thermals and soars.

Look at me! it says, *This is what it means to be free!*

⁂

The sound of Lilah's laughter greets me at the gate. It is the giggle of a woman much younger. Both she and Ewan Bevan are hard at work in the back garden, a pair of teenage boys at their service. Today they plant fruit trees, apple and plum, so Lilah informed me this morning.

"We're just in time," I hear Ewan say. "October to March is the best time for planting these beggars."

I stand for a moment, a secret spectator, listening to the ease of their chatter. They are comfortable in each other's company, that much is certain, and I am pleased for her.

But am I really? Truth be told, I am a little envious of the way she has settled into life here. The way in which she has formed friendships despite her increasing years, while I can call no one a friend, not Mrs. Jones the Draper who has taught me to sew, and certainly not Gruff Lewis, despite the fact that he has mellowed somewhat.

Lilah's ease highlights my unease. The only person I have got to know here is my dead sister. What if Ewan should ask Lilah to marry him? What then? I would be left to live at Parrog House alone, my scrawny bones rattling around the house like Miss Havisham from Dickens's *Great Expectations*. A wealthy spinster, one who grows increasingly embittered and mad.

Oy, stop the nonsense, Lilah would say if I told her how I feel. Then she would swear her allegiance and vow never to leave my side. And it would not be a lie, because I know she puts my welfare before her own. She always has. How spiteful of me to keep her prisoner. How selfish.

But all I have to look forward to is knowing that each month I will be visited by the ghosts of the past, be it in the form of my mother, sister, or something as yet unseen. Perhaps it will be my grandmother's turn next. What a joy that will be.

I hurry up the path, eager to get inside before any of them spot me. I am not in the mood for polite conversation. Instead, I shall sit in the sewing room and stare out to sea, counting the days until my next trial.

XXXII

WHEN A LETTER FROM VERMONT ARRIVES A WEEK later, my heart skips a beat, and then I realize it cannot be in answer to my most recent one. Indeed, it is Helena who writes…

> *Dearest Aunt Grace,*
>
> *I hope you are well. That is all the small talk you will hear from me, because this is a letter of confession.*
> *Aunt Grace, I have done a bad thing. A very bad thing, indeed.*

I wander over to the window, so that I can read the words more plainly by the light.

> *The other night, I overheard Daddy talking to Mother about a letter he'd received from you. I could tell by the hushed tone of his voice that the contents upset him, and so, instead of going to my room, I sat on the stairs and listened.*
> *However, I was able to gather very little. He said something about a sister who died during childhood, and about how you had written, demanding to know more.*
> *"Then tell her," I heard Mother say. "Perhaps it will be for the best."*
> *As is typical of Daddy, he insisted he would prefer to let things lie, but I knew the matter irked him. He was not the same afterwards, distant, self-absorbed.*
> *Well, of course, curiosity got the better of me, and now this is where the confession comes in…*

I could not stop thinking about it, so one afternoon, while he was at work, I went into his study and found the letter.

So, it is true, then? There was a third child. A girl named Caitlin.

Really, Aunt Grace, I know it was wrong of me to snoop, but I would love to know what happened to her. After all, I am part of this family. Perhaps you can write to me in secret and tell me what you have discovered.

Please do not think too badly of me. I feel certain you will understand. We are both so very inquisitive, aren't we?

Your loving niece,
Helena

Oh, Helena, you have no idea how much heartache surrounds the mystery of Caitlin's death. One day all will be revealed, for I am writing everything in a journal for your eyes only. But not now. You will not learn of it now. You must wait until you are a little older, because despite your obvious maturity, some of the detail is far too gruesome for such young ears.

Of course, I will not tell her this. Instead, I will reply with the scantest of detail. Jonathan has asked that I say nothing of the matter to Helena, and I will not betray him. However, nor will I lie to her. Omission is not the same as a lie, or so they say.

When Mrs. Jones calls to see how I am getting on with the embroidery I am glad of the distraction.

"You did well there," she says, holding the piece close to her face and examining it. That moon wouldn't have been easy to stitch, I bet. Not with those shadows."

I am pleased she thinks so, but it is of little consequence. This last week or so, since learning of my grandmother's illness and discovering the link between my own state of mind and the moon phases, I care about little. Numb: that is the best word to describe how I feel. Numb, but at the same time in constant turmoil about the inevitability of the future. No one on this earth can stop the tides from turning, so no one can halt the torment of monthly visitations. In the end, just like Mother, my mind will become so burdened by past events that I will be in a perpetual state of anguish. That is not how I wish to live my life.

I want to finish the tapestry, though. It will be part of my legacy.

Mrs. Jones and I while away an hour or so, watching the lull of the ocean and the skiffs sailing by.

"How best might I capture the feel of the sea?" I ask. "On the clock face, the sea is turbulent, but I'm not sure I can capture the same feeling in thread. It's easier to show the water's turbulence in paint."

"Hmm," she picks up a pencil and a blank sheet of paper and begins to sketch. "You could go with something quite abstract and create overlapping scrolls in different shades, but it's getting the water to look realistic that's tricky."

She turns the paper towards me. "You'll need to bring out the texture, Grace, but at least a textured finish doesn't have to be as neat." She smiles and points at her hand-drawn waves. "See here, by using a variety of stitches: French knots, scrolls, stem stitch, we can layer them up to create waves."

"I see."

"How about we make a start in that corner? Then you can carry on without me."

⁂

After she leaves, I decide to go for a walk. The fresh air should help clear my head, if nothing else. For early March it is fairly mild, though still too cold to go without a coat.

Over the last few weeks, I sense the girl close by, even when she does not show herself. She is like one's own shadow, so much so that I have grown accustomed to her presence. At least she does not taunt or threaten me, not yet, not like the woman who followed Mother. A silent companion, that is how I would describe her, and yet I know that one day she will reveal herself fully, and the two of us will finally meet.

Low tide. No sooner do I set foot on the sand than I realize the sea has left behind some of its cargo. Not treasure, though. Instead, a bloom of jellyfish lie dotted around, hardly more than six feet between them. Translucent and shaped like umbrellas, their stinging tentacles burrow in the sand. I cannot tell if they are dead or alive. I stand close to one specimen, the size of a dinner plate, and watch for any sign of

221

life. In the centre of the jelly mound, four circles are visible, purplish in colour. No brain, no blood or heart, instead they absorb oxygen through the skin. The creature is incapable of thought, and yet I sense it watching me. I shiver, and move further down the beach, counting as I go.

By the time I am adjacent to the boat-shed, I have counted no less than thirty-four, and there are so many more I did not count. Bran hears me approach and comes running out of the shed and onto the beach, barking and jumping. Within seconds, Gruff appears and calls the dog to heel.

I wave a hand in warning. "Jellyfish," I shout. "They're everywhere."

He hears me, and ties Bran's lead to a post before coming to meet me. I have stopped in front of a jellyfish and use the opportunity to study it so that I do not have to make eye-contact. I have always been like this. If I have not seen someone in several weeks, I struggle to relax in their company.

He takes one glance and says, "Moon jellyfish. Common as muck." His grin is wide, but the label moon jellyfish startles me and I do not smile back.

"You all right?"

I nod and look down again.

"For a moment there I thought you'd been stung."

"Why are they called that?" I feel vulnerable now, as if the sea has provided an omen. Have they come because I am here? A plague of plankton to punish the youngest daughter.

"Look here," he says, pointing at a large specimen. "It's like a full moon, see? Though its proper name is *Aurelia aurita*."

"And you know that how?" I am on the defensive, as is so often the case when under duress.

He laughs, and the skin beneath his eye puckers further. "Grace, I have lived by the sea all my life. Are you questioning my knowledge?"

I shake my head. "No, I am sorry. It's just—it's just the sight of so many washed ashore has unnerved me, that's all. Are they dead?"

He folds his arms. "They might be. It's difficult to tell, but even if they are, you shouldn't touch them. They can still sting, you know, weeks after they die."

I shudder at the thought. Dead, and yet still able to cause pain.

"Would you like to know more about them?"

I am not sure I would, but feel it is polite to listen, especially considering my earlier retort. "I suppose."

"Well, often a jellyfish is called a Medusa because of its appearance. The trailing tentacles resemble her hair, see." He watches my face, keen to note my interest. "And did you know that jellyfish are older than dinosaurs? In fact, they're the oldest multi-cellular creature on the planet."

I wait for him to continue, certain there is more to come.

"But wait for this…the best thing about them is that they are capable of cloning themselves. How incredible is that?"

"Really?" It is truly fascinating. "How on earth are they capable of such a thing?"

He glances away for a moment. "It's to do with the way they reproduce." He flushes, except for the scar which remains white as bone. "I shan't go into detail, but in a way they might be called immortal."

"Immortal? How so?"

"Because an adult medusa can revert back to polyp stage. While medusas are dying of old age, clones of their polyps are thriving on the seafloor. Therefore, they're immortal. Incredible, isn't it?"

He is in his element. Talking about this creature has taken years off him, ironed the creases on his face. He looks so much younger, now, than Jonathan. My brother with his starch-collared office job and all the stress that goes with it. For a moment, I get a glimpse of how good this life could be, this outdoor life, immersed in nature, and I long for a second chance. Tears spring to my eyes, and I stare down at my feet.

"Grace, have I upset you?"

"Not at all." I take a handkerchief out and dab at my eyes. "It's the wind, that's all." He knows differently, though. I see it in his one good eye.

"Listen," he says, nodding towards the sky. "If this weather keeps up, how about that boat ride? I meant it, you know, when I offered."

He sees me hesitate, then adds, "Lilah, too, of course, as long as she's not seasick." He grins, so I know he is joking.

"Actually, it was me who got seasick on the ship over, not Lilah. That woman is strong as an ox, I tell you."

"Well, think about it then, and let me know."

The sound of Bran barking alerts us to his state of confinement.

"I'd better get back to work. I'll never have this skiff ready on time otherwise."

And with that we say farewell, and I make my way back to Parrog House, stepping over immortal creatures with the venomous tentacles of a gorgon. Turn me to stone, I think. Right here, in front of the harbour. Let me watch over the sea for an eternity.

That night, I dream of the sea. Standing in front of the gate of Parrog House, I watch it roll out on an ebbing tide. Each wave is a hiss of warning, like that of a snake. The moon shines down on black sand, highlighting discarded treasure. This time it is not jellyfish she has left behind but a writhing mass of starfish. Five-fingered creatures that flex and falter in their attempt to return to the sea. But their mother does not want their company. This is why she has left them behind: innocent, helpless creatures that will die without her protection.

Without hesitation, I run onto the sand, bare feet sinking in the wet mass. Armful upon armful, I gather them up, sensing their suckers slither up my arms. Their own arms are scarred, raised white lines criss-cross over the limbs, just like Gruff's. I must return them to the sea. I must save as many as possible. Like the jellyfish, these creatures are also capable of regeneration, capable of detaching a limb to escape a predator if need be. But I am not a predator. I only wish to help.

Time and time again, I run to the shore, wading as deep as my thighs before letting go of my catch, but the more I save, the more there are when next I turn around. I sink to my knees on the sand, realizing the futility of the task, and turn my head skyward. Cloudless. Stars from the heavens, not those from the sea, wink and twinkle without a care in the world.

XXXIII

THE THING I AM MOST SAD ABOUT IS THAT MY BELOVED grandfather clock has now become my jailer. Each and every day, I watch it move a little closer to the next full moon, and it fills me with dread. It seems to know I fear it, because the moon's eye peeps solemnly from behind the left-hand globe, widening with each passing day. Its mouth is open, too. *Oh*, it seems to say, *I do apologize, but there is nothing I can do to stop it!*

At times I am tempted to revisit the clockmaker and ask him to remove the click spring again, but apart from not wanting to embarrass myself, it would do no good. Like Mother, I would find another way of counting down the days. There is no way to escape the inevitable, and just one more day until its entire face is revealed. What delight might it offer this time?

By the time nine o'clock arrives, I am so nervous that I turn to the drinks cabinet. I have drawn the curtains to block out the moon, but I know it is there.

"Nightcap, Lilah?" I say, holding aloft the wine decanter. Blood-red Bordeaux, with a bouquet of blackcurrant and earth. It reminds me of Christ and The Last Supper.

"Ooh, you're a temptress," she says. "But why not?"

We sit awhile, sipping in silence.

"Garden's almost planted," she says. Her knuckles are calloused—her nails short and jagged. A worker's hands. Five days out of seven, she and Ewan have toiled in the garden, and she has enjoyed every minute of it. "Come summer we'll have beans and beetroot, potatoes, and radish. Even some fruit, with a bit of luck, though Ewan reckons it'll take at least two years for the apple trees to bear fruit."

I try to muster up some enthusiasm, but my thoughts are elsewhere. "All we need now is a serpent," I say, encircling the rim of my glass with a finger.

"Pardon me?" She frowns.

"Sorry, Lilah. The wine, the apples. So many biblical references."

She shakes her head, perplexed. "If you say so." She finishes her wine, then says, "Anyway, I'm off to bed if that's all right with you. I'm worn out."

The sitting-room feels too large without her, too much space for too few bones. My face is flushed from the wine, yet I pour another and wait.

✠ ✠

"I really think it's time you went to bed." I jolt awake in the armchair, expecting to see Lilah standing there. But it is not Lilah; it is Father.

"Father?" My heart lurches. I have longed to see him again, and now he has come. But it is not me he addresses, for sitting on the armchair opposite mine is Mother. She is dressed head-to-toe in black, as is Father. The crepe of her mourning dress rustles at his words, and her eyes are hollow. I have never seen her looking so poorly, except during those last few days.

I turn my head in Father's direction. His face is drawn, the weight of the world sits on his shoulders.

"You go on up; I am not ready," she says.

He walks over to her and places one knee on the floor as though about to propose. His moustache twitches. "Please, Marta. Come to bed. You have not slept in over a week."

Caitlin's funeral, I realize. This is the scene I am witnessing.

She stares through him, untouched by his gesture and the compassion in his voice. "How can I sleep when my child lies cold in her grave?"

Her words cut like a knife. I see it in the way he faces the ground and in the sag of his shoulders. I want to run to him.

I want to take him in my arms and comfort him, but just like on previous occasions I cannot move.

He shakes his head. "She was my child, too, you know. Do you not think I feel the same?"

His words fall on deaf ears. She does not move a muscle, even her starched gown is silent.

He gets to his feet, far older than his years, then runs his hands through his hair. "You shouldn't have gone to the grave," he says. "I knew it was too soon."

She looks at him then, eyes like daggers. "You would not allow me to witness her put in the ground yesterday, and still you have the nerve to tell me it is too soon!" Every word is spat like venom.

So Caitlin was buried the previous day, then. The air is thick with grief. If I were to wave a knife, it would leave behind jagged patterns of pain.

"Well, if you had to go, then at least you could have waited for me," he says. "I would have accompanied you if you'd insisted."

How typical of Mother. She must have waited for him to be otherwise engaged then gone to the graveyard alone.

"I needed to see for myself," she says, her voice a hoarse whisper. "And in any case, I was not alone." She waits for a few moments. "*She* was there, too." She trembles now, I see it in her hands and in the way her teeth chatter. She is terrified, and in that moment, I feel a surge of great pity.

"Who?" he asks, feebly, though I can tell by his voice he already knows the answer.

She leans towards the side table and picks up her purse. Black beads glint like the eyes of a serpent. Here comes the snake, I think.

"She gave me this." She opens her purse and holds it out for him to see. He glances at her, undecided, so she gives the purse a little thrust to encourage him to look inside.

I am on my feet, the compulsion to see what is inside the purse has freed me of my paralysis.

The purse is lined with pale green silk, like dewy grass. There on the bottom is a sexton beetle. Its squared body hunkers low, as if it is trying to hide. But its orange and black markings give it away. She reaches inside and prods it with her index finger. Despite being cooped up for most of the day it is still alive, though on its last breath it would seem. It ambles forward, hardly able to put one foot in front of the other, sniffing the air with its antennae.

"Oh, good god, Marta!" Father places a hand to his mouth. "Whatever is the matter with you?"

She snaps the purse shut. "It's for our daughter. That's what *she* told me."

"Our daughter is dead, for heaven's sake! When will you accept the fact?"

I am trembling from head to toe. My skin is clammy, and I feel close to fainting.

Mother says nothing for a few moments, then, "I don't mean Caitlin…it's for our other daughter."

He paces the room, head in hands, then returns to stand in front of her. He bends and grips her forearms, and she winces. "We do not have another daughter, Marta."

She looks him in the eye, no malice now, no bitterness, just fear and sadness. Then she pulls one hand from beneath his grip and places it against her stomach. "But we will have, soon. I thought it would end with Caitlin, but I was wrong."

It is me she refers to. I am the daughter in her womb. In my mind, I conjure the date on Caitlin's headstone: December 8th 1873. I was born August twelfth the following year. Mother was carrying me when Caitlin died, though it seems she did not realize it at the time.

A jay's feather for Jonathan, a delicate white shell for Caitlin, and now the sexton beetle for me. Why do I represent the most horrific of the three? The beetle is the undertaker of the insect world, often found in graveyards. I shudder at the thought, but at least now I understand why Mother kept the items all those years.

❧ ❧

I am certain that lack of sleep is adding to the sense of disorientation, but how can one sleep after witnessing something like this?

Having analysed the conversation between Mother and Father, I am now certain that mental affliction runs in the female family line. Grandmother, Mother, me. It cannot be a coincidence. In all likelihood, Caitlin, too, would have suffered had she lived. Her tendency towards petulance and sleepwalking were already in evidence.

I thought it would end with Caitlin. Those were Mother's words. She must have been devastated to discover she was carrying another child, especially a girl. Perhaps that is the reason we never really bonded, not like a mother and daughter should. Or was she afraid of loving me too deeply because she knew the inevitable torment I would suffer?

What kind of future awaits me? I am in no doubt other than my condition will worsen. At least Mother had all of us to support her. Who do I have? Yes, there is Lilah, but she is twice my age. What will become of me once she has gone or when she is too old to look after me? I say this not out of self-pity but out of genuine concern, knowing all too well what the future holds: life in an asylum.

After Father died, I researched possible treatments for Mother, studied everything from Duchenne to Charcot. In comparison, Doctor Reynolds is an innocent puppy. In fact, I am surprised he allowed me to get away with just a tonic, though I rather suspect he leans toward pelvic manipulation and vibration therapy, given his suggestion of the possible link between my unmarried status and my moods. I have no intention of allowing such a thing to happen.

But what will he suggest when my affliction worsens? Bed rest and tonics would be replaced with electro-convulsive therapy, or worse still, something I read about recently—the surgical removal of part of the brain's cortex.

And so it is with a sense of dismal inevitability that I wash and dress and make my way downstairs.

"You all right, Grace?" Lilah asks when I appear in the kitchen. "You don't seem yourself these last few days."

"I'm fine, just a little tired."

"Have you been taking the tonic?" She eyes me suspiciously.

"I have, but in truth I have little faith in such things. Think about it, Lilah. How many tonics did Mother take over the years? They did nothing to help her, did they?" I have been trying to hide my feelings from her these past weeks, but after such a disturbed sleep I cannot manage it today.

She slumps down on a stool, head in hands. "I'm worried about you, Grace." She gestures for me to sit, too, and I oblige. "Perhaps you ought to see the doctor again, ask him for something stronger, something to help you sleep."

My fists are clenched beneath the table, not out of anger, but because I am so afraid. My whole body is stiff with fear, like an iron rod. I look her in the eye.

"Listen, Lilah, I want you to think about what happened to Mother. Consider the numerous doctors Father paid in the hope that one of them might make her well, or at least ease her symptoms. Nothing worked, did it?"

Her eyes cloud with tears and it startles me. Lilah is tough as old leather, I have never seen her cry.

"But you're not sleeping, and if you don't sleep then how can you hope to get better?"

"I am sleeping. I just dream a lot, that's all."

A silent pause follows, one that seems to hang in the air, expectantly. "Grace, you might think you're sleeping, but you walk the boards half the night. You talk in your sleep, cry out at times. It is all I can do to stop myself from coming to comfort you."

Her words come as a shock. I did not think I had walked in my sleep for some time. I swallow hard. "How often? When was the last time?"

Her sigh is the quivering kind, almost a sob. "Every night, just about. Every night for the last few weeks. Since I'm half-deaf I've been afraid to sleep these past weeks in case you get into danger. I hear the floorboards creak, and your mumbling. Like a whine, your voice is at times." She leans across and takes my hand, though mine is limp and cold. "Sometimes I get out of bed to check on you, but you are not a child, and you know what they say about sleepwalkers…don't wake them, they say. It's dangerous."

My breath comes quick and shallow. "Is that the reason the front door is bolted at the top at night?"

She nods and her chin quivers. "You must understand, after what you told me about your sister, I was afraid." There is a pause, and then she says, "How do you know about the door? I unbolt it first thing in the morning, hoping you won't find out."

"The other day, when you and Ewan were working in the garden and I went to town. I noticed the front door was bolted at the top. How do you even reach it, Lilah?"

She looks sheepish. "I climb on a chair, of course."

I give her hand a little squeeze. "Well, that's dangerous. A woman your age should not be climbing chairs."

She looks at me then, and I see love reflected in her eyes.

"Oh, Grace," she says, "I'd do anything to keep you safe. Anything. You're like a daughter to me."

Her words are a punch to the stomach because I know how this must end. "I am so afraid, Lilah. If it hadn't been for us, and you in particular, Mother would have ended her days in an asylum. That is not an exaggeration."

She closes her eyes and sighs. She knows I speak the truth.

"I cannot bear the thought of it happening to me, Lilah. I would rather die."

"Oh, Grace, don't say that. Why would such a thing happen to you? You are not sick like your mother. You've learned of so much tragedy since arriving here, Grace. First your sister, then your grandmother. It's bound to affect you."

I remove my hand from hers and lean back. "It's more than that, Lilah, trust me. Far more. There are things I have not told you, because I don't like to worry you."

She pinches her mouth and shakes her head, but her eyes do not leave mine.

"All this time, I lived in hope, just as you have been doing, that my…eccentricities, shall we say, were simply that. However, I am now convinced I have inherited Mother's madness, and that she inherited it from her mother. Things will only get worse, Lilah. I know it."

She shakes her head. "No, Grace, you don't know that. Give yourself—"

I raise a hand. "I do know it, Lilah, and I am terrified. But I am also still able to apply logic, and I know this much…no matter what the doctors say, or what the medical examiner said after Mother died, there is more to our sickness than meets the eye. It is not simply a matter of brain deterioration; it is something else. Something no one would ever believe, even if the evidence were laid out before them."

When I entered the kitchen a few minutes ago, it was not my intention to unburden myself like this; but talking about my feelings has been somewhat cathartic.

"Listen, Lilah." I take her hand in mine again. "I want you to know this. No matter what happens to me, you must live your own life. Too long you have sacrificed your own happiness for the sake of our family, and it is not right."

"I would do it all again. Where do you think I'd be now if it wasn't for you? Out of a job and homeless."

I manage a smile. "Do me a favour, Lilah. Marry Ewan Bevan...that is if he asks you, of course."

She turns the colour of boiled beetroot. "Get away with you. How can you say such a thing?"

Both of us laugh. "I mean it, Lilah. If that is what you want, then do it. Life is very short, you know."

XXXIV

Jonathan's letter arrives on the morning of Lilah's sixtieth birthday, and though I am tempted to open it, I must wait until after tea, otherwise the contents might sour the occasion. I hold the envelope in both hands, imagining what lies within. Is it a sixth sense that suggests he confesses all, or is it the envelope's weight? This is no flimsy gesture of politeness, but rather it suggests several sheets. I place it next to the silver trinket box and join Lilah in the kitchen, a waft of cinnamon and apple there to greet me.

In typical Lilah fashion, she has baked her own cake.

"Today, I pay homage to my mother who gave birth to me sixty years ago," she says, dabbing the sweat on her forehead with a handkerchief. "Since we'll be eating chicken for tea, the cake must be dairy-free, in accordance with kosher rules."

She rarely mentions her Jewish heritage, nor does she usually abide by its rules, so the announcement takes me by surprise. I say nothing though, assuming she feels a little nostalgic on this special day.

I sniff the air and wrap my arms around her. "It smells delicious. Happy birthday, Lilah, and may you enjoy many more in this house." Her body is warm and soft, comforting to hold.

"Now all I need do is double this age and I'll be on par with Moses," she says, her voice quivering a little with emotion.

I let go of her. "Really? Moses lived to be a hundred and twenty?

She winks. "According to the Torah, he did."

"Come with me," I say, taking her by the hand and leading her out of the kitchen in the direction of the back door.

"Where are we going?"

"Wait and see."

Ewan has not let me down, he promised he would come after dark and deliver the gift. There, a few steps from the door, stands a wild cherry tree, root-ball attached and ripe for planting.

Her hands fly to her mouth and she gasps. "A cherry tree. Oh, Grace! Thank you."

"It's a wild variety, so it's best you don't eat the berries. Leave them for the birds."

She nods. "I prefer that. You know how I love to feed the birds."

The tree is in bud. Pure white balls lie curled within bright green receptacles, all except for one which has opened early. Lilah gently strokes the open flower. "Look," she says, "it's opened in time for my birthday."

Her joy brings a lump to my throat. "Would you like to know why I chose it?"

She takes a deep breath and nods.

"I chose it because the cherry tree symbolizes the importance of appreciating the time we spend with our loved ones." My voice cracks, and I take her hand. "Lilah, thank you for coming to Wales with me. I hope you know how much I appreciate you, even though I don't always show it."

We hug then, both of us shedding a few tears on one another's shoulders.

"And thank you for bringing me. You are my daughter, you know that, don't you?" We look at each other for a few moments, knowing no more needs to be said. "Come on," she says, drying her eyes on her sleeve. "Daft pair, we are. Let's go put the kettle on."

⚘ ⚘

As I dress for Lilah's tea party, Jonathan's letter whispers to me.

Come, open me now and allow me to spoil things for you, but I dig in my heels and turn my face away from its pallid complexion.

At three o'clock on the dot, Ewan arrives carrying a gladsome bouquet: roses, daffodils, begonia, in every shade of yellow. He kisses Lilah on the cheek and the hall is filled with the scent of spring.

He is joined a few minutes later by Mrs. Jones and her daughter, followed by Aelwen and Lowri from The Ship Afloat.

Between us, Lilah and I have prepared a delicious spread, and we while away a few hours with our guests in the front parlour. I am happy for Lilah, glad to be able to show her some appreciation after all she has done.

The last guest leaves just after six, and the clock seems to sigh with relief. Like me, it is impatient to devour the contents of the letter.

Once everything is cleared away, I turn to Lilah and say, "I'm going up to change and maybe have a lie down."

"Good idea," she says, fanning her face with a napkin. "I'm exhausted, but thank you, Grace. I don't think I've ever enjoyed myself so much."

※ ※

The letter opener splices through the dried gum, leaving behind jagged tears, a sign of things to come.

Inside sit three sheets of paper which have been written on both sides. I take a deep breath and prepare myself.

The opening paragraph pays no heed to polite enquiry; instead it cuts me to the quick, taking tiny pieces of me with it.

Dear Grace,

I read your letter with sadness in my heart and indecision in my thoughts. As you will see from the date, I needed to set your words aside for some time to allow their flavour to mature, though I have to admit I returned to sniff their bouquet on several occasions.

My first inclination was to deny all knowledge of what you have discovered and to act dumb. However, in the end I decided that the time has come to bear my soul and share with you my memory of events as I perceived them at the time.

You will not like it, Grace; you will not like it one bit.

I turn the page, my mouth dry as the desert:

As far as our grandmother is concerned, I was just three years old, going on four, when she died and therefore have few memories of her. You are right in thinking we shared her home. Parrog House belonged to our grandparents originally. Also, whoever it was that suggested she was a formidable character was correct.

I remember the sound of her voice—cold as winter—and her pale grey eyes, but little else. If you don't mind me saying so, you resemble her, though you are far more kind.

She was tall, willowy, with hip-length hair pulled tight against her head. At night she would release it from its pins and allow it to tumble all the way down to her hips. Then, she would take a brush and run it through the whole length a hundred times whilst scowling and muttering at her reflection in the mirror.

She was mad, too—quite mad, and I have always believed it was she who caused Mother's decline, not because her madness was inherited, but because of her fierce dominance.

You also asked about the significance of the jay's feather and the seashell. I am afraid I cannot help on either score, Grace. I remember something about a silver box (or was it you who brought that to my attention?), but I cannot say I remember those items.

You mentioned Gruff Lewis, the shipwright, and his role in Caitlin's death. As children, Gruff and I were the best of friends. As different as chalk and cheese, it was his earthiness and also his bravery that attracted me. Well, that and his dog. (I jest, Grace.)

I was rather more timid than Gruff, rather less inclined to swim out of my depth or climb to great heights on rocky cliffs. It did not surprise me to discover it was he who tried to save our sister. After the event, our family shunned him. Mother could not bear to look at him, saying his scars reminded her of what had happened, and I was never allowed to play with him again.

I remember him with fondness and wish our parting could have been more amicable. Life is so unfair, Grace. His scars and the loss of his sight bear testament to the kind of boy he was. No doubt, he is just as brave as a man.

Why did I not write to him? Guilt, Grace, a simple matter of guilt. It was I who should have saved our sister, not Gruff. It was I who had the opportunity to do so, and I have never forgiven myself.

I am shocked at his words. How could Jonathan have saved her?

And now, Grace, now I must address that which has eaten away at my conscience all these years. I never imagined admitting this, either in writing or in speech, because I can barely admit it to myself, never mind to someone else. I hope that in sharing this with you, not only will it answer some of your questions, but it might also help me to put the matter to rest once and for all.

Are you ready?

Am I? I ask myself as I turn the page. I am not certain. Should I throw the letter onto the fire and pretend it never arrived? That way I could remain in blissful ignorance, but despite the temptation I continue to read.

You have discovered much about our family, Grace, I'll give you that, but there are some things you do not know. The night Caitlin died...I could have prevented it if only I had listened to my instinct. I have blamed myself ever since and always will.

Often have I reflected on it, but I was just a child, and the memories of children are not always reliable. Suffice it to say that over time Mother had grown increasingly sick, particularly after the death of our Grandmother. Instead of it setting her free and allowing her to be mistress of her own house, it made her worse. Of course, she would have been in mourning, but it was more than that, much more.

Young though I was, I remember her collapsing to the floor on hearing the news, understandably so, given the cause of Grandmother's death. It is not every day that a close fami-

ly member hangs themselves, is it? So, when you fainted the night Mother died, the memory came flooding back, and I was so afraid. Afraid that you, too, might become ill.

Anyway, I digress…soon after Grandmother's death, Mother started hearing voices and seeing things which weren't there. She became irrational, manic, and often as cold as the grave. She was full of fear, too, and whenever Father had to go away on business she would insist that either Caitlin or I sleep in her room. Which brings me to the night in question, the night Caitlin died.

As you already know, it was a few days before Christmas. I recall the sense of anticipation, tinged with uncertainty, for nothing felt certain back then.

I slept in one of the bedrooms on the upper storey—the one next to the playroom, overlooking the sea. It was gone midnight when a sound outside woke me, the squeal of a gate, I thought. I got out of bed and looked out of the window but saw nothing, so I went back to bed. I could not sleep afterwards. Something seemed amiss, though I did not know what it was. I knew that Caitlin slept in Mother's bed that night. This is why I say I should have listened to my instinct, Grace, but I didn't, and I have regretted it ever since.

I remember the clock chiming the quarter hour, and the half hour, before eventually it chimed one o'clock. Still, I tossed and turned, certain something was amiss.

Then came another sound. A scream, like the cry of a wild animal. I jumped out of bed and ran to the window.

Mother stood in front of the gate, facing the house. Her hair hung down in straggly clumps, and she tore at it with one hand. She wore a coat, though, I remember that, so whatever reason she had for being outdoors in such cold weather and so late at night, at least she'd had the sense to dress.

I put my hands on the glass and pressed my nose to the window to try and see more clearly, but all it did was mist the glass. I remember the iciness on my palm as I wiped away the condensation. She stood there still, facing the house, something hanging from her right hand. I was about to open the window and call to her when she screamed again.

I can see her now, Grace. She stood stock still and raised the object in her hand skyward. I recognized it then. The thing that dangled from Mother's hand was Caitlin's doll, Vio-

let. And I tell you this, Grace…Caitlin never went anywhere without Violet.

Back and fore from the window to the bedroom door, I ran several times, desperate to go and see what was happening, but I was afraid. You see, Grace, as much as I loved Mother, I was also afraid of her, especially when she was…shall we say, perturbed.

Eventually, I heard the front door open and close, then a pause as she took off her coat, followed by the sound of her feet on the stairs. I ran across the landing and tiptoed down the narrow stairs towards the first floor. I peeped through the keyhole, expecting to see Caitlin. We could have faced Mother together then. But Caitlin wasn't there. How could she sleep through such a din, I wondered.

Mother paused on the landing, trembling and muttering incomprehensible words before entering her bedroom. I listened for several minutes, expecting to hear Caitlin's voice, but all I heard was the sound of my own heart in my ears and a distant moan.

And that, Grace, was that. No sooner did I manage to fall asleep again than someone was knocking on the door and asking if Caitlin was at home.

You know the rest, Grace, except for one small, seemingly insignificant detail: the doll. When next I saw it in the playroom, the back of its head was smashed.

It is true that Caitlin sometimes sleepwalked, Grace. Did she do so that night? Who knows? All I know is what my instinct tells me, and that is that our own mother played some part in our sister's death.

I told no one. Not then or now. Not the police, not Father, or even Eva.

Why? Perhaps you were right about the jay's feather. Maybe it has always been my role to protect the family, no matter the cost.

Yours,
Jonathan

P.S. After Caitlin died, not once did Mother visit the upper storey; not even after you were born. She hired a nanny who nursed you in the back room up there, but she never visited you, nor did she come to watch me at play. I believe she liked to imagine Caitlin might still be alive up there. That if she didn't face it, she could imagine her sleeping in her old bedroom and playing in the playroom. Perhaps this is why she barricaded the place when we left, so that Caitlin could not get out. Who knows? I know you asked me in a previous letter, but I was not then ready to tell you, Grace.

Please forgive me.

⊰ CHAPTER ⊱

XXXV

I HAVE SPENT THIS PAST WEEK PUTTING MY AFFAIRS IN order. The embroidery is finished, the words, *Love is a moonlit path of memories* stem-stitched in threads of silver and pearl where sea and sky meet. Mrs. Jones says I have done her proud—such a sweet sentiment. Wrapped in pale blue silk, the finished piece sits in a file, alongside my journal and last will and testament at the solicitor's office. The tapestry will be posted to Helena soon. As for the journal, she is to open it when she turns twenty-one, some eight years from now.

In the will, I bequeath all my worldly goods to Helena, with a clause attached stating that Lilah must be allowed to reside at Parrog House for the remainder of her days, whether or not she marries, as long as she wishes to do so. I have also set up a fund to cover Lilah's day to day living costs. When she is old enough, Helena may choose to come and live in Wales, or she may choose to sell the house. That will be her decision, though I spend many an hour imagining her here.

My journal is an open-hearted document explaining everything I have discovered about our family and also the reasons I have chosen to take the moonlit path. I hope that in time she will be able to forgive me.

Which brings me to the matter of Gruff Lewis. From him, too, I seek forgiveness. In my will, I have bequeathed him enough money to purchase a brand-new skiff, one with all the bells and whistles. It is the least I can do.

Tomorrow is Saturday, just two days remain before the next full moon, and the weather is set fair. If he is free this Sunday, I shall ask him to take me out on his boat. I wish to see the coastline in all its glory before the next full moon.

For the first time since we met, I feel no trepidation as I approach the boat-shed. Quite the opposite, in fact. This is the first time I have felt excited in years.

As is usual, I am greeted by his dog, Bran, though today instead of barking at me he wags his tail and hurries towards me like a long-lost friend. I bend down and ruffle his ears.

"Good boy," I say, breathing in his scent.

Gruff appears at the door, wiping oily hands on an old rag.

"To what do I owe the pleasure?"

He wears a collarless shirt, open at the neck, and a lop-sided grin that suits his personality. Only now do I know a moment's hesitation.

"I wonder, are you free tomorrow? If so, I'd like to take you up on the offer of that boat trip." I nod towards Dinas Island in the distance, my feet planted firmly on the ground.

He takes a step back, and his good eye widens.

"I had intended giving this a second coat." He gestures towards a small rowboat that bobs in the shallows. "But for you I will make an exception."

How typical of him, I think, not to succumb without a little protest. I admire him for it, though.

"Will Lilah be joining us?"

"No, just me and you, and Bran of course. That is, if he usually accompanies you on such voyages." The dog barks at the sound of his name, just one quick yelp. Then, to hide my embarrassment I add, "Though Lilah will no doubt provide a delicious picnic."

"Oh, well in that case." He laughs, and the corners of his eyes wrinkle unevenly which makes him all the more charming. "Shall we say eleven?"

⚕⚕

Lilah stares open-mouthed when I tell her of my plan. She considers my words for a moment, gasping like a fish out of water, then she breaks into a smile.

"Good for you," she says, hands clasped together. "One life, Grace…one life. I'll say no more."

⚕⚕

"Goodness me, Lilah, this will sink the boat."

The basket she hands me is filled to the brim: slices of cold roast beef, wrapped in waxed paper, cheese and cress sandwiches, homemade scones with butter and jam, and bottled ginger beer to wash it down.

"Just go and enjoy yourself," she says, and her eyes sparkle.

The basket is so heavy that I have to set it down three times on my way to the boat-shed. I spy Gruff in the distance and wave, and he hurries to relieve me of its weight. Today, there is not a spot of grease or grime on him. Dressed in dark green tweed and a white-collared shirt, he looks quite dapper, especially in his captain's hat. He doffs it as he greets me, and I see he has attempted to tame his unruly curls with a little pomade.

He takes the basket from me and says, "Well, at least we won't go hungry. Good old Lilah."

As we reach the bay, I notice the beach has been washed clean. No sign of the jellyfish now, the sea has claimed them once again. Bran is already waiting in the boat. Ears pricked, he watches us approach, panting all the while. He turns full circle and whines as we draw close. Gruff sets the basket down in the hull then reaches for my hand.

"Steady as you go," he says. "If you get your feet wet now, you'll be uncomfortable for the rest of the day."

I sit at the stern, and he takes up position in the bow, facing me. Bran sits between us, sniffing the basket.

"You ready?" Gruff asks, taking up the oars.

I am so excited that I cannot speak, so instead I nod, several times. I feel more alive and carefree than I have done in years, decades, even. The drag of the boat against the water feels dense, as if we row through treacle. A different

243

sensation to that of the liner that brought me to Wales; more primeval, somehow.

No sooner are we out of wading depth than the wind whips at my face and tugs at my straw sailor's hat. I sit with one hand on top to prevent it from flying away.

"Take it off," Gruff calls. "Your arm will ache if you sit like that for too long."

I do as he says, pinning the hat between my feet.

Around the rocks we sail, and the coastline opens up in front of my eyes. I gaze up at the cliffs, towards the coast-path, the place where I first encountered Gruff, and Bran. I remember the words we shared that first day, both of us determined and wary of each other. The sensation of looking back at someone else's life is strong. Was that really me, or is this who I am?

A company of gannets swoop and dive in the air, riding the thermals, while a strop of razorbills stand upright on the rocks, unimpressed by their antics. Round another jagged strip, I sight the little inlet where I stopped to read all those weeks back.

I angle my hand against my eyes to get a better view. "I walked this far," I say. "It seems like a lifetime ago."

Gruff points towards the rear of the little beach which backs onto woodland.

"From here, it's possible to cut up into the woods and climb all the way up to the top road. You can walk back to Newport from there, but it's a fair step."

He rows past the inlet and heads farther out to sea. The wind picks up again, and the waves do battle with the boat.

This is our domain, they seem to say. *Do not test us too far.*

Little do they know what I have planned.

"First stop, Aberfforest Beach," Gruff shouts above the wind, yet still his words are carried off into the distance. "Great spot to see baby seals, come September," he says. "Perhaps we can come again."

I know a moment's regret, then. Today I will absorb every single detail, right into the core of my being, for it will be the one and only time.

"From there, we'll sail onward to *Cwm yr Eglwys*, then on to Dinas Island, though it's not really an island, not in the truest sense."

I look at him quizzically.

"What is it, then?"

"It's a promontory, only partially detached from the mainland. Formed during the Ice Age, it was. We'll picnic up on the cliff and watch the birds, or, if you're hungry by the time we reach *Cwm yr Eglwys* we'll eat there." He stands for a moment and gives a little bow. The boat rocks, and I let out a squeal which he finds amusing. "The day belongs to you, Grace Morgan," he says. "I am at your service."

⁂

By the time we return to The Parrog, the light is fading. We step out of the boat, Gruff first, then me. He holds my hand in his as I climb. My feet are unsteady and my head sways from the motion of the waves.

Lilah's picnic basket is as spent as my energy, but I am sated in more ways than one.

Bran senses the time to say goodbye has come. He sits at Gruff's side with his head tilted. I bend down and smooth his chest, feeling his heart beating beneath the warm fur.

So much life.

Then I raise my head and look Gruff in the eye. "Thank you," I say. "This has been the best of days. I mean that from the bottom of my heart." Then I lean in and place my lips against the puckered skin on his cheek. The smallest of kisses.

⊰ C H A P T E R ⊱

XXXVI

I SIT IN FRONT OF THE ARCHED WINDOW ON THE LANDING, staring out to sea. All is calm and quiet, even the gulls have gone home to roost. It is close to midnight, and the full moon sits just left of centre-stage, enveloping me in cool blue light. As usual on a clear night, its starry servants swoon, each vying for the moon's attention. It has rolled out a shimmering path of moonlight. It glistens on the water, rippling with the gentle ebb and flow of the tide, but only the brightest star will be given permission to walk it.

The distant sound of Lilah's snores drift from the bedroom. She will sleep deeply, I am certain, especially after the nip of brandy I added to her night-time cordial. Dear Lilah, her skin cool and scented with rosewater as I kissed her goodnight.

"Whatever was that for?" she had said.

"For everything, Lilah. For everything."

The grandfather clock in the hall downstairs chimes midnight, and my heart skips a beat. She will come soon, I am certain. These last few weeks she has barely left my side—a ghost of a girl, dressed in grey, yet as familiar as my own reflection. I wait, and I watch.

At two o'clock, I am roused from sleep by a change in the air. No sound, no footsteps or voices, just a whoosh of wind against my skin. I open my eyes and face the window, my back stiff and sore from having slept with my knees curled beneath me.

The moon has travelled west as I slept. It sits, now, a little higher in the sky, a little smaller, but of course it has not really diminished in size. It merely wants me to follow, that is all. *Come this way,* it says. *Follow the light.*

She is there now, the girl in grey, a little less shadowy, a little more distinct than on previous occasions. She stands on the path in front of the gate, looking out to sea.

I slip off my shoes and tiptoe across the landing. In the hall, I put on my coat, though I know it is pointless. Still, old habits die hard and Lilah would not want me to be cold. The clock face watches my every move, its pendulum ticking away the seconds. I cast my gaze over the painted harbour scene one last time, then step out into the night.

"You have come," she says, her back to me still. "I knew you would."

Her shadow is long and sinewy. I stand on it and wait for her to turn around. I know what I will see, though. Deep down I have known it all along.

"Are you ready?" she whispers, and her voice is the sound of an Aeolian harp, gentle and resonant.

From deep inside I hear myself whimper. It is the softest of sounds, like the hum of a bee.

Then she turns to face me, and I stare at my own image. A *doppelgänger,* though not quite. She is half of me, and I am half of her, though we are two bodies. Grey complexion, blue-tinged lips, eyes hollow and shadowed. She allows me to drink in her image while she stands there, a small smile playing about her lips.

"Do you understand, now, why Mother wrote the word *Wherever*?" she says.

I say nothing, for I am struck dumb.

"One cannot escape one's problems, Grace. Wherever one journeys, one's problems go, too. And do you know why? It is because we cannot run away from ourselves."

She sighs, and her breath is the wind on the water. "The jay's feather—Jonathan. The dreamer who fixes his sights on the sky and refuses to acknowledge its limits, and the protector of truth, of course."

My eyes have not left hers, not once.

"And Caitlin, our sister, the child who lived and died beside the sea. A shell of her former self, a delicate mineral." She rubs the fingers of her right hand together, as though sprinkling the finest ash, then she takes my hand in hers, though hers is not quite solid, and together we walk the path towards the boat-shed.

"And then, of course, there's you; or should I say us?" She stares into the distance. Only then do I notice her footsteps are silent.

"The sexton beetle, the one who burrows in the earth and bears the burden of reaping death." Her words carry on the wind like flakes of snow. You were never meant to be, you see. *We* were never meant to exist. It was supposed to end with Caitlin."

We have reached the boat-shed. Its door is closed and bolted. It is no more than a black shadow against a backdrop of night sky. Hard to believe that hours earlier it was so full of warmth and life.

But it is not the boat-shed we have come to see. Gruff's rowboat bobs in the water, its belly empty and cavernous. The sea licks at the hull, oily-black. Wooden oars, out-stretched like a pair of arms, welcome us aboard.

My feet are sodden by the time I step inside. Ice-cold water creeps up my calves, and I shiver from head to toe.

"You know," I say, helping her into the boat. "There are still some things I don't understand."

"Such as?" Her expression is whimsical, not a care in the world.

I take a deep breath and prepare my words. "Such as who tormented Mother? Did Mother murder Caitlin? And why do the visitations occur during a full moon?"

She tuts in quick succession. "Oh, my dear girl," she says, her dilated pupils an infinite space. "I thought by now you would understand."

She lowers herself onto the wooden bench, and only then do I realize I have taken the seat at the bow. The oars are already in my hands, eager to set off.

"It's like this, Grace. Each and every one of us has two sides, do you understand?"

I nod and begin to row.

"One good side; one not so, and that is true of everybody. But, of course, that is oversimplifying things."

Her hair whips about her face like Medusa's serpents. Untethered and wild.

"In our family it goes a step further." She laughs then, full of mirth. "What an inheritance! We are cursed, you see. As the last female dies, the next in line inherits the curse. Do you remember how you fainted when Mother died? It wasn't a faint, not really. It was the split, the moment of separation."

She looks at me to see if I am following. My shoulders burn with the effort of rowing, yet I continue to guide the boat along the moonlit path.

"So, in answer to your first question, Mother tormented herself, or at least one half of her did."

Caitlin's drawing springs to mind: the two women, identical, one smiling, one crying. Of course! Then there was the matter of Mother's denial when Caitlin insisted it was she who gave her the jay's feather. Now I understand why she denied it. She was not there. And the woman on the beach, the one who gave the shell to Caitlin. Which Mother was that?

"The evil side, you mean? Mother's evil side tormented her?"

Her laugh is haughty.

"No, Grace, you are quite mistaken. The evil side is the ever-present one, or at least the *potential* evil side, shall we say?"

I shake my head in denial. Yes, I knew we were cursed; but we are not evil.

"That word, Grace—potential. That is what matters most. In ourselves we recognize that potential, don't we? Come now, don't pretend to be a saint."

She leans back against the stern, stretches graceful limbs towards the sky, and yawns.

"Mother recognized it in herself, eventually. But then she had children to consider, didn't she? Our grandmother, on the other hand, well let's just say she had very little conscience. Her other self, the good half remember, found it necessary to drive her to distraction before she was willing to put an end to her life. I'm sure you've heard the tales." She shakes her head. "Quite wicked, by all accounts."

As we row past Parrog House, I look up at the windows and picture Lilah fast asleep, in blissful ignorance. How thrilled she was to have been given a bedroom overlooking the sea. My heart lurches, but I row ever onward, following the moonlit path.

"And my second question," I say, turning my attention back to the girl in grey, my other self. "Did Mother murder Caitlin?"

Sea mist wraps her in wispy strands, causing her to appear and disappear momentarily. Her sigh is Poseidon's breath. "Grace, when will you understand? Despite all that I have told you, you seem to forget that I was not there back then. *You* were not there. How could I possibly know the answer?"

I think for a minute. "But you knew about our grandmother. If you knew that, then how do you not know this?"

She grows fainter now, a spectre surrounded in mist, and her voice is distant.

"No, Grace. *You* knew what our Grandmother was like. You have been told about the things she did. All I know is that her suicide was a necessarily evil. Her other self, her good self, would have hounded her until she carried it through."

She stands and wraps me in her arms, and I feel the beat of her heart and mine meld into one. "I, of course, have not found it necessary to torment you to such an extent. A little encouragement here and there was all that was required, and I am grateful for that."

A tight band constricts my chest. The toil of rowing and the brittle air have thickened the walls of my lungs and rendered me breathless. My head swims and her vision fades to grey. I can row no further. One by one, I cast the oars into the sea and watch as they separate, drifting off in opposite directions.

The harbour is far in the distance now. A speck of yellow lamplight from The Ship Afloat the only sign of its existence.

She has not yet answered my final question, so I ask again.

"And the moon?" It shrouds us in light, silver-blue and ice-cold. It whips the waves into a frenzy so that the boat rocks and lurches, dousing me from head to foot in spray.

"The moon," she says, gazing up at it. "A full moon symbolizes clarity, the ability to see things otherwise hidden. It also represents completion, which is why you have chosen this night, Grace."

I look to the skies. The moon smiles down on us, large as life, its expression pensive. It, too, has been on a long journey. It is closer now, almost within reach.

The girl in grey is all but shadow, a vague outline of limbs and body, celestial almost.

"If I die, you die, too. Does that not matter to you?"

Her voice floats on the breeze, no more than a whisper.

"I am tired, Grace. So very tired."

And then she is gone. Atomic specks of ash flutter in the moonlight before settling on the sea with a hiss.

I am close now, so close. Curled like a foetus inside the hull, the cool light of the moon tints my skin blue, like a newborn baby.

And the waves carry me into Mother Moon's waiting arms.

FINIS

A Note on the Type

The text of this book is set in Baskerville, a serif typeface designed in the 1750s by John Baskerville (1706–1775) in Birmingham, England, and cut into metal by punchcutter John Handy. Baskerville is classified as a transitional typeface, intended as a refinement of what are now called old-style typefaces of the period, especially those of his most eminent contemporary, William Caslon.

Baskerville's typeface was part of an ambitious project to create books of the greatest possible quality. Baskerville was a wealthy industrialist, who had started his career as a writing-master (teacher of calligraphy) and carver of gravestones, before making a fortune as a manufacturer of varnished lacquer goods. At a time when books in England were generally printed to a low standard, using typefaces of conservative design, Baskerville sought to offer books created to higher-quality methods of printing than any before, using carefully made, level presses, a high quality of ink and very smooth paper pressed after printing to a glazed, gleaming finish.

Chapter headings are set in Scotch Modern, a serif typeface designed by Nick Shinn and released through Shinn-Type in 2008. Recontextualizing the 10-point type of a scientific report published in 1873, Shinn expresses massive respect for the readability of a much-maligned genre, the Scotch Modern. He has produced sleekly refined, micro-detailed vector drawings by eye, without the usual reliance upon scans for tracing. This style of Modern typeface was popular during Victorian times and differs quite a bit from other Modern styles like Bodoni and Didot. Scotch Modern has lavish serifs that make it instantly recognizable.

Composed by Clever Crow Consulting and Design
Pittsburgh, Pennsylvania

Acknowledgments

As writers we spend the majority of our time alone, furiously bashing away at the keys until something acceptable takes shape in front of our eyes. The journey can seem a lonely one, and yet there are many who help us along the way.

First of all my thanks to my husband, Tony. Without your encouragement and wisdom this book would not exist. You are my first reader, my harshest critic, my best friend, and my life.

Immense thanks and appreciation to Christine Scott and Dave Neal of Nosetouch Press for believing in this story. Your professionalism and friendship along the way have meant so much.

To my fellow Nosetouch authors, especially Coy Hall and C.W. Blackwell, for your comradeship. I appreciate you more than you know.

A huge shout-out to my fellow writer and good friend, Tim McGregor, for your frank and ever-so-supportive beta-read of this novel, as well as my other work. I truly cannot thank you enough.

To the horror community at large, of whom there are too many to mention...you are all incredible and inspire me every day!

Last, but not least, to each and every reader, my appreciation always. Without you, my work would have no purpose.

About the Author

Catherine McCarthy is a spinner of stories with macabre melodies. She is the author of the collections *Door and Other Twisted Tales* and *Mists and Megaliths,* and the novella *Immortelle* (Off Limits Press).

Her short fiction has been published by Nosetouch Press, Brigids Gate Press, Gallery for the Curious, Dark Recesses Press, and Black Spot Books.

When she is not writing she may be found hiking the Welsh coast path or huddled among ancient gravestones reading Machen or Poe.

Discover more at catherine-mccarthy-author.com or on Twitter at serialsemantic.

Nosetouch Press is an independent book publisher
tandemly based in Chicago and Pittsburgh.
We are dedicated to bringing some of today's most
energizing fiction to readers around the world.

Our commitment to classic book design in a digital
environment brings an innovative and authentic
approach to the traditions of literary excellence.

We're Out There™

NOSETOUCHPRESS.COM

Horror | Science Fiction | Fantasy | Mystery
Supernatural | Gothic | Weird